THE GHOST
WHO CAME FOR CHRISTMAS

HAUNTING DANIELLE

THE GHOST OF MARLOW HOUSE

THE GHOST WHO LOVED DIAMONDS

THE GHOST WHO WASN'T

THE GHOST WHO WANTED REVENGE

THE GHOST OF HALLOWEEN PAST

THE GHOST WHO CAME FOR CHRISTMAS

THE GHOST OF VALENTINE PAST

THE GHOST FROM THE SEA

THE GHOST AND THE MYSTERY WRITER

THE GHOST AND THE MUSE

THE GHOST WHO STAYED HOME

THE GHOST AND THE LEPRECHAUN

THE GHOST WHO LIED

THE GHOST AND THE BRIDE

THE GHOST AND LITTLE MARIE

THE GHOST AND THE DOPPELGANGER

THE GHOST OF SECOND CHANCES

THE GHOST WHO DREAM HOPPED

THE GHOST OF CHRISTMAS SECRETS

THE GHOST WHO WAS SAYS I DO

THE GHOST
WHO CAME FOR CHRISTMAS

BOBBI HOLMES

The Ghost Who Came for Christmas
(Haunting Danielle, Book 6)
A Novel
By Bobbi Holmes
Cover Design: Elizabeth Mackey

Copyright © 2015 Bobbi Holmes
Robeth Publishing, LLC
All Rights Reserved.
robeth.net

ISBN 978-1-949977-05-9

To my readers, who've made this journey possible.
Thank you and Merry Christmas.

ONE

Spending the holidays with strangers wasn't Chris's idea. It was Trudy's. Chris could feel her watching him. She sat on the cushioned bench seat at the table while he shoved his meager belongings into the worn duffle bag. He had left the cabin door open. They could hear the seagulls from outside and the occasional sound of a boat's horn. The floor beneath them lightly swayed.

He paused a moment and looked at her. "You know, I'm going to freeze my butt off in Oregon. It's practically cold enough to snow."

Trudy shrugged. "It's supposed to be cold at Christmastime. Don't you want a white Christmas?"

"Not particularly. Thankfully, it's not *that* cold. I looked up the weather for the area. The average low for this time of year is around thirty-eight degrees, with a high of forty-eight."

"That's not much different than here."

Chris let out a snort and resumed his packing. "Not if you consider twenty degrees warmer no different." He zipped up his bag.

Trudy watched Chris. "Thank you for doing this for me."

"Did I have a choice?" he asked.

"We all have a choice."

Chris laughed. He knew that wasn't true, and so did Trudy.

"Will you miss me?" She flashed him one of her rare smiles.

Chris studied Trudy for a moment, seriously considering her question. He suspected she had been a beautiful woman in her youth. Now, her pale skin reminded him of a rippling pond. He wondered what color her gray hair had once been. Blonde, he guessed, considering her blue eyes.

"Miss you? I suppose I will. As much as I'd miss an abscessed tooth or a splinter in my big toe."

"That's hardly flattering!" Trudy scolded.

"I didn't mean it to be." Chris grabbed his wallet and cellphone off the table and shoved them into his back pockets as he glanced around the sailboat's cabin, looking for any stray belongings.

Before Trudy could respond, the sailboat dipped slightly and then righted itself. A voice called out, "Chris, you ready?"

Chris picked up the duffle bag and looked toward the open cabin doorway. Ken Palmer, who had just jumped onto the sailboat from the dock, stood on the boat's deck, peeked inside the cabin, and looked around. For a man in his early seventies he was still agile, which he credited to the fact that he spent all his free time at the docks, either working on his sailboat or helping his friends work on theirs. Ironically, his free time didn't include actual sailing.

"You all packed?" he asked.

"I think I have everything." Chris started for the doorway, the duffle bag now slung over his shoulder.

"Goodbye, Chris, and thank you again for doing this," Trudy called out.

Chris paused a moment and looked back at Trudy, giving her a nod goodbye before making his way out of the cabin.

Ken climbed off the sailboat first, followed by Chris, who fumbled a bit with his duffle bag, careful not to drop it in the water. When Chris stepped onto the boat slip, he paused a moment and looked around, mentally saying goodbye to his home of the last six months. For a Friday, it was fairly quiet on the docks, but it wasn't quite 9 a.m. He had already said his goodbyes the previous day. Taking a deep breath, he hoisted his duffle bag back over his shoulder and hurried up the dock, catching up to Ken.

"I saw the new owner up at the office a few minutes ago," Ken said when Chris reached him. Both men continued to walk up the dock toward the ramp leading to the parking lot.

"He stopped by the boat thirty minutes ago. I already gave him the keys," Chris explained.

"I still can't believe Tad sold the boat." Ken shook his head and dug his hand into the front pocket of his work pants, searching for his truck keys.

Chris shifted the weight of the duffle bag from one shoulder to the other. "Doesn't surprise me. He hasn't used it for the last year, what with the divorce and all."

Ken pushed through the gate leading from the dock to the parking area. "Yeah, but now where are you going to live?"

"I'll figure out something." Chris shrugged. "I want to thank you again for taking me to the airport this morning."

"Hey, no problem. You coming back to Dana Point after Christmas?"

"There's no reason to." Chris stopped by Ken's truck and waited for the older man to unlock it. "With Tad selling the boat, no place for me to stay."

"If you want, I could ask around. Someone might be looking to rent out their boat." Ken climbed into the driver's seat.

Chris tossed his duffle bag into the back of the truck and then got into the passenger side of the cab. "Why would I want to rent something?" Chris laughed. "Tad let me crash there for free."

"You got to stay somewhere." Ken slipped a key into the ignition and turned on the engine.

"I suppose, but it was time for me to move on anyway." Chris slammed the door shut and buckled his seat belt.

"You said you're going to Oregon?" Ken asked as he drove the truck out of the parking lot and headed for the highway.

"Yes. Flying into Portland, and I plan to rent a car there. Staying at a bed and breakfast on the coast, a little town called Frederickport."

"Never heard of it. You said you're staying through Christmas?" Ken glanced briefly at Chris and then looked back down the road.

"Yeah." Chris leaned back in his seat and looked out the side window.

"Is this some family get-together?" Ken asked.

Chris shook his head. "Nope. I don't have any family in Oregon, at least not that I know of."

Both hands on the steering wheel, Ken started to chuckle.

Chris glanced over to Ken. "What's so funny?"

"I get it. This is a little romantic holiday getaway. I should have figured it out when you said you were staying at a B and B.

My wife has been trying to get me to stay at one of those for years."

Chris shook his head. "No. I'm not meeting anyone." *Well, at least no one I know personally.*

"You going by yourself?" Ken frowned. "What about that cute little gal who was always hanging around the sailboat? The little blonde whose parents own *Weekend Warrior*."

"You mean Bridget?" Chris glanced briefly at Ken.

Ken nodded. "Yeah, I think that's her name."

"Bridget is practically jailbait."

"Practically, but I'm sure she's at least eighteen. And by the way, she was always mooning over you...damn...I'd love to be your age again!"

Chris laughed and shook his head. "Not really interested in schoolgirls, Ken. She's a nice girl, but not my type."

Ken narrowed his eyes and glanced over to Chris. "Umm...you do like girls, don't you? I mean...well, if you don't, that's okay with me. After all, I have a nephew who prefers...well...you know..."

Chris flashed Ken a smile. "I like women all right. I just prefer one who isn't looking for a meal ticket."

"Guess as long as you remain homeless, you won't have to worry about that," Ken said with a laugh.

"I guess not." Chris smiled and leaned back in the seat.

After a few moments of silence, Ken asked, "So this trip to Oregon, it's just you. All alone for Christmas?"

"I won't be alone, Ken. I assume there'll be other people staying at Marlow House."

"Marlow House?"

"It's the name of the bed and breakfast."

"Can I ask you something?" Ken asked.

Chris thought the question amusing, considering Ken had practically just asked him if he was gay. "Sure, ask away."

"Whatever gave you the idea to book a room at this bed and breakfast for the holidays?"

"I...I saw a brochure on the place; it looked interesting," Chris lied.

"While I can't say I'd choose to stay alone at some B and B, I have to admit I rather envy your freedom to be able to just up and go wherever you want, whenever you want."

"Yeah, I'm one lucky guy," Chris said dryly. Still leaning back in his seat, he closed his eyes and thought about Marlow House and his real reason for going there.

WITHOUT A SOUND, Walt appeared in the kitchen and found Danielle standing at the counter, about to dump an open bag of walnut pieces into a stainless steel mixing bowl. "I assume you're making more cookies?"

Startled, Danielle let out a squeaky yelp and looked up into Walt's blue eyes. "You scared me! Don't sneak up on me like that!" She turned her attention back to her cookie batter.

"Sorry. But why are you so jumpy?" Walt leaned closer and peeked into the bowl.

"I'm not jumpy. I just didn't expect you to pop in like that." Danielle grabbed a wooden spoon off the counter and started to stir the batter. "And yes, chocolate drop cookies. My grandma's recipe."

"I wish I could have one." Walt sighed, leaning back against the counter. Waving his hand, a lit cigar appeared between two of his fingers. "It's been decades since I've enjoyed a cookie."

Danielle paused a moment and looked at Walt. "Maybe you can't eat one of these, but wouldn't it be possible to…well, conjure up one like you do a cigar?"

"I'm a spirit, Danielle, not a witch."

"I think the proper term is *warlock*."

"Warlock?" Walt frowned.

"Yeah, you know, a guy witch." Danielle grinned.

Walt shrugged and took a drag off his cigar. "Well, in either case, I can't just conjure up food like some magician or wit—warlock."

"Well, I'm sorry about that." Danielle sounded sincerely contrite. "One thing I love about Christmas is the baking—cookies and pie and homemade pumpkin bread." Closing her eyes briefly, she let out a satisfied sigh before opening her eyes again and resuming her task.

"Danielle, you like all those things even when it isn't Christmas."

"True that. Which is one reason a bed and breakfast is an ideal business for me. I can do all the baking I want, and someone will be around to help me eat it."

"So who's helping you eat this? Don't your guests start arriving tonight?" Walt glanced around. "Where's Lily, by the way?"

"She's over at Ian's."

"I thought it sounded awful quiet around here."

"Enjoy the solitude now, because we're going to have a full house all the way to the New Year."

"I don't know if I mentioned it, but the Christmas tree looks beautiful. You and Lily did a wonderful job decorating it. Although I don't know why you just didn't use the Christmas lights I had in the attic. They were brand new."

"Walt, they were brand new when you bought them ninety years ago. I'm afraid they would probably burn down the house if I tried to use them."

"I suppose you have a point." Walt watched Danielle and then added, "The Christmas tree brings life to the living room. Since you moved in here, I don't think I've seen you go into that room a half a dozen times."

Danielle shrugged. "I always thought the parlor felt more intimate, and there's something cozy about the library. The living room —well, is just sort of large and impersonal."

"It doesn't feel that way now." Walt smiled.

"No, no, it doesn't. Although, I'll have to think of something to do with the room when Christmas is over and we take the tree down. Otherwise it will go back to being a big ol' lonely room."

Walt waved his hand and the cigar vanished. "You didn't answer me; do your guests start arriving tonight?"

"Just one. I guess he's flying in from California to Portland and then renting a car and driving here. I'm not sure what time he'll actually get here."

"He's coming alone?" Walt frowned.

"Yes. His name is…" Danielle stopped stirring the batter for a moment and tried to remember the man's name. "Chris, Chris Johnson."

"Any relationship to Joanne?"

"I doubt it. He didn't mention anything and neither did Joanne. Johnson is a pretty common name."

"So he's not coming with a wife? Is he meeting someone here?"

Danielle grabbed a small scoop and began spooning up balls of cookie dough, strategically placing them on a cookie sheet. "No. Just him."

"Don't you find that…odd?"

Danielle shook her head. "Not particularly. Maybe he has family or friends in Frederickport."

"You really need to start asking prospective guests more questions," Walt scolded.

"Oh, Walt, you worry too much! Everything is going to be just fine! After all, it's Christmas!"

TWO

"I just heard it on the news. Clarence Renton is dead," Cleve Monchique announced from the open doorway of Peter Morris's office.

Peter looked up and waved him in. "Shut the door." Strewn across his desk were papers. He hastily shoved them into an empty manila file folder, which he then set aside. When Cleve reached the desk, Peter motioned to one of the empty chairs facing him.

"What are they saying?" Peter asked.

Cleve sat down. "That he hanged himself in his cell. The guards found him this morning."

"Any talk of foul play?"

Cleve shook his head. "No. But they did say it was currently under investigation."

"That's to be expected. I'm just happy to have that out of the way. Let's hold off a few days before we file his will with probate. I don't want to seem too anxious to cash in on poor Clarence's untimely death," Peter instructed.

"That's what I thought too."

Peter glanced at his watch. "Richard Winston is supposed to be here any minute. I don't want you to mention anything about Clarence around him."

Cleve glanced to the closed door. "Did he know Clarence?"

"I doubt it. While he's bound to hear about Clarence's death—

considering the notoriety of the case and his connection to Earth-bound Spirits, I'd prefer to avoid the topic. It would only confuse Richard, especially now, when he has a job to do."

"And you think he's the one to do it?"

Peter picked up the file folder. Opening it, he plucked out a news clipping from amongst the papers. He looked at it a moment; it was about Danielle Boatman. "She's a very wealthy woman." He leaned across the desk and handed the clipping to Cleve.

Cleve took it from Peter, studying the picture of Danielle Boatman in the article. "And she's a very attractive woman."

"What makes her especially attractive: she has no family. No one. The poor dear is all alone in the world. She and Richard have a lot in common." Peter grinned, showing off straight white teeth, a stark contrast to his bottle-dyed black hair.

Cleve leaned forward and set the scrap of paper back on the desk. "Her friend—Lily Miller—it's my understanding that she's come into a considerable sum of money now that the lawsuit has been settled."

Peter shook his head. "That one will pose more of a challenge. Remember, she comes from a large family, and they appear to be close. She's also seeing Jon Altar. Or Ian Bartley, whatever he chooses to be called these days. I just hope they don't get in our way with Boatman. People like that are too skeptical—they don't have an open mind. They're the types who'll continue repeating the same mistakes and never move onto where we're going—where Clarence went."

Cleve moved uneasily in his chair, his right hand restlessly combing through his hair.

Peter leaned back and narrowed his eyes, studying the younger man. "You need to get over it, Cleve. We had no choice. It was for a higher good. You know that."

"Yes...yes, I do." Cleve looked down.

"And Clarence is in a better place now. As for Lily Miller, I don't see the point in wasting our time on her right now, considering her friend is perfect for us. Danielle Boatman needs us. She's a beautiful, vulnerable woman, and without our help, some unscrupulous man will swoop in and take advantage of her. It's our duty, Cleve."

RICHARD WINSTON'S need to wear six-hundred-dollar shoes was not a matter of choice, but of habit. He had learned as a young child it was easier to go along with the wishes of his controlling mother, Rachel Winston, rather than attempting to assert any independence. Even from the grave she continued to exert influence over his wardrobe.

While he continued to dress the part of a Winston, his rebellion had begun. Peter Morris's Earthbound Spirits provided a new road for him to travel, one to contentment and peace—unlike the road he had inherited from his parents, paved with deceit and lies.

When he arrived at Earthbound Spirits' offices, Peter Morris was there to greet him. "Please, take a seat, Richard. So glad you were able to make it in today."

"Thank you for seeing me, Mr. Morris." Richard grinned eagerly and took a seat, anxiously glancing around the office. "Thought I'd be seeing Mr. Monchique today, not you, sir."

Peter smiled and leaned forward, his elbows resting on his desk. "You have a very important assignment, and I wanted to see you personally."

"I just want to do my part," Richard insisted. "Whatever I can do to help."

"Are you ready for your little holiday trip?" Peter asked.

"Yes, sir. I check into Marlow House tomorrow morning. I have a reservation through New Year's."

"Have you asked her about the Christmas open house?"

"Mr. Monchique and I discussed that. We decided I should casually bring it up in conversation after I get there. It'll sound more natural."

Peter sighed. "I suppose that'll work. But you'll need to call me and let me know what she says."

Richard nodded. "Yes, of course."

"Very good, Richard. Excellent. Danielle Boatman needs us."

"There's just one thing…" Richard nervously cleared his throat.

"What's that?"

"I feel a little hypocritical…it being Christmas and all, since I no longer celebrate Christmas."

"Didn't you tell me Christmas wasn't very important in your family? I understand some members have a difficult time relinquishing their notion of Christmas and all its traditions—the drivel we've been fed over the years by retailers out to make a buck. Sentimental nonsense. Christmas has nothing to do with our spiritual growth. If anything, it hinders it."

"There was nothing sentimental in how my parents celebrated Christmas." Richard turned his head slightly and gazed out the window. It looked out to the ocean. "Like you said, it was simply an opportunity to make more money."

"Then what is it?" Peter asked.

"I imagine the other guests at Marlow House will be there because of what the brochure promised—an old-fashioned Christmas."

"And the problem?"

Richard shrugged and looked from the picture window back to Peter. "While I agree it's nothing but nonsense, I'll feel a little like Scrooge…"

Peter laughed. "What, like you're there to take away their Christmas?"

"I suppose, in a way."

"Put your mind at rest. I don't expect you to interfere in any of Marlow House's scheduled Christmas festivities—after all, I plan to attend the Christmas open house, remember? Our point is not to convert whoever is in residence at Marlow House over the holiday—just to reach its proprietor. I'm certain this holiday will be a stark reminder to the poor girl of how alone she really is."

"What do you mean?" Richard frowned.

"Danielle Boatman has no family. I don't believe the void, the void many people feel so keenly this time of year, can be filled with strangers. She needs a new family. She needs Earthbound Spirits in her life."

DANIELLE STOOD at the kitchen counter, spooning dark chocolate frosting over her cooled chocolate drop cookies, when her cellphone began to ring. Gingerly setting the now frosted cookie onto the platter, she set the spoon back into the bowl of frosting and licked her fingers before picking up the phone.

Danielle checked to see who was calling before she answered. "Hey, Chief, a merry Christmas and ho, ho, ho to you," she said cheerfully.

"Have you been listening to the news?" the chief asked.

"The news? No. I'm listening to Christmas carols. What's up?"

"It's Clarence Renton, he's killed himself."

"What?" Danielle hastily walked over to her iPod and turned off the Christmas carols, giving her full attention to the phone call.

"They found him this morning. He hanged himself in his cell."

"What does his cellmate say?"

"His cellmate was in the infirmary for the night, claimed to have stomach cramps. Renton was alone."

"What about the guys in the other cells around him?"

"All claiming they didn't hear anything. Which, of course, would support suicide."

"Yeah, like a bunch of convicts really want to rat out someone who might sneak into their cell during the night and slit their throats."

"You don't believe it was suicide?"

"I don't see Renton as the type to kill himself." Danielle paused a moment and then groaned. "Oh crap…"

"What's wrong?"

"You don't think he's going to show up here, do you? Dang, he is absolutely the last person…ghost…I want to see."

"You would know more about that than me. Aren't you always telling me you don't see everyone you know who dies—or that you can't control who you can see?"

"That's what I'm afraid of. I really don't want to go through another Stoddard episode." Danielle groaned.

"If he stops by, you might want to ask him if he really killed himself."

"Talk about putting a damper on the Christmas spirit," Danielle grumbled. She grabbed a chocolate-frosted cookie, sat down at the kitchen table, and shoved the cookie in her mouth.

"I just thought you'd want to know."

Biting off a large chunk of the cookie, she responded with her mouth full. "Yeah, thanks."

"Are you eating something?" he asked.

"Uh-huh, cookies," she said, taking another bite. She grabbed a glass of milk off the table and took several gulps.

"From what I understand, Renton rewrote his will a while back and left Earthbound Spirits everything," the chief told her.

"That figures, considering he was so closed-mouthed about Isabella's will."

"I was always a little surprised you never sued Renton for embezzling from your aunt's estate, and never filed a civil suit for killing Cheryl."

"It wouldn't have brought Cheryl back. Anyway, after the courts looked into those bogus charities Renton set up, most of that money went back to my aunt's estate." *And to me.*

"True, but still, from what I understand, Renton was by no means a pauper."

"Yes, and now whatever he had goes to Earthbound Spirits. I still don't understand why those guys are still in business. I figured after trying to pass off Isabella's old will as the current one and blackmailing Darlene, someone would have gone to jail, and they would have lost their nonprofit status."

"I told you, we couldn't prove anything. A little difficult to haul Darlene's ghost into court to testify about the blackmail," the chief reminded her. "There was no way to connect those photographs we found to Earthbound Spirits."

"I suppose you're right. But if I ever see those lying jerks again…"

THREE

Patricia Morgan held the prize letter in her right hand and her landlord's eviction letter in her left. She studied them each a moment longer before tossing them both onto the kitchen table and glancing up at the wall clock. She would need to leave in thirty minutes to pick her daughter up at school.

Jessica believed they would be buying a Christmas tree this evening; after all, it was the beginning of Christmas vacation, and Patricia had been promising her for weeks they could get a tree as soon as school was out. Normally, they bought the tree after Thanksgiving, but just days before Thanksgiving this year, Patricia had lost her job at the preschool.

It wasn't anything personal—after all, the entire staff had found themselves instantly unemployed when the owners of the preschool forgot to file their corporate income tax for over five years straight. It was easier for them to simply close the school as opposed to coming up with the exorbitant fees they now faced.

Had Patricia known she was about to lose her job, she would never have spent her savings on the new transmission for her old car. She would love to have those thousand plus dollars back in her bank account.

It wasn't as if she was completely destitute. She had the regular social security payments from her late husband and a pittance of an unemployment check coming in. She had believed she would have

14

found a job by now, yet none of the local preschools were hiring. She considered getting a part-time job in retail; after all, it was the Christmas season, and many stores hired seasonal employees. Yet that would mean leaving Jessica home alone during Christmas break —and paying for a sitter would probably eat up whatever pay she might earn from the temporary job. One thing Patricia had liked about working at the preschool—it enabled her to have school holidays off with her daughter.

Picking up the prize letter, she reread it.

"Congratulations, Patricia Morgan. You and your daughter have won a two-week, all-expenses-paid Christmas holiday at Marlow House Bed and Breakfast located in Frederickport, Oregon, on the northwest coast. Your name was submitted by an anonymous member of our nonprofit organization. Enclosed is a money order to cover additional expenses and gift tax, and airline tickets for you and your daughter. Your room has already been paid for at Marlow House, which will include breakfast and dinner. Additional Christmas gifts—valued at over $10,000—will be delivered to you and your daughter on Christmas Eve at Marlow House, so we hope you will make the trip or forfeit the additional prizes. Merry Christmas from Benevolent Charities, a nonprofit serving the needs of American families."

Tossing the letter back onto the table, she picked up her cellphone and dialed the number on the letterhead for Benevolent Charities. The call went to a message machine—as it had the last ten times she had dialed it.

Standing up, she walked to the kitchen counter and picked up a piece of paper she had left there the night before. Unfolding the paper, she looked at the numbers she had scribbled on it. Since she did not own a computer—she couldn't afford the monthly Wi-Fi fee, not to mention the initial cost of purchasing a computer—she had stopped by the library and looked up Marlow House Bed and Breakfast. According to its website, it was a real place. Of course, she understood anyone could create a fake website. She had also jotted down the numbers for the Frederickport Chamber of Commerce as well as the airline's phone number.

She had already checked with the airline, and the tickets were legit. When she had first received the letter two weeks earlier, she had taken the money order to her bank, and they assured her it wasn't counterfeit, and she could deposit it. Reluctantly she did, yet she hadn't spent any of the money. She had heard horror stories of people being scammed with fake checks, only to have them bounce after they spent the money and were left having to repay the bank.

Considering her options, she picked up her cellphone and looked at it a moment. It seemed everyone had one of those smart-phones except her. Jessica called hers a dumb-phone—one of those twenty-dollar throwaway phones with prepaid minutes. She dialed the Frederickport Chamber of Commerce. The call lasted only a few minutes. They assured her Marlow House Bed and Breakfast was a legitimate business, and the phone number she had for them was correct. Her next call was to Marlow House Bed and Breakfast.

"NOW WHAT ARE YOU MAKING?" Walt asked when he popped back into the kitchen and found Danielle dumping a bag of choco-late chips into a bowl.

"I'm making chocolate chip cookies." Danielle stopped what she was doing and looked over at Walt, who had just taken a seat at the kitchen table. "I was going to come look for you after I mixed this up." Danielle wiped her hands on her apron and abandoned her baking, joining Walt at the table.

"Anything particular?"

"Yes. I wanted to tell you about the two phone calls I got a little while ago. The first one was from MacDonald."

"The chief?"

"He told me Clarence Renton is dead. They say he committed suicide. Hanged himself in his cell."

Walt cringed. "Those things can be faked."

"You would know."

"Does he really think Renton killed himself, and why?"

"I guess there isn't anything to indicate foul play, but the more I think about it, I just find it hard to believe someone like that would take his own life."

"Danielle, the man was facing the rest of his life behind bars." Walt glanced around the room. "You haven't seen him, have you?"

"No. And I don't want to. I hope he's moved on."

"You mentioned a second call?" Walt reminded her.

"Yes, from one of the guests who is supposed to arrive tomorrow —Patricia Morgan. It was the strangest call."

"Strange how?" Walt summoned a lit cigar and took a puff.

"She told me who she was and wanted to know if we had her reservations and if we received the full payment."

"And?"

"Then she wanted to know how long the reservation was for and if she would owe anything else once she arrived."

"I thought you told me she already paid for the two weeks?"

"She did. But she kept asking me—over and over again—and then told me that she was on a tight budget, and if she arrived and I expected any more money, she wouldn't be able to pay me."

"Perhaps she's had a bad experience somewhere before."

"Yeah, maybe. Now that I think about it, once Lucas got us reservations for a place in Vegas, paid up front, and when we got there, we were charged something called a resort fee. Really made Lucas angry. Perhaps that's what she was worried about." Danielle stood up.

"You mentioned before she's coming with a daughter?" Walt asked.

"Yes. I'm putting them upstairs in the Green Room because it has twin beds."

"Seriously, Danielle, you're still going with the room colors?"

"Yeah." Danielle sighed and sat back down in the chair. "But I've decided I sorta hate the color thing. Seemed like a good idea at the time."

Walt laughed. "I'm glad you finally agree with me! Maybe we can think of something a little more original and fitting for Marlow House."

"After the holidays. Colors are okay for now. But you're probably right. And when I decide to redecorate, my hands will be tied by the room's name."

"I suppose you could really confuse the guests and decorate a room red, then call it the blue room." Walt smiled.

"Funny." Danielle rolled her eyes and stood up again, going back to her cookie batter.

"So how old is the daughter?" Walt asked.

"I believe she said she was seven." Danielle added ingredients to the bowl. "She also asked me something else that was odd."

"What was that?" Walt fiddled with his cigar, watching the smoke rise and disappear.

"She asked me if I was familiar with Benevolent Charities."

Danielle stirred the batter and added a liberal splash of vanilla extract.

"What's that?" Walt waved his hand and the cigar vanished.

"I have no idea. I've never heard of it before. She told me she tried to find it online and couldn't find anything about it."

"Why was she asking you about some charity?"

"I have no idea. Like I told you, it was a strange conversation." Danielle shook her head.

"Maybe she wasn't asking you for information about the organization—maybe she wanted to find out what you already knew about it before she asks you for a donation."

Danielle stopped stirring the batter, leaving the wooden spoon sitting in the bowl. "You know, I never considered that. Although, it didn't sound that way." She picked up the jar of vanilla and put its cap back on. "She arrives tomorrow. If she starts hitting me up for a donation, I guess I'll have my answer."

Walt silently watched Danielle for a few moments. Finally, he asked, "Just how many kinds of cookies are you intending to bake?"

Danielle stopped what she was doing and looked over at Walt and smiled. "I guess this seems a little silly, doesn't it?"

"Silly? No. It's just that I imagine one or two types of cookies would have been enough for your guests. But I've lost count of the different cookies you've already baked this week."

Danielle silently considered Walt's question for a moment, her dark eyes glistening with unshed tears. "When I was growing up, Aunt Susan, Cheryl, and Sean would come over to our house, and we would spend hours baking. Most of the recipes were passed down from my grandmothers." Danielle smiled softly and added with a chuckle, "Of course, Cheryl didn't do as much baking as she did eating. I remember one year she got so sick eating raw cookie dough."

"I can rather see that." Walt smiled, his eyes studying Danielle's whimsical expression.

"We would also make graham cracker houses every year."

"Graham cracker houses? What's that?"

"It's like mock gingerbread houses, but we use graham crackers instead. Lets the kids get right to the decorating. Sean loved that. I think that was his favorite. He would always come up with the wildest-looking houses, usually several stories tall—which he ended up gluing together with a hot glue gun so they wouldn't collapse. That was a trick Mom taught him."

"I don't know what a hot glue gun is, but it sounds interesting. I have an idea there's also a story behind that." Walt nodded to the apron Danielle wore. It boasted an appliqué Santa, its cheeks yellowed from age.

Danielle glanced down at her apron and smiled softly. "We each had our own Christmas apron, even Dad and Uncle Carl. When I packed up Cheryl's things, I found her apron—along with her parents' and Sean's. I brought them back with me. Kind of surprised she kept them after all these years."

"Sounds like you have some good memories."

"Yes, I do. But that's really all I have left of my family. Memories."

FOUR

Danielle was just taking the last batch of cookies out of the oven when she heard the doorbell ring. Hurriedly, she used the spatula to move the hot cookies from the cookie sheet to the wooden cutting board on the counter, trying her best not to misshape the still-soft cookies. She glanced up at the wall clock. It was almost 6 p.m. She had been baking most of the day.

"It's Joe," Walt announced as he appeared in the kitchen.

"Well, he'll just have to wait," Danielle said as she moved the last cookie to the wooden board. "I wonder what he wants?"

"Have you done anything to get yourself arrested again?" Walt teased.

"Funny ghost," Danielle said under her breath as she placed the now empty cookie sheet back into the hot oven. Turning the oven off and shutting its door, she headed for the front entry, wiping her hands on her Christmas apron along the way.

When she opened the front door a few moments later, she found Joe Morelli standing on the front porch. Instead of wearing his police uniform, he wore street clothes: tan slacks and a pullover sweater.

"Evening, Joe," Danielle greeted him.

"The chief asked me to drop this off." Joe held up Danielle's old iPhone and grinned. His gaze swept over her, silently noting the dark tendrils escaping her once tidy fishtail braid, the smattering of flour across the bridge of her nose, and the colorful Santa Claus apron covering her black stretch pants and hip-length red T-shirt.

"Thanks. I was beginning to wonder if I was ever going to get it back. Aren't I supposed to sign for it or something?" Danielle took the phone from Joe and looked at it, turning it from side to side.

"He said you can do that the next time you stop by the office. I guess he trusts you." Joe leaned into the doorway and sniffed. "Someone has been baking."

"You want to come in and have a cookie? I just took the last batch out of the oven. They're still warm."

"I thought you'd never ask." Joe grinned and stepped into the house, letting Danielle close the door behind him.

"I also wanted to talk to you about John Smith," Joe said as he followed Danielle down the hallway to the kitchen.

"He's bringing you the iPhone? A rather transparent ploy to see you," Walt said when he suddenly appeared, walking next to Danielle. "And what more can be said about Smith? The man is in prison, where he belongs."

Silently, Danielle glanced to Walt and smiled and then asked Joe, "Do we have to talk about Smith? It's Christmastime. It's bad enough I had to testify in his trial the week before Thanksgiving." Danielle walked into the kitchen and headed for the counter, grabbing two glasses out of the overhead cabinet.

"At least the jury came back with a quick verdict." Joe took a seat at the table and watched Danielle.

She held up the glasses and looked at Joe. "Milk or coffee? Or maybe you'd rather have a beer or some wine?"

"Too late for coffee, it would keep me up all night. I've done beer and cookies before, but I think homemade cookies call for a glass of cold milk."

"I agree." Danielle poured two glasses of milk and set cookies on a plate before joining Joe at the table.

"If you feed him homemade cookies, he's going to get the wrong impression. When a woman offers a man her homemade cooking, they naturally assume she wants one thing, *him*," Walt warned just before vanishing.

Danielle resisted her urge to let out a snort in response to Walt's comment, but instead glanced around the room, looking for him. She suspected he had retreated to the attic. Joe had already grabbed a cookie and taken a bite when she asked, "What is this about Smith?"

"It's not bad news," Joe explained. "Do you remember that Vancouver case where authorities were convinced Smith was their man?"

"Sure, and the case fell apart. What about it?" Danielle picked a chocolate chip cookie up off the plate and took a bite.

"A new witness has come forward. With Smith already locked up for his attempt on our lives, the witness is more willing to talk."

"If this means Smith will be locked up longer, that's terrific news." Danielle paused a moment and frowned. "Will we have to testify again? I would assume our testimony on how he held us at gunpoint would help this other case. Lets the jury see he's capable of murder. But crap, I really don't want to go through that again."

"I have a feeling the DA may work out some sort of plea bargain with Smith to take the death penalty off the table. If they do, there would be no reason for us to testify. But we'll have to see."

Danielle sighed. "I would like all that to be behind us."

"It has been one hell of a year…for all of us." Joe paused a moment and then added, "The chief told me he already called you about Renton."

"Yeah, well, I'd rather not think about Renton or Smith. I'd rather drink to a better year." Danielle lifted her glass of milk in a mock toast.

"As long as it comes with cookies, works for me." Joe grinned.

They finished off the plate of cookies. Finally, Joe looked up at Danielle and said, "I'm really sorry I didn't listen to Lily and get over to Presley House sooner."

"Yeah…well…let's just put that behind us too." Danielle smiled.

"But it really was your credit card. If someone hadn't been using it…I mean, what were the chances of that happening at the same time you get trapped at Presley House?"

Danielle shrugged. "When you first told me about the credit card, I assumed someone had gotten ahold of my account information, maybe from some previous purchase. I figured my card was still in my purse. But when I checked later, it wasn't."

"Yeah, you told me."

"The only thing I can think of, it must have fallen out of my purse. Back when all of that was going on, I remember dropping the purse in a restaurant and some stuff fell out. I thought I got everything, but obviously I didn't."

"I just wish we could have caught the person who was using your card."

"They had quite a shopping spree before the card was cancelled."

Joe glanced over to the counter where Danielle had set the iPhone. "What're you going to do with your old phone?"

"I'm donating it." Danielle sipped her milk.

Joe picked up a napkin off the table and wiped his mouth. "You could sell it on eBay."

Instead of responding, Danielle just looked at Joe, her lips almost turning into a smile.

He glanced up into Danielle's dark eyes and shrugged. "Yeah, I guess there's no reason to do that. You don't need the money. Of course, that doesn't stop you from baking cookies for a bunch of strangers."

"Oh, stop, Joe. I like running the B and B. And I like baking." Danielle stood and picked up the empty plate, taking it to the sink.

"I didn't notice any other cars out front. I assume you don't have anyone staying here now."

"Actually, we're booked up through the New Year. No one is here right now, but I'm expecting someone…" She paused when she heard the doorbell ring. Grinning, she looked over at Joe. "How is that for timing?"

Joe watched as Danielle quickly removed her Christmas apron and tossed it on the counter before running her hands over her hair in an awkward attempt to tidy up.

"You might want to remove the flour on your nose," Joe said with a chuckle as he stood up and snatched the two empty glasses off the table to carry them to the kitchen sink.

"Flour?" Danielle lifted her hand to her nose and unsuccessfully attempted to wipe away the evidence of her recent baking. She startled when Joe stepped in front of her and reached out, his hand gently brushing off her nose and cheek.

"I can't leave you alone for a minute!" Walt snapped when he suddenly appeared in the kitchen, a look of disdain on his face.

Startled by Joe's gesture and Walt's sudden appearance, Danielle stepped back, muttered an awkward thank you to Joe, and flashed

Walt a glare before giving her nose a final wipe with her hand. She turned to the door and rushed from the kitchen.

WHEN DANIELLE REACHED THE FOYER, she paused for a moment by the mirror hanging over the cherry wood entry table. She took a moment to tuck a few stray tendrils back into her braid and straighten her red shirt before turning toward the front door. Joe followed her back to the entry, but paused quietly at the parlor door, watching her. The bell rang a second time just as Danielle was about to open the door.

The man Danielle found standing on her front porch was nothing like she expected. For some reason, she had imagined that Chris Johnson—assuming that was who this man was—would be more in line with Will Wayne, an older gentleman, alone and seeking company for the holiday.

This man—whom she guessed was close to her age, perhaps a little older—looked like someone who would be spending his Christmas vacation on a cruise ship with other singles instead of tucked away in a little bed and breakfast on the northwest coast. And considering his looks, Danielle imagined he wouldn't be lacking the attention of the women. She couldn't wait until Lily got a look at this one.

Dressed in faded jeans, a powder blue dress shirt, and suede jacket, the man carried a duffle bag over one shoulder. He broke into a wide smile the moment his eyes met hers. His gaze swept over her, and his smile broadened.

"Well, hello," he greeted her, his blue eyes twinkling. "I sure hope I'm at the right place. I'm Chris Johnson; I've a reservation. This is Marlow House, isn't it? I didn't see a sign."

Danielle opened the door wider and stepped to one side. "You're at the right place. Welcome. I'm afraid we don't have a sign yet. I'm your host, Danielle Boatman."

Chris put out his hand and shook the one Danielle offered as he made his way into the house. Once inside, he glanced around and immediately spied Joe standing to one side, silently watching.

"Hello." He flashed Joe a smile. "Are you Mr. Boatman?"

Joe stepped forward and shook Chris's hand. "No. I'm a friend of Danielle's, Joe Morelli." Joe gave Chris's hand a final firm shake while adding, "Sergeant Joe Morelli."

"Sergeant? Are you in the military?" Chris asked when the handshake ended, a smile still on his face.

"Joe's with the local police department," Danielle explained, flashing Joe a disapproving glance for his less than friendly demeanor.

"Nice." Chris dropped his duffle bag to the floor and glanced around the foyer. "Never hurts to be on good terms with the local cops."

"And what do you do, Mr. Johnson?" Joe asked.

Chris's gaze swept over the room before looking back to Joe. He studied him a moment. "I try to enjoy life, Sergeant Morelli."

"Does that pay well?" Joe asked.

Chris laughed. "You would be surprised."

"Thanks for bringing me my iPhone," Danielle interrupted. "I know how busy you are, Joe." Danielle started walking to the door, preparing to show Joe out. Unfortunately, Joe seemed quite content where he was standing.

"You offer the boy a cookie and he starts getting all territorial," Walt announced as he appeared the next moment, standing between Joe and Danielle. "I warned you this would happen if you encouraged him."

CHRIS'S EYES widened when a man wearing a vintage pinstriped suit materialized, standing just a few feet away. Resisting the urge to voice an expletive, Chris withheld comment, his gaze shifting from Danielle to Joe. By Joe's lack of reaction and the way he seemed to be looking through the man, who was clearly criticizing him, Chris surmised Joe could not see the apparition. Yet by Danielle's body language and the way her gaze shifted between Joe and the man, Chris assumed she could both see and hear him.

Very interesting, Chris told himself. *It seems Marlow House has its own ghost—and I believe Danielle Boatman can see and hear him.*

FIVE

"So is he your boyfriend?" Chris asked after Joe said his goodbyes and stepped out onto the front porch, closing the door behind him. Chris remained standing in the foyer with the chatty ghost and Danielle.

By the way the spirit was yammering on about the cop, Chris was fairly certain he already knew the answer: Joe was not her boyfriend, but not from lack of trying. That was not only obvious by the ghost's nonstop tirade but also by the unfriendly police officer's possessive attitude toward Danielle, which did not seemed to be reciprocated.

"You hear what he's asking you?" the ghost asked Danielle. "Not only are you sending the wrong message to Joe, the way you're behaving toward Joe makes others think you and he are in a relationship. I told you he's all wrong for you, Danielle. Haven't you learned that already? If you give him the chance, he'll hurt you again."

Chris noted the flash of annoyance Danielle gave the nagging spirit before she turned to him and said, "No, he's just a friend. What made you think he was my boyfriend?"

"It's really none of my business. I shouldn't have said anything."

"No, that's okay. I was just curious why you thought he was my boyfriend."

"It's not so much I thought he was your boyfriend…"

The ghost, now silent, stood between them. Chris could feel the apparition studying him.

Resisting the temptation to shout *boo* to the spirit, Chris told Danielle, "It's not that *you* acted like he was your boyfriend, just the opposite, in fact. Seemed you were a little annoyed with the guy. But him, well…maybe he was just being protective, and I was reading him all wrong. You did say he was a cop, and I'm a stranger staying in your home."

Chris wanted to laugh at the ghost's sudden scowl. He caught the satisfied smirk Danielle flashed her ghost friend. At least, Chris assumed he was her friend. By the way the ghost was behaving, it was obvious Joe-the-cop-dude wasn't the only protective male hovering around Danielle Boatman.

"Joe and I are just friends, but I suppose he is a little protective of me, considering that he did save my life." Chris didn't miss the mischievous grin Danielle flashed the spirit.

"Oh, please. He didn't save your life. If I hadn't intervened, both you and Joe would be on this side with me." The apparition vanished.

"Is he the cop who saved you from the hit man?" Chris asked. "I read about it online."

"And you still decided to spend Christmas here?" Danielle stepped to one side as she opened the door to the downstairs bedroom, where Chris would be staying.

"I'll confess, I read up on Marlow House before making the reservation. Sounds like this is a lively place." Chris flashed Danielle a grin and walked into the room.

"I hope you don't expect anything too exciting during your stay here. If I have my way, this will be a nice, quiet Christmas."

Chris walked into the bedroom. "That would suit me just fine, a drama-free Christmas." He was about to toss his duffle bag onto the bed when something on the center of the bedspread caught his eye.

"Max!" Danielle shouted when she saw what had captured Chris's attention. The cat—all black save for the white tips on his ears—raised his head, opened his eyes, and yawned. He looked at Danielle and then turned his attention to Chris.

"I'm sorry about this. I don't know how he got in here. I try to keep Max out of the guests' bedrooms." Danielle walked over to the bed and scooped up the cat, who immediately rested his chin on her shoulder and began to purr. "I hope you aren't allergic to cats."

"Not at all." Chris reached out and scratched behind Max's ears. "He's welcome in my room anytime. I like cats."

"He does seem to be partial to this bedroom." Danielle pointed to another door. "This room has a private bathroom, through there. It's the only guestroom on the ground floor."

Chris tossed the duffle bag onto the bed and looked around. "Nice."

Max began to squirm. Danielle set him on the floor. He immediately walked to Chris and began winding in and out around his ankles.

"I think he likes you," Danielle said, looking down at her cat. "But if he gets in your way, please feel free to put him out of your room."

"I assume there are other guests?" Chris asked.

"There will be. We have several arriving tomorrow; they'll be staying in the upstairs bedrooms. And then there's Lily; she lives here full time."

"Lily? I think I read about her too. Is she the one that rich guy tried to pass off as his niece? When she was in a coma?"

"You really did read all about this place."

"When I was considering staying here for the holiday, I looked you up online. I was surprised how many news articles popped up when I typed in *Marlow House*."

Danielle groaned. "Not exactly the publicity I was looking for."

Chris laughed. "I imagine not. But don't worry about it, this place is beautiful, and I'm anxious to get the grand tour."

"I'll be happy to give it to you now, unless you'd like to freshen up."

"Freshen up?" Chris chuckled.

Danielle blushed. "I guess that does sound like a funny thing to say to a guy."

"Just makes me think of all sorts of retorts about getting fresh. Which I should probably save until we know each other better." Chris grinned.

Danielle smiled and quickly changed the subject. "We don't normally provide dinners, but during the Christmas holiday, your room will include breakfast and dinner. Both meals are served in the dining room, with breakfast being served from seven to nine and dinner from five to seven."

Chris glanced at his watch and smiled. "Looks like I have a few more minutes to make dinner."

"I wasn't sure what time you were getting in—"

"No," Chris interrupted. "I was just teasing. I ate something in Portland. I didn't think I'd make it here in time for dinner."

"Well, we do have lots of cookies in the kitchen—and home-made pumpkin bread—and if you would like a sandwich later, I have plenty of lunch meat and sliced cheese, along with some bread I picked up at the bakery."

"It all sounds good. Maybe you could just give me a tour for now, and we can swing by the kitchen for some of those cookies."

Before Danielle answered, Chris heard the front door open and then what sounded like male and female voices, followed by the barking of a dog. Just as Chris looked up to the open door leading into the foyer, Max dashed out of the room. Chris spied a golden retriever coming from the direction of the front door. The dog raced down the hall, chasing the cat, and by the sound of it, the cat and dog were headed up the stairs.

"I think a dog just got in your house and is after your cat!" Chris started for the doorway, yet paused when he heard Danielle laugh.

"That's just Sadie. Those two are old friends. Well, maybe not friends exactly."

When Chris and Danielle reached the doorway, they came face-to-face with the man and woman attached to the voices Chris had heard moments earlier. While he had never met the pair, he instantly knew who they were: Ian Bartley, also known under the pen name Jon Altar, and Lily Miller.

"We brought you something to eat," Lily announced, holding up a sack for Danielle to see. Her gaze immediately went from Danielle to Chris, flashing him a friendly smile.

If Chris wasn't mistaken, he would swear Lily's green eyes noticeably widened when her gaze set on him. For just a moment she stood speechless, staring. Finally, she said, "Hello, you must be the new guest. I'm Lily Miller and this is Ian Bartley. We brought enough for you too, by the way."

"Lily, Ian, this is Chris Johnson. He arrived a few minutes ago. I was just showing him his room."

"Nice to meet you, Chris," Ian said as he shook Chris's offered hand.

"Pleasure's mine. I'm a fan," Chris announced. He and Danielle now stood in the foyer with Ian and Lily.

Ian raised his brow, silently asking, *Really?*

"It seems as if Mr. Johnson—" Danielle began.

"No, it's Chris, please," Chris interrupted.

Danielle smiled and then continued, "Seems *Chris* came across most of those online articles about Marlow House, which I assume includes the articles by Ian."

"I confess I did a little Internet stalking to find out that Jon Altar is actually a pen name for Ian Bartley," Chris admitted.

"I hope when you say *stalking*, you mean it in the most benign way," Lily said, only half teasing. She lifted the sack back in the air again and motioned for the three to follow her to the kitchen, which they did.

Lily paused just before she reached the kitchen door and turned to Ian. "Why don't you take Chris into the dining room, and Dani and I'll get some plates and bring out the food."

"I don't want to take your food," Chris said. "I had something to eat in Portland."

"Oh, don't be silly." Lily grinned. "When you see what we brought, you'll want some. Like I said, we brought plenty."

"OH MY GOD, he's freaking gorgeous!" Lily said when she and Danielle were alone in the kitchen.

Danielle chuckled. "Yeah, he is rather hot."

"Hot? Oh please, talk about the understatement of the century. Where did you find him?"

Danielle opened an overhead cabinet and took out four plates, setting them on the counter. "I didn't find him. He's a guest, Lily, not some guy I ordered from a dating service."

"Well, duhh, I know that. But dang, girl, is he an actor or something? Underwear model?" Lily opened the sack and began removing the cartons of Chinese takeout.

Danielle giggled. "Underwear model? Yeah, I could so see that. I wouldn't mind seeing him in—"

"Is this any way for two young ladies to act?" Walt reprimanded when he suddenly appeared in the kitchen. "Lily should be ashamed of herself. I thought she promised her heart to Ian."

"Look out, Lily, Mr. Prim and Proper just popped in and does not approve." Danielle giggled again as she opened a drawer and pulled out some silverware.

"Walt?" Lily glanced around the room.

"Who else?" Danielle shrugged.

"I really don't understand young women these days." Walt paced the room in a fit of agitation.

"You're doing it again," Danielle reminded him.

"He's doing what?" Lily glanced around, wishing she could see and hear Walt.

"He's rewriting the good old days—when women were proper and buttoned down and would never consider peeking at a hunky guy wearing just his boxers." Danielle tossed the silverware onto the counter with some napkins.

"Didn't Walt live during the Roaring Twenties?" Lily asked.

"*Exactly.*"

Walt stopped pacing and looked at Danielle. "Well, he isn't *that* good looking."

Danielle looked over at Walt and cocked her brow. "Seriously? You can stand there and say that with a straight face? Even if I put a sack over his head, he would still look great—those broad shoulders; he's obviously athletic. The perfect height, not too tall."

"That's just because you're short," Walt spat.

"*Humpf.* That was not nice."

"What did he say?" Lily asked.

Ignoring Lily's question, Danielle said, "He sort of has that boyish hunky look going for him. Sandy-colored hair that needs a trim, vivid blue eyes, nice smile. Good teeth. Rather yummy."

Narrowing his eyes, Walt glared at Danielle. "As you know, Angela was quite beautiful. Some said a beauty beyond compare."

"Your point?" Danielle asked.

"I married her, Danielle. How did that work out for me?" Walt disappeared.

Danielle let out a sigh and glanced around the kitchen. Walt was gone.

"What is it?" Lily asked.

"Walt was just reminding me that even the prettiest face can have a black and ugly heart."

"True…" Lily picked up the tray holding the cartons of Chinese food. "But it's still fun to look."

SIX

"Who's that?" Chris asked when Danielle showed him through the library after dinner. He stared up at the massive portrait —an obvious likeness to the resident ghost. He glanced from the portrait to the spirit lingering nearby, watching him.

"Walt Marlow," Danielle said as she stepped up to the portrait, standing next to Chris. She looked up at the painting.

"He's the one who was murdered in the attic?" Chris asked, glancing over to Walt, who continued to stare in his direction.

"Yes. His grandfather built this house—founded Frederickport." Danielle glanced briefly from the portrait to Walt. "His grandfather was Frederick Marlow."

"Kind of a nerdy-looking guy, wasn't he?" Chris remarked.

"What does he mean by that?" Walt scowled.

"Umm…no…I don't think so," Danielle stammered. She glanced nervously to Walt and back to his portrait.

"Maybe it's just that suit he's wearing. The way he's standing. Rather effeminate."

"What in the hell is *that* supposed to mean?" Walt roared.

"I don't see that at all," Danielle said.

The corners of Chris's mouth twitched; he resisted the urge to laugh. "And the woman? Is that his sister?"

"No. It was his wife, Angela Marlow. She was killed the day before he was murdered, by a hit-and-run driver."

32

"Walt Marlow is also the one who stole the Missing Thorndike," Ian said from his place on the sofa, where he sat with Lily, sharing a plate of homemade cookies.

Lily, who was no longer munching on cookies, listened attentively to Chris's comments about Walt, her eyes nervously darting about the room.

"The way you say that makes me sound like some sort of common thief," Walt grumbled before summoning up a cigar. "And what does he mean I look effeminate? If he's not careful, I'll knock him off his block and show him effeminate!"

Still standing in front of the portrait, Chris's gaze moved from the painting to Ian and then to Walt Marlow's spirit. By Ian's and Lily's body language and reaction to Walt's presence, Chris surmised that neither one could see Walt, yet it was obvious Danielle could.

Curled up under Walt's feet was Sadie, Ian's golden retriever. Chris had already heard Walt issue verbal commands to both Sadie and Danielle's cat, Max. By the animals' reactions, he was certain they too could see and hear Walt, which didn't surprise Chris. Nor was he surprised the animals understood the spirit—and the spirit understood the animals—on a level superior to normal human animal interaction. He had witnessed that before.

"Damndest thing," Ian said abruptly. All heads turned in his direction.

"What?" Lily asked.

"Can you smell that, Chris?" Ian asked.

"Smell what?" The only thing Chris noticed was Walt's cigar smoke.

"Sometimes, I swear I smell cigar smoke in this house," Ian explained. "It comes and goes."

Chris looked over to Ian, where he sat on the sofa with Lily. He caught a brief exchange between Lily and Danielle—Lily, while popping a piece of cookie in her mouth, flashed an impish grin to Danielle.

"Yes, I think I smell something," Chris finally admitted. *I'm not sure if I'm more surprised over the fact Ian can smell the cigar smoke or the fact Lily obviously knows something. I don't think she can see him…Whatever it is, I hope it doesn't interfere with what I came here to do.*

Danielle walked to the sofa, snatching the now empty plate from Lily. "You know these old houses, funny smells." She set the empty plate on the desk and took a seat on one of the two empty chairs facing the sofa.

"Funny smells," Walt scoffed. "I prefer to think of it as my way of making my presence known."

Chris stepped away from the portrait, a slight smile on his face as he sat in the empty chair next to Danielle.

Ian's interest in the sporadic whiffs of cigar smoke quickly dissolved when Lily changed the direction of the conversation and asked Chris what he did.

"I enjoy sailing," Chris said with a smile. He glanced from Ian and Lily to Danielle.

"I think she was asking what you do for a living," Walt said. He moved to the sofa and sat on one of its arms, facing Chris. "You avoided that question earlier when Ian asked it in the dining room."

"I dream of sailing sometimes," Danielle said.

"Don't change the subject," Walt scolded. "Find out what he does for a living. If you insist on welcoming strangers into the house, you need to at least try to learn as much as you can about them."

"Have you ever been sailing?" Chris asked Danielle.

"Only in a dream I had once—it seemed real—but no, I've never actually been sailing." Danielle sighed and leaned back in her chair.

"It felt real to me too, Danielle. Isn't that all that's important?" Walt asked in a soft voice.

Chris frowned, suppressing the urge to stare at Walt. *What was he talking about? It felt real? What does he mean—that's all that's important?* Instead, he said, "Until this morning I was living on a sailboat."

"You live on a boat?" Lily perked up.

"Well, I did. For the last six months, down at Dana Point. It was a friend's boat. He sold it, so time to move on."

"The man is homeless," Walt said with a scowl.

"I'm afraid I'd get seasick," Ian said.

"I have to say, I never slept better than I did on that boat. It was probably the movement on the water."

"Sort of like being rocked to sleep?" Danielle teased.

Chris smiled over at Danielle. "Yeah, pretty much."

"Oh please, Danielle, are you flirting with him?" Walt stood up and shook his head. "I don't know why you and Lily think he's so good looking. He's nothing special. You need to listen to what he's saying. The man is homeless. I bet he doesn't have a job."

"Will you be returning to Dana Point after the holidays?" Danielle asked.

Chris shook his head. "No, time to move on."

"So you don't have a job you have to go back to?" Lily asked.

Walt smiled. "Good girl, Lily, at least you know how to ask the right question. Let's see what he has to say about that."

Smiling at Lily, his eyes darting to the end of the sofa where Walt sat, Chris shook his head. "I have no reason to return to Dana Point."

Danielle stood up. "Why don't we take this discussion in the living room? We have that beautiful tree in there, and it seems a shame not to enjoy it."

Fifteen minutes later, they sat in the living room. Pine scent from the fresh-cut tree filled the air, triggering memories of Christmases past and overshadowing evidence of Walt's cigar smoke. Danielle poured them each a glass of wine and had just finished serving the beverages when the doorbell rang. She went to answer it, taking her glass with her.

When Danielle opened the door, it was Heather Donovan, her neighbor from down the street, standing on the doorstep. The young woman wore her long black hair pulled into two buns instead of pigtails, the ends of her hair sticking out of the buns like jagged swords. Clad in a bright green sweat suit, Danielle thought she looked like a cast member from *Grinch*.

"Merry Christmas!" Heather greeted her, holding up a small colorful foil sack.

"Merry Christmas to you too!" Danielle returned, raising her wineglass in mock salute. "Please, come in!"

"I wanted to stop by and bring you this," Heather said as she stepped into the house and handed Danielle the sack.

"A gift? How sweet. Would you like a glass of wine?"

"I'd love one." Heather hesitated a moment and asked, "Do you have company? I don't want to just barge in."

"It's just Lily and Ian and our new guest. Please, come join us." Danielle led the way back to the living room, now carrying the gift sack and glass of wine.

Once in the living room, both Ian and Chris stood up. Danielle was about to introduce Heather to Chris when Heather cocked her head to one side and interrupted by saying, "Do I know you?" She stared at Chris.

"I…I don't think so," Chris said hesitantly. He then added with a bright smile, "I'm sure I would remember you."

"This is our neighbor Heather Donovan. Heather, this is our guest Chris Johnson."

Heather shook her head. "No, that's not right."

"You aren't Heather Donavon?" Chris asked with a mischievous grin.

"No, I'm Heather Donovan," Heather said seriously. "But you… no, the person I'm thinking of…Chris…no, not Johnson."

Ignoring Heather's puzzled expression, Danielle poured her neighbor a glass of wine and handed it to her, directing her to an empty chair. Heather pointed to the sack Danielle had left on the table while pouring the wine. "Open it," she urged.

"It seems Heather came bearing gifts," Danielle said when she picked up the sack.

"It's actually for Marlow House," Heather explained as she took a sip of her wine.

Danielle pulled an electrical gadget from the sack and looked at it.

"It's a diffuser," Heather explained. "You fill it with water and then add a few drops of essential oil—look in the sack, you'll find a bottle of oil."

Danielle set the diffuser on the table and then pulled out a small vial of oil from the bottom of the sack. She looked at it, reading the handwritten label.

"My sister uses essential oils." Lily spoke up. "When we were there for Thanksgiving, she used one of those with a holiday fragrance, smelled a little like scented candles."

"This is to get rid of any spirits," Heather explained.

"Spirits?" Chris spoke up, unable to resist his impulse to glance over at Walt, who sat silently on the edge of the sofa's armrest.

Heather nodded. "These old houses sometimes attract spirits that just don't want to move on. I figure you can never be too careful. It's my own blend. I was going to use it on…well…that turned out not to be necessary…so I figured you might want to use it here at Marlow House, just in case." Heather smiled.

"Umm…well…thanks…" Danielle slipped the bottle back in the sack.

"Go ahead, try it now," Heather urged.

"What did I ever do to her?" Walt grumbled.

"I think maybe later." Danielle glanced over to Walt. "I know essential oils typically have their own unique scent, and I'm really enjoying the Christmas tree. Puts me in the holiday spirit."

"Oh…of course…well, you can try it later." Heather smiled and took another sip of her wine. She looked over at Lily. "Are you going to spend Christmas with your family?"

"No." Lily shook her head. "Ian and I went down there for Thanksgiving. But we're going to spend Christmas here, and Ian's sister's going to join us. She'll be here on Christmas Eve."

"That's nice…having family…" Heather looked down in her wineglass.

"Heather, you're more than welcome to spend Christmas with us," Danielle told her.

"I appreciate the offer, but I'm going to spend Christmas in Vancouver with some friends. That's one reason I stopped by. I wanted to let you know I won't be able to make your open house. I'll be gone through the New Year."

———

CHRIS FELT as if he and Danielle had a chaperon—*Walt Marlow.* Not long after Heather said her goodbyes and left, Ian and Lily made an excuse that they were going back to Ian's house to watch a movie. Chris suspected they weren't actually going to watch a movie, but wanted to be alone.

Sadie left with Ian and Lily, while Max napped under the Christmas tree. Chris helped Danielle carry the dirty dishes and glasses back to the kitchen while Walt silently trailed behind them, occasionally interjecting with negative comments about Chris.

"So tell me, what's the story with Heather? Essential oils to ward off ghosts?" Chris took a seat at the kitchen table and tried to ignore Walt's presence, focusing his attention on Danielle.

"Well…" Danielle squirted a little soap into a wineglass as she considered her answer.

"This should be good." Walt chuckled. "Although I'm not sure why she thinks Marlow House needs her voodoo. It's not like she can see me like she did him."

"I'm surprised she didn't mention it when she was here," Danielle went on. "But Heather's working on a book—I guess you might call it a real-life ghost story."

Chris lifted his brows. "Ghost story?"

"She inherited an old house—a couple blocks away from here. Locals call it Presley House, and some claimed it was haunted."

"Haunted?"

Walt laughed. "I love how you tell the story as if it were just a legend. That crazy ghost almost got you killed in that fire."

"I went over there, managed to get myself trapped in a hidden room—and then Lily came looking for me, and she got trapped. Some teenagers broke into the house for a Halloween prank and ended up burning the place down after one of them was careless with a candle. Had Heather not shown up when she did…"

"Oh my god, that sounds horrible. Were you hurt?"

"Nothing major."

"So what is this about a ghost?" Chris asked.

"Heather's writing all about it. Basically she claims those old stories were true—the house was haunted and that she saw the ghost just before the house burned down."

"Did you or Lily see it?" Chris asked.

Danielle's gaze shot up and looked Chris in the eyes. "Of course not. I can't see ghosts."

SEVEN

Sadie's barking brought Ian into the living room. There he found the golden retriever's wiggling butt sticking out from under the curtain's hem, her tail wagging wildly while the rest of her remained hidden as she looked out the front window.

"Sadie, what's all the commotion?" Ian grabbed hold of the curtain and yanked it open so he could look outside. It was Saturday morning—five days until Christmas.

Ian glanced up and down the street, yet saw nothing to warrant the dog's enthusiastic outburst. Giving a little whistle, Ian made a snapping gesture with his fingers. Reluctantly, Sadie stopped barking and sat down, her tail still wagging. She looked up at Ian and then back out the window.

"I still don't see what you're barking at." Ian looked up and down the street. There were no cars parked nearby, aside from his, which was in the driveway, and Chris's rental car parked across the street. There were no walkers or joggers in sight, no stray animals.

Looking over at Marlow House, he smiled when he spied the Christmas wreath hanging on the front door. He thought about how the Christmas lights had looked the night before. He had helped Lily hang a half a dozen or more strands of lights on the mansard roofline of Marlow House before they took off for California to spend Thanksgiving weekend with Lily's family.

Sadie let out a little whimper, distracting Ian from his thoughts of Christmas decorations and reminding him that she had been barking just moments before. Ian, still holding onto the curtain as he held it to one side, glanced down at his dog.

"What is it, Sadie? Was it Max? Did you see him outside? Is he tormenting you?" Ian smiled and then looked back up out the window. To his surprise, he saw a woman standing at the gate of Marlow House, a suitcase in her hand. Ian frowned. "Where did she come from?" He looked up and down the street again. Since there were no cars parked nearby and he hadn't seen a vehicle drop her off, the only explanation he could come up with was that she had arrived by foot. Yet he couldn't understand how he could have possibly missed seeing her walking up the street toward Marlow House. He had only looked away for a split second. Scratching his head in confusion, he released hold of the curtain and let it fall back in place.

"I think I need a cup of coffee."

DANIELLE STEPPED out into the hallway from the dining room and took a deep breath. She loved the smell of Christmas—pine trees, cookies, and cinnamon. Closing her eyes for a moment, she thought about her late husband, Lucas. How couldn't she? After all, today was the first anniversary of his death. He had died last year on December 20—killed in a car accident with his lover.

She heard Lily's laugh coming from the dining room. Opening her eyes, Danielle glanced back toward the sound. Lily and Chris lingered with Joanne at the dining room table. They had just finished breakfast. Danielle suspected they were sampling the pastry tray she had left on the table, while they had more coffee.

If Lily remembered today was the anniversary of Lucas's death, she hadn't mentioned it. Danielle suspected her friend did not want to put a damper on her Christmas spirit. After all, Danielle had once believed it would be impossible for her to ever again enjoy her favorite holiday.

The pain she had experienced last Christmas was excruciating and she honestly believed she would never again decorate a Christmas tree or bake her grandmother's Christmas cookies. But then, she had moved into Marlow House and something inside her had changed. It was as if she had come home, and all she wanted to do was fill the house with laughter and love. She wanted to celebrate life. Danielle wanted Christmas back.

She forgot why she had come into the hallway and was about to return to the dining room when she heard the doorbell ring. Thinking it was a little early for her next guest to arrive, she wondered if it was Ian, and then she wondered why he hadn't simply entered through the side gate as he normally did.

When Danielle opened the front door a moment later, she found not Ian standing on the front porch but a young woman, suitcase in hand. Danielle had three more guests arriving that day—one was a man, who obviously wasn't the person standing at her door. Another was a woman, yet that woman had a seven-year-old daughter, and not only was there no little girl in sight, this woman didn't look old enough to have a seven-year-old child. Not unless she was thirteen when she'd had her.

"Hello, how can I help you?" Danielle asked.

"This is Marlow House, right?" The woman held up her hand; in it was a crumbled piece of newspaper. Danielle immediately recognized it. It was the ad she had placed in an Oregon paper for Marlow House, advertising an old-fashioned, traditional Christmas holiday.

"Yes, it is. How can I help you?"

"I'm here for the old-fashioned Christmas holiday." She handed the crumpled paper to Danielle and started to walk into the house.

"I'm sorry," Danielle said, handing the paper back. The woman froze. "But we're all full for the holiday."

Tears filled blue eyes as the woman shook her head in denial. "No, please, you have to have a room. I have nowhere else to go. I can pay. Honest."

Danielle peeked her head out the door and looked toward the street. The only car she saw was Chris's rental car.

"How did you get here?" Danielle asked. "Where's your car?"

"I was dropped off. Please, I won't take much space. You can put me anywhere. I'll sleep on the couch."

"I'm really sorry, but all our rooms are taken. I'm sure I can get you a room at one of the hotels. They're usually not busy this time of year."

"You don't understand." The woman shook her head again. "It's Christmas, and I don't want to spend it alone. Not again. Not this year. I saw your ad, and I thought…well, maybe this year will be different. Maybe this year I won't be alone."

The woman's heartfelt words felt like a slam to Danielle's gut. Staring into her blue eyes, Danielle thought for a moment she was looking at herself. She understood the woman's pain—her loneliness.

Impulsively, Danielle said, "There's a sofa bed in the attic. But you'd have to walk down the stairs to use the bathroom at night."

"That would be perfect!"

"And it isn't very comfortable. I had it in my house before I moved here, so…"

"Oh, that's fine! I can sleep anywhere, I promise. You don't know how much this means to me!"

Danielle opened the door wider, welcoming the woman in. "My name is Danielle Boatman. I'm the owner of Marlow House."

"Nice to meet you, Danielle. Can I call you Danielle?" Now in the entry hall, the woman set her suitcase on the floor and looked around.

"Yes, and you are?" Danielle closed the front door.

"My name…my name is Anna Williams."

"You're putting someone in the attic?" Walt asked when he appeared a moment later.

Ignoring Walt, Danielle pointed toward the living room. "Why don't you wait by the Christmas tree and I'll have Joanne prepare the room for you."

"Thank you, that would be wonderful."

"And then we can go into the parlor, and I'll check you in."

"Thank you, Danielle. You have no idea how much this means to me."

"I think I'll keep an eye on this one," Walt muttered as he followed the woman into the living room.

CHRIS WAS on his way back to his room when he glanced into the living room and spied Walt sitting on a chair, watching a young woman. She sat quietly on the sofa, glancing around the room, oblivious to the fact she was being watched by Marlow House's resident ghost.

Stepping into the room, he called out, "Hello, you must be the new guest Danielle said would be staying in the attic…" He paused when she looked his way and their eyes met. He knew those eyes.

"Hello, and you are?" she asked.

Chris stepped closer and extended his hand. "Chris…Chris Johnson. And you are?" They briefly shook hands.

"I'm Anna Williams. Are you a guest here too?"

"Yes, yes, I am." Chris forced a smile.

"I suppose we're all going to spend Christmas together. Won't that be nice?" Anna smiled at Chris.

The sound of a bell jingling came from the direction of the Christmas tree. They both looked toward the sound and watched as Max leisurely strolled out from beneath the branches of the evergreen.

"A cat?" Anna asked.

"Meet Max," Chris introduced.

Walt looked down at the cat Anna was now petting. "Yes, Max, there is another one, and this one Danielle is putting in the attic. You know what that means? Right, it means I'm being kicked out of the attic during the duration of her stay. No, Danielle has asked me not to go into the guests' bedrooms when they're there. Privacy, Max. No, I can't be lurking in a woman's bedroom like some peeping tom."

Max responded with a loud meow.

"I wonder if he's hungry?" Anna asked.

"Come on, Max, let's go see the attic one last time—before she officially kicks us out."

The moment Walt vanished and Max strolled from the room, Chris leaned forward and hissed, "I know who you are, but why are you here?"

"Oh, Chris, you did recognize me! What was all that—"

"Listen to me, *Anna*. He could come back any minute."

"He?" Anna glanced around the room.

"You didn't see him?"

"What are you talking about? Him who?"

"It seems Marlow House has its own ghost, and I'm fairly certain Danielle Boatman can see and hear him. What I can't figure out is why didn't you see him?"

Anna looked around. "Are you telling me there was a ghost in here?"

Chris nodded. "He just left. So unless you want to ruin everything, you need to be careful because maybe you can't see him, but he can obviously see you."

Anna frowned. "This could complicate things."

"Fortunately, from what he was saying——"

"He was talking to you?"

"No. He was talking to the cat."

"But he doesn't have to talk out loud to communicate with the cat."

"Maybe not, but he obviously likes to think out loud. What I was about to say is I don't think he'll be going into the attic while you're there. Something about an arrangement he has with Danielle about the guests' rooms."

"Now that would really complicate things."

"You still need to be careful. What did you say to convince her to give you a room? She came into the dining room and asked Joanne—the woman who works for Danielle—to help her fix up a place in the attic for an unexpected guest. Joanne and Danielle's friend Lily seemed quite surprised Danielle was willing to let you stay in the attic."

Anna smiled. "Oh, it wasn't difficult to tap into her vulnerabilities."

EIGHT

Walt stood by the Christmas tree and watched Anna absently tap her right toe to the melody of "Rudolph the Red-Nosed Reindeer." She sat on the living room couch, flipping through the latest version of *Country Living Magazine.*

Christmas carols had been streaming nonstop through the living room speakers since Anna had checked into the attic room and returned downstairs. The volume was low enough that it didn't prevent conversation. Yet at the moment, Anna was alone in the living room, and there was no one for her to talk to. That wasn't entirely accurate—she wasn't alone. Walt was in the room with her, but she could neither hear nor see him, so conversation was out of the question.

The first time Walt had heard the song, he had asked Danielle about this Rudolph character. He had never heard of him before, which wasn't surprising, considering Rudolph was born about fourteen years after Walt died.

Anna began to hum along with the song as she tossed the magazine onto the coffee table and picked up another, beginning to flip through it. Walt couldn't put his finger on it, but he thought there was something a little odd about Marlow House's newest guest. She looked normal enough—a young woman whom he guessed was barely twenty years old, if that. It wasn't her appearance he found odd; though she was dressed rather conservatively for her generation, if he compared her attire to what he saw on television and in Lily's *People* magazines.

She was actually a pretty thing, with white-blond hair cut into soft curls falling to her shoulders and clear blue eyes. *Maybe it was her eyes*, he thought. It was the way they looked at Chris earlier. They reminded him a little of Angela's eyes—not how he first saw Angela—but later, after she had revealed her true nature. Walt found that disturbing.

He also wondered where she had come from. According to Danielle, Anna's ride had dropped her off in front of Marlow House, yet she couldn't quite explain who that ride was. As much as he tried, Walt couldn't get Danielle to see how peculiar it was—someone just being dropped at the front door without any prior arrangement and willing to take any room—even a sofa bed in the attic. All Danielle could see was a young woman all alone for the holidays.

Lunchtime had come and gone, and while Danielle had said the rooms only included breakfast and dinner, she had offered Chris a sandwich, which he had accepted. At the moment, Chris sat outside with Danielle on the back patio, talking. Judging from the way they were bundled up in jackets, Walt guessed it was cold outside and suspected the reason Danielle had invited Chris outside for hot tea and cookies was so that Walt couldn't listen in to their conversation.

Anna had declined a sandwich, saying she had eaten a big breakfast that morning. Walt was somewhat relieved to know the woman had already paid for her room—through New Year's Eve, with cash—and so far, she hadn't been peeking in drawers and closets, looking for something to pilfer.

Ian had taken Lily out for lunch, and they hadn't yet returned. Instead of leaving Sadie at Marlow House, Ian had left his dog at his house across the street. Walt hated when he did that. Max was upstairs, sleeping on Danielle's bed—the cat seemed to spend most of his life sleeping. Also upstairs was Joanne Johnson, attending to her housekeeping duties.

The sound of the doorbell interrupted Walt's thoughts. Anna stood abruptly, tossing the magazine back to the table as she looked toward the doorway and straightened imaginary wrinkles from her skirt with the palms of her hands. Walt wondered if Danielle would come inside now to answer the door, or would Joanne hear the doorbell and come downstairs to answer it?

A moment later, Anna dashed from the room. Walt followed her into the hallway and to the entry. Without hesitation, Anna opened the door.

Standing on the front porch was a young man, a suitcase by his side. Walt surmised this man was around Chris's age. *Does Danielle really need a houseful of men?* Walt asked himself in disgust.

Upon seeing the young man, Anna let out a gasp, her right hand flying to her mouth. "Bobby!"

Walt thought the man looked a little taken back by Anna's outburst. He stood there for just a moment staring at the woman when his frown quickly turned to a smile—one that seemed oddly fake to Walt. He said, "Umm, I'm Richard Winston. Are you Danielle Boatman?"

"Oh, no." Anna shook her head and nervously glanced behind her. "I'm Anna Williams. Danielle is outside, having tea with another one of the guests. But please, come in; I'll let her know you're here."

Anna showed the man to the living room and then rushed outside to get Danielle.

"YOUR ATTIC GUEST seems a little unstable. I think she just frightened your newest guest," Walt told Danielle as she and Chris walked into the kitchen from the outside patio, Anna by their side.

Danielle glanced over at Walt as they made their way through the kitchen.

"When Anna opened the front door, she acted like she knew him. Called him Bobby," Walt explained.

"Anna, have you tried one of Danielle's chocolate drop cookies?" Chris called out to Anna, who seemed intent to tag along with Danielle back to the living room.

Anna paused a moment and flashed Chris a questioning frown.

Lifting the lid off one of the cake pans sitting on the kitchen counter, Chris picked up a cookie and offered it to Anna. "Really, you must, they're amazing. They remind me of chocolate cake—but better."

Glancing from Danielle, who was just walking out the doorway, and back to Chris, Anna let out a sigh and walked over to the counter.

"What is it?" She looked at the cookie in his hand. "You know I don't want that."

Chris returned the cookie to the plate and covered it with the lid. He glanced to the doorway through which Walt and Danielle had just exited. "What did you do, *Anna*?"

"I didn't do anything. Richard is here. I want to go." Anna started to turn around toward the door when Chris stopped her.

"Didn't I tell you to be careful about what you say because you won't know if Walt Marlow is in the room."

"Is he here now?" Anna looked around.

"Of course not. I certainly wouldn't mention him if he was. But he could come back at any moment."

"I don't understand what the problem is, then," Anna said impatiently, anxious to go to the living room, where she had left the new arrival.

"You weren't alone when you answered the door and let Richard into the house. You obviously said something to make Walt suspicious, because he said something to Danielle just a moment ago."

Anna glanced down sheepishly then looked up to Chris. "I'm sorry. I guess I got excited when I first saw him—I couldn't help it."

"And that's one reason you shouldn't be here. You're too emotional. Too involved."

"I just want to see him...see her." Anna looked over to the door again.

"I'm beginning to wonder why I'm even here." Chris let out a sigh and took a seat at the table.

"You can't leave, Chris. I need you," Anna begged.

"I'm not going anywhere. But if I cough—that means he's in the room with us. So whatever you do, don't say anything you don't want reported back to Danielle."

"Okay, I promise. If you cough, I'll be on my best behavior. Can I go now?"

"In a minute. You need to understand that when I'm not with you, you have to always assume he's there watching you."

"I'll be more careful, I promise."

Chris stood up. "I have one more question."

"What's that?"

"How did you come up with the name Anna? Did you just pick it out of a hat or what?"

"It's my middle name."

"I thought your middle name was Ann."

"Close enough. I just think Anna sounds more feminine than Ann." Anna smiled.

By the time Anna made it back to the hallway, Danielle and Richard were no longer in the living room but halfway up the stairs leading to the second floor. Anna assumed Danielle was showing him to his room. Instead of following them upstairs, she went back to the living room.

<hr>

DANIELLE HATED ADMITTING Walt was right. There *was* something a little peculiar about her holiday guests. First, she assumed those coming to spend Christmas at Marlow House would be couples—maybe elderly couples who didn't have family to spend Christmas with or young couples who preferred not to spend Christmas with family. She certainly never imagined young singles would make up the majority of her guest list. She also never imagined they would stay for so long—registering the weekend before Christmas and staying through New Year's Eve.

One perk—something that seemed to annoy Walt—was that both male guests were pleasing to the eye. Maybe not to Walt's eyes, but Danielle was fairly certain Lily would find Richard good looking. Not as hot as Chris, but frankly, who was?

Danielle found something peculiar—while Chris and Richard dressed nothing alike, how they dressed reminded her of her late husband, Lucas. Chris's manner of dress reminded her of the Lucas during their early years together, before the financial success of their marketing company. Back then, Lucas wore casual yet trendy clothes. His clothes didn't look as if they came off the discount rack, but neither were they pretentious.

Richard looked as if he shopped at the same stores as Lucas had —after the marketing company started making money and Lucas started spending more than they made.

"So what brings you to Marlow House for Christmas?" Danielle found herself asking as she opened the door to the bedroom Richard would be staying in. "Will you be visiting family or friends in Frederickport?"

Pausing at the doorway, Richard smiled at Danielle. "No, I don't have any family here. A friend of mine—Peter Morris—recommended Marlow House since I was coming to Frederickport."

Danielle stared at Richard for a moment before asking, "Peter Morris? Not the same Peter Morris from Earthbound Spirits?"

"Yes, are you familiar with the organization?" He walked into the bedroom, glanced around, and set his suitcase on the floor next to the bed.

Danielle followed him into the room. "Yes, a little."

Looking to Danielle, Richard's smile broadened. "I've known Mr. Morris for several years; he's a wonderful man, often misunderstood."

"Yeah…well…perhaps you didn't hear about the little issue the organization had regarding a deceased member's will?" Danielle immediately regretted the comment. *Learn to hold your tongue, Danielle. No reason to talk politics or religion with the guests, or to point out one of their friends should probably be behind bars.*

"I assume you're referring to Isabella Strickland? She was a friend of mine."

Danielle hadn't expected that. "You knew Isabella?"

"Yes. We first met when I joined Earthbound Spirits. We became close back when she was still active with the group. But then she began having doubts—something that's quite natural and part of the process."

NINE

I f the man at the car rental company was correct, Patricia should reach Frederickport by 6:30 p.m. According to the brochure, dinner was served from five to seven, so she hoped that meant she and Jessica could still get something to eat if she arrived before seven. While Jessica had recently eaten the last of the peanut butter sandwiches she had prepared for the trip, Patricia hadn't had any food since they had left home. *Home*; it wasn't exactly home anymore. They had no home.

With both of her hands on the steering wheel, Patricia glanced in the rearview mirror at her daughter, who sat in the backseat. It was dark in the car, so she couldn't see anything.

"How are you doing back there, kiddo?" Patricia called back to Jessica.

"Are we almost there?"

"Pretty soon, honey. You've been a really good girl on this trip."

"I wish you would've let me sit up in the front seat with you."

"I told you, it's safer for you in the backseat."

"Becky's mom lets her sit in the front in their car." Jessica squirmed in her seat, trying to loosen the seat belt.

"I guess Becky doesn't have a mean mom like you do," Patricia called back.

"Can I at least take my seat belt off?"

"What do you think?" Patricia spied the turnoff to Frederickport up ahead. They were almost there.

WALT WAS SERIOUSLY CONSIDERING USING his ghostly powers to turn off Danielle's Christmas carols—*permanently*. While her guests seem to be enjoying the festive tunes, he had been listening to holiday music since the first of the month. Fortunately, it was only playing in the living room, but unfortunately, that was where everyone was sitting, and if he retreated to the parlor or library to escape the music, he would miss the action. Walt had discovered he rather enjoyed observing the guests. People often behaved in the most peculiar fashion when they didn't know they were being observed. Walt wondered—*Does this make me a voyeur?*

Ian and Lily sat at a small table at the far side of the living room, playing cribbage—a game Walt had taught Lily. Anna and Richard sat in the two chairs facing the couch. Anna kept trying to engage Richard in conversation, yet he seemed preoccupied. Danielle sat with Chris on the sofa. Walt suspected Chris might be allergic to either Sadie or Max—or both, since the man always seemed to be coughing whenever Walt entered the room.

"Danielle, I noticed several Portland area phonebooks stacked up in the parlor, I wondered if they're current," Anna asked.

"No, I keep meaning to put them out to be recycled. But if you need a current phonebook for that area, there's one in the library."

"No, but I was wondering, can I have the old phonebooks?"

"Sure, I suppose so."

"Your Christmas tree is beautiful," Anna told her. "I can't remember the last time I had a live tree."

"We used to have artificial trees when I lived in California," Danielle explained. "Down there, live trees just died too quick."

"I love the smell of pine," Anna said.

"Me too," Danielle agreed.

"Your family?" Chris asked.

Danielle glanced to Chris. "My family what?"

"You said *we used to have artificial trees*—I wondered who you meant. Your parents?"

"No. My parents died a number of years ago—when I was still in college. I meant my husband and me."

"You're married?" Anna asked.

Danielle shifted uncomfortably on the sofa. "A widow."

"Oh, I'm sorry," Anna said. "How long's it been?"

Before Danielle could reply, Lily turned abruptly from her cribbage game and looked at Danielle. "Oh my god, Dani. I'm sorry. I didn't even think about what today was. It's the 20th, isn't it?"

"What's today?" Ian glanced from Lily to Dani.

"A year ago today, Dani's husband was killed in the car accident," Lily explained.

"I'm so sorry," Anna apologized. "I shouldn't have—"

The doorbell interrupted Anna's apology, sparing Danielle from enduring the uncomfortable shift in the conversation. Sadie, who had been napping by Ian's side, lifted her head and let out a short bark. Ian silenced her, telling her to stay. Danielle jumped up from the sofa and left to answer the door.

Walt followed Danielle into the hallway. "Why didn't you say something?" he asked as they headed toward the front door.

Danielle glanced over to him and then looked back to the open doorway of the living room, where Lily and Ian remained with her guests. "I suppose a part of me wanted to see if I could do it," she said in a whisper.

"Do what?" Walt frowned.

"Get into the Christmas spirit again. I used to love this time of year. But since my parents died, it's been harder and harder—and then last year—"

"I'm sorry, Danielle." Walt reached out to her, his hand passing through her wrist, yet not before she felt the briefest of contact. Danielle looked down at her wrist and then smiled sadly at Walt before making her way to the front door and opening it.

Standing at the front door was a tall, slender woman and a young girl. Several suitcases sat next to them on the porch. The woman, her blonde hair pulled back into a careless bun and held in place with a clip, looked to be in her mid-forties, perhaps younger. Red edged her tired blue eyes, and had she put on makeup that morning, it had since faded away.

Danielle's mother would have described her as *pleasant looking*, an expression she used when she felt a woman was neither homely nor a great beauty.

The girl by her side bore a remarkable resemblance to the mother—at least Danielle assumed it was the mother. However, the child was quite stunning, with brown eyes and raven-black hair curling wildly to her shoulders. By the child's mussed hair, it was obvious to Danielle the girl had recently been sleeping in the car.

"I'm hoping this is Marlow House. It's so dark out, and I didn't see a sign." The woman then glanced to a piece of paper in her hand. "But it does seem to be the right address."

"Yes, this is Marlow House. I'm afraid we don't have a sign yet. You must be Patricia Morgan?" Danielle opened the door wider.

The woman picked up the suitcases by her side. "Yes, and this is my daughter, Jessica."

"Welcome to Marlow House. I'm your host, Danielle Boatman."

Just as Patricia and Jessica stepped into the house, Sadie came racing out from the living room to greet the new arrivals.

Jessica's eyes widened when she spied the golden retriever charging in her direction. Instead of being afraid, she dropped to her knees and opened her arms while saying, "Oh! You have a dog!"

Without hesitation, Sadie accepted the child's invitation and in the next moment covered her face with kisses while Jessica wrapped her arms around Sadie, resting her head against the furry face.

"Jessica loves dogs. I was going to ask if she was friendly...but I guess that answers my question," Patricia said with a laugh.

"Sadie is the unofficial greeter around here." Danielle grinned. "And yes, she's friendly. We also have a cat, which is mentioned in the brochure. I figure it's best to let people know up front before they make a reservation, in case they have an allergy."

"I...I must have overlooked that when I read your brochure."

"Is there going to be a problem?" Danielle glanced from Patricia to the child, who was still loving on Sadie.

"Dogs don't bother me, but I'm allergic to cats."

"Oh my, we usually mention Max when someone makes a reservation. If it helps, I don't let Max in the upstairs guestrooms, where you'll be staying."

"I'll be fine," Patricia assured her. "As long as I don't pet or hold the cat, I'm usually okay."

"I'm really sorry about that," Danielle apologized, showing Patricia and her daughter into the parlor to check in.

After showing Patricia and Jessica to their room to leave their luggage and freshen up, she met them downstairs in the kitchen. The rest of the household had eaten dinner prior to Patricia and

Jessica's arrival. Instead of feeding the latecomers in the dining room, Danielle felt the kitchen was a cozier setting.

Forty-five minutes later, Lily found the three in the kitchen, sitting together at the table. Danielle and Patricia each sipped a cup of eggnog while Jessica finished up her dessert, a piece of homemade apple pie.

"I was wondering where you disappeared to," Lily said when she walked into the kitchen.

Danielle stood up from the table. "Lily, I'd like you to meet our new guests, Patricia Morgan and her daughter, Jessica."

"Hello, nice to meet you both," Lily greeted them, her eyes settling on Jessica. "What grade are you in, Jessica?"

"Second." Jessica smiled up at Lily, showing off a missing front tooth.

"No kidding? I teach second grade." Lily took a seat at the table.

"Are you staying here for Christmas too?" Patricia asked.

"Currently, I'm living here," Lily explained. She looked over to Jessica and added, "I suppose I should have said I used to be a second grade teacher. I had to take a leave for medical reasons, so I'm currently not teaching. But I hope to get back to it someday." Lily flashed Jessica a smile and gave her a wink.

"Patricia mentioned earlier that she's allergic to cats, so we need to make sure Max doesn't sneak into her room, like she did Chris's," Danielle told Lily.

"Chris?" Patricia asked.

"He's another guest here," Danielle explained. "He's staying in the downstairs bedroom, and that seems to be the only guest room Max loves to invade."

"I like cats. Where is he?" Jessica asked.

Danielle looked over to Jessica. "Last I noticed he was napping under the Christmas tree, which seems to be his new favorite place."

"I want to see the Christmas tree! And the cat!" Jessica pushed her plate aside and got off the chair.

Lily glanced over to Patricia, a concerned frown on her face. "I hope your friend mentioned the cat to you. He promised he would."

Patricia, who was still sitting down despite her daughter's energetic attempt to pull her from the chair so she could see the Christmas tree and cat, looked over to Lily. "Friend?"

"Yes, the one who made the reservation for you. I told him Marlow House had both a cat and dog—something we always tell people before they check in. Well, technically, Sadie doesn't live here, but this is her second home."

"I still don't understand what you're talking about. What friend?"

"Mom, please, I want to see the Christmas tree and cat!" Jessica tugged on her mother's arm.

"Shhh…in just a second, Jessica," Patricia scolded, looking back to Lily.

"The person who made the reservation for you and paid for the room. He explained it was for you and your daughter, and when I told him about the animals, he said that wasn't a problem. I asked him to please check with you; I have friends who can't even be in the same room with a cat. He promised he'd let you know, and if there was a problem, he'd call me back. I assumed that since we never heard from him again, there wasn't a problem."

"I don't know about any of that." Patricia shook her head. "I didn't know the person who made my reservation."

"What do you mean?" Danielle asked.

"I assumed you would know." Patricia glanced from Danielle to Lily. "I won my trip here."

"What do you mean you won your trip here?" Lily asked.

"Someone from Jessica's school put our name in for some drawing—the prize was a holiday getaway here—to Marlow House. I assume whoever made the reservation was from Benevolent Charities."

"Benevolent Charities? Isn't that the organization you asked me about when you called to confirm your reservation?" Danielle asked.

Patricia nodded. "Yes, I wanted to make sure it was legit. I called the Frederickport Chamber of Commerce, and they vouched for you. I asked you about the organization. I just figured you had some agreement with them to respect their anonymity."

"No." Danielle shook her head. "Until you mentioned the group on the phone, I had never heard of them before."

TEN

Danielle sat at a booth at Pier Café, eating lunch with Adam Nichols. It was Sunday afternoon, four days until Christmas.

"I was surprised you wanted to meet for lunch. Grandma tells me you have a full house." Adam picked up his burger and took a bite, his eyes still on Danielle, who sat across the booth from him, absently stirring her iced tea with a straw.

Danielle shrugged. "Everyone's been fed. They're all doing their own thing. Lily's at the house." *And Walt.*

"So what did you want to talk to me about? I don't think you asked me out to lunch to simply enjoy my company." Adam took another bite of his burger.

Danielle dropped the straw back into the glass and looked up at Adam and smiled. Picking up the glass, she took a sip from the straw. Setting the glass back on the table, she flashed Adam a smile. "Aw, come on, you know your grandma would be thrilled if we surprised her with a Christmas wedding."

Startled by Danielle's quip, Adam began choking on his food. Dropping his half-eaten burger to the plate, he grabbed his glass and took a swig of water while still struggling to breathe normally.

When he finally stopped choking, he looked across the table and glared at Danielle, who clearly found humor in his discomfort. "Hell, I haven't even seen you naked yet."

Danielle cringed. "Now you're just being gross."

"Hey, you started it!" Adam reminded her.

"Well, yeah, but if we can't find humor in your grandmother's matchmaking attempts…and anyway, wouldn't kissing come before getting naked? No wonder your grandmother is having such a hard time getting you married off. You don't seem to know the order of things."

"So are you saying you want to kiss me?" Adam asked with a grin.

"Eww, you're getting gross again." Danielle picked up her sandwich and took a bite.

"Okay, then tell me why you asked me to lunch today, or was it just to mock me? Destroy my fragile male ego?"

"Now you're almost making me feel guilty." Danielle set her sandwich back down on its plate. "I say almost because I know there's nothing fragile about your male ego."

"I think I'll take that as a compliment." Adam took a sip of his beer.

"Please do." Danielle grinned and then got serious. "I wanted to ask you something about Isabella."

"Isabella? What about her?"

"Did you get to know any of her friends from Earthbound Spirits?"

"A couple, why?"

"One of them is spending the Christmas holiday at Marlow House."

"Really?" Adam took another sip of beer.

"His name is Richard Winston; I wondered if you knew him."

"Richard or Rick?" Adam asked.

"He introduced himself as Richard, but he might go by the nickname Rick. Does it matter?"

"I remember meeting a Rick and a Richard that belonged to the group. I don't think I ever knew their last names. The group wasn't big on last names. I doubt Isabella even knew what they were. It had something to do with distancing themselves from their previous lives." Adam picked up his burger again and started eating.

"Well, he knew her last name. But that might just be because of everything that was in the press when her body was found."

"Describe what your Richard looks like."

"Well, *my* Richard looks about thirty-five. Nice looking, light blond hair, blue eyes, not quite six foot, on the thin side. Not the athletic type. Looks like he would be at home working on computers."

"Oh, you mean nerdy looking?"

"Nerdy? No, not at all. I said he was good looking. Dresses pretty nice too. On the expensive side."

Nodding, Adam picked up his napkin and wiped his mouth. "I know which one. He does go by Richard. From what I recall, he was from Bend, or maybe it was Grants Pass." Adam shrugged. "Whatever. Just remember he wasn't from Frederickport. Isabella used to drag me to some of their events—trying to convert me. I remember meeting him, if he's the same one I'm thinking of. Sort of quiet, got the impression he came from a wealthy family, yet never found out which family exactly. Not that I bothered checking him out. So what's he doing staying at Marlow House?"

"He came to stay for Christmas. According to him, Peter Morris recommended the place."

"If he's a member of Earthbound Spirits, his reason for staying at Marlow House has nothing to do with Christmas," Adam said.

"Why do you say that?"

"For one reason, they don't celebrate Christmas."

"They don't?"

Adam shook his head. "Nope."

"That time I met Morris and his sidekick, they explained what they believed. Now that you mention it, there was no mention of God per se, and certainly no mention of Jesus. So I don't know why I'm surprised."

Adam shrugged. "I remember Isabella had a hard time with that."

"What do you mean?"

"Christmas was her favorite time of year, and having to give up Christmas for her new religion was a little rough on her."

"Well, a lot of people who don't identify as Christians celebrate Christmas. And some people who identify themselves as Christians don't celebrate it. I suppose it means something different to everyone. So why couldn't she still have Christmas?"

"With Earthbound Spirits, denying Christmas is almost a show of faith. And members like Isabella, those who are reluctant to leave behind Christmas trees and other holiday traditions, are instructed to donate the money they would normally spend on Christmas to Earthbound Spirits. The rationale being, that money is being spent on helping guide other souls to their ultimate destination."

"If that money helps feed the homeless or starving children, then maybe they have something," Danielle said.

Adam laughed. "Earthbound Spirits never fed any starving people. That's not their gig. In fact, according to Morris, starving people are simply reaping what they sowed from their misdeeds in previous lives. And to interfere by feeding them—well, that spoils the lesson they're here to learn, and basically you would be interfering with their progress if you gave them food. Tsk-tsk."

"Are you serious?" Danielle frowned.

"Yep. Pretty much." Adam pushed his now empty plate to the edge of the table.

After a moment of silence Danielle asked, "Did you hear about Renton?"

"Yeah, I heard about it on the news. Never saw Clarence as the type to take his own life."

"That's pretty much what I thought too."

"Can't say I felt all that bad when I heard the news. After all, he did try to frame me for your cousin's murder. And I can't imagine you cried any tears for him yourself."

"No, but like you, I don't see him as someone who'd take his own life. Did you know he got involved with Earthbound Spirits?"

"Yeah, I remember hearing about that. I can't remember if you told me or if Grandma did."

"Apparently, Renton left his estate—what's left of it—to Earthbound Spirits."

"Interesting." Adam finished the last of his beer and then set his glass back on the table. "Maybe he did kill himself."

"Why do you say that?"

"Not only does Earthbound Spirits not believe in Christmas—they encourage suicide in some situations. Of course, that's not widely known outside the group. Morris tries to keep that little bit out of the press."

"They encourage suicide? In what situation? The terminally ill?"

Adam shook his head. "No. They believe we're here on this earth to learn lessons, and when we finally realize that's the purpose of this life, when we die, then we move onto the ultimate, more perfect life to live out our eternity. If we die without realizing that, we get reborn and do it all over again."

"Like the movie *Groundhog Day*?" Danielle asked.

"Pretty much."

"So once someone embraces Earthbound Spirits, they're encouraged to just end it and move on?"

"Yes…and no. They're taught that once they've embraced the *truth*, they have a responsibility to guide others to the same realization."

"Like missionaries?"

Adam nodded. "Of course, they're encouraged—quite rigorously—to leave whatever they have to Earthbound Spirits so the group can then go on to help more people discover the—as they call it—*eternal truth*."

"So what is this about suicide?"

"In certain situations, primarily when they can no longer help convert more people to Earthbound Spirits, they're free to move on. With Renton locked up in prison, there wasn't much he could do to help the group. So perhaps—if he sincerely believed—he figured it was his way of breaking out of prison and moving onto paradise."

"Why does that make me think of suicide bombers?"

"I suppose it's the same mentality."

"So what reason does Peter Morris have for sticking around? If he truly believes this, why doesn't he just call it a day and move onto the next world?"

Adam laughed. "Because Peter Morris, according to his devoted followers, is making the ultimate sacrifice. He's postponing moving onto paradise—something he could do by simply ending his own life here—but he chooses to stay in this imperfect world. I believe Isabella compared him once to the captain of a ship who makes sure all of the passengers get on the lifeboat before he does."

"I can't believe Isabella once fell for that." Danielle shook her head.

"You would have had to have known Isabella to understand."

I did know Isabella. Danielle picked up her tea and took a sip. *Of course, that was after she died.*

"If Richard didn't come to Marlow House to spend Christmas, why do you think he came? There are plenty of places to stay in Frederickport this time of year, without choosing one decked out for the holidays."

"Did he mention why he's in town? Visiting family, friends? Maybe some Earthbound Spirits function going on?" Adam asked.

"He said he didn't have any family in town. And he didn't mention doing anything specific while here."

"Didn't you say Peter Morris recommended Marlow House?"

"Yes, that's what he said."

Adam considered the question for a moment and then looked up at Danielle and smiled. "I can only think of one reason why he's here."

"Why?"

"He's here for you."

"For me?" Danielle frowned.

"If I'm not mistaken, Danielle Boatman, I believe you're about to get recruited by Earthbound Spirits."

"Recruited? Are you telling me Richard intends to convert me to his wackadoodle religion?"

"I would be sorely disappointed in you, Danielle, if he actually succeeded. But yes, I believe that's exactly what he intends to do. After all, you said yourself, Peter Morris recommended Marlow House. Morris doesn't go around giving travel tips unless there's something in it for him."

"Uggg…" Danielle slumped down in her seat.

"Richard admitted being friends with Isabella?"

"Yes, when I brought up the issue of the will. Of course, I didn't mention any names, but he knew who I was talking about."

"What did he think about that? The fact that his beloved leader tried to cash in on Isabella's death and fraudulently claim her estate."

"He obviously believes what Morris sold the court—that he didn't realize Isabella had made a new will leaving everything to her uncle."

"Whatever you do, don't say anything to Grandma about one of your guests being a member of Earthbound Spirits."

"Why?"

Adam chuckled. "Grandma would have an absolute fit. She's grown very fond of you, and if she thought you were in danger of being sucked in by that cult, she'd probably insist I drive her over to Marlow House so she could personally evict this Richard character. Trust me, you do not want to rile the protective-mother side of Grandma."

Danielle grinned at the thought.

Adam frowned. "Why are you smiling like that? I was serious."

"Oh, I know you were." *It's just sort of a nice feeling to know there's someone out there—someone beyond Marlow House—who actually cares what happens to me.*

ELEVEN

Lily was about to step out of the kitchen when she heard Jessica tell her mother, "But I'm hungry, Mom."

"I know, sweetie, but I don't want you to have any more cookies."

Jessica groaned. "But I didn't have any lunch. Can't we at least go get a hamburger?"

"That's why I wanted you to eat all your breakfast. I told you we only get breakfast and dinner here. We have to be careful with our money. But if you're hungry, I'll go to the store and pick up a loaf of bread and some peanut butter. I should probably do that anyway. That way I'll have something to give you for lunches."

"Mom, I'm sick of peanut butter!"

Lily stepped back from the kitchen door and then began whistling a Christmas tune before taking a step back toward the door again and bursting into the hallway.

"Hi!" Lily greeted them cheerfully, pretending to be surprised to find Patricia and Jessica standing in the hallway. "Have you seen Danielle?"

"I don't think she's back yet," Patricia told her. "She mentioned something about meeting someone for lunch."

"Oh darn," Lily groaned. "I forgot about that. I was hoping she'd want to split a sandwich with me." Lily then paused a moment and looked from Patricia to Jessica. "Hey, would one of you want to share a sandwich? I'm not really hungry enough to eat a whole one."

Jessica perked up. "What kind of sandwich?"

"Well, what's your favorite?" Lily asked.

"Grilled cheese."

"Wow, what a coincidence! That's what I was going to have. You want to have one with me?"

"Sure!" Jessica paused a moment and then looked up at her mother. "Can I, Mom?"

Patricia smiled. "Yes. But why don't you go wash your hands first."

Without another word, Jessica raced for the downstairs powder room to wash her hands.

"Thank you," Patricia told Lily when they were alone. "You heard us, didn't you?"

Lily shrugged. "No big deal. I was going to have lunch anyway. But you know, you're more than welcome to make Jessica sandwiches for lunch while you're here. We have plenty of cold cuts in the fridge, and Danielle doesn't mind. Honest."

Neither woman noticed Richard, who stood in the shadows of the hallway, listening to their conversation. Before Jessica returned from the powder room, he silently made his way back up the stairs.

An hour later, Jessica, who was no longer hungry, crouched down and peered under the Christmas tree. All she could see of Max was his golden eyes staring back at her.

"Here, kitty, kitty…" Jessica said for the third time, determined to coax the cat out from his hiding place.

"Come on, Max, be a sport. The kid just wants to say hello. She's not going to hurt you," Walt called out from where he lounged against the sofa, keeping an eye on Marlow House's holiday guests.

Max responded with a loud meow.

"Oh, come on, Max," Walt scoffed. "Don't exaggerate."

"Jessica, leave the poor cat alone. He'll come out when he wants to," Patricia scolded. She sat in a chair next to Anna while Chris lounged silently on the sofa, flipping through a magazine, seemingly oblivious to his surroundings. When no one was looking, he would peek over the top of the magazine and look over at Walt and then at the women.

Anna stared at Jessica. "Your daughter has such beautiful hair."

"Thank you. She gets that from her father."

Anna reached out, leaned toward Patricia, patted her knee, and then leaned back in the chair again. "It must be difficult for you, raising the child all alone."

Patricia shifted uncomfortably in her chair. She looked over at Anna. "Jessica is a good girl. I'm very blessed. But yeah, it's rough sometimes. And I hate knowing as each day goes by she forgets more and more about her father. He was such a good father."

"I didn't mean to pry." Anna glanced over to Chris, who looked at her and rolled his eyes before turning his attention back to the magazine.

Walt, who had moved to the other side of the room, caught the exchange and frowned. He turned to Chris and then looked over to Anna.

"What is with you two?" Walt asked. "Is there something going on?"

"I just understand how difficult it is to raise a child on your own. It's not easy, especially if you don't have any family support," Anna said.

Patricia tilted her head slightly as she studied Anna. "Do you have children?"

"Oh me?" Anna shook her head. "I was thinking of my mother. She raised me and my brother alone—after our father was killed in an accident. It wasn't easy on her—and when she died—well—there was no family to step up and help."

Patricia abruptly stood. "I think I'll go to my room for a while. I've a little bit of a headache coming on."

"I'm sorry, perhaps if you take an aspirin?" Anna suggested.

"Yes, I think I'll do that. Jessica, come."

Jessica looked up from her place on the floor. "I wanna stay down here."

"I'm sure she'll be okay." Anna flashed Patricia a smile.

"I don't want to impose on anyone," Patricia said. "Jessica, now."

Reluctantly, Jessica got up from the floor and went to her mother.

Chris set the magazine on his lap and looked over at Patricia. "I hope you feel better."

"I'm sure I will. The last few days have just been—well, a little overwhelming."

After Patricia and Jessica left the living room, Anna looked over to Chris. "I think I may have scared her off."

In response, Chris coughed into his fist. Anna's gaze moved around the room before she slumped back into the chair and closed her eyes.

Lily was just stepping out of the kitchen when she ran into Patricia and Jessica again. This time, Jessica was pleading with her mother to let her stay downstairs. She didn't want to go upstairs while her mother took a nap.

"Jessica, why don't you sit on the stairs for a moment. I'd like to speak to your mother for a second," Lily suggested.

Jessica looked to her mother, who gave a nod. With a heavy sigh, Jessica plunked down on a step. Propping her elbow on a knee, she rested her chin on a balled fist.

"I didn't want to say anything in front of your daughter," Lily began. "But I'd be more than happy to keep an eye on her while you take a nap."

Patricia glanced down the hallway toward the living room. "Anna made that offer…but well…"

"You really don't know Anna, right?"

Patricia nodded.

"I know you don't know me either, but I really was a second grade teacher—and I guess you could say I'm part of the staff here." Lily smiled.

"Can I ask you something?" Patricia asked.

"Sure."

"Why did you quit teaching?"

"I was in an accident a few months ago and had to give up my class—at least for this year."

"I really don't want to impose."

"Don't be silly. I'd be happy to keep an eye on her while you're upstairs. And anyway, there's a batch of cookies that needs decorating, and I was thinking of putting Jessica to work on them."

After Patricia went to her room, Lily took Jessica into the kitchen to decorate Christmas cookies. When Richard found Lily and Jessica at the kitchen table thirty minutes later, the two females were busy decorating cookies, yet judging by the evidence smeared on the young girl's face, not all of the frosting was staying on the cookies.

"Looks like you two are having fun," Richard greeted them as he walked to the table.

"I just hope Jessica doesn't get sick from all the frosting she's sneaking, or her mother might kill me." Lily laughed. In one hand she held a star-shaped sugar cookie and in the other a dull knife dripping with frosting.

Jessica, who sat across the table from her, spread white frosting over a cookie. She looked up at Richard and smiled. When her gaze met his, he froze a moment, unable to look away. Lily noticed Richard's sudden change of demeanor. "Is something wrong?"

Richard shook his head and glanced away from Jessica. "It was just something about her smile—her eyes. It reminded me of someone."

"Who?" Lily set the cookie down on a plate.

Richard shook his head again and sat down at the table. He grabbed a cookie, and instead of decorating it, he took a bite.

"Hey! You aren't supposed to eat them!" Jessica protested.

Lily laughed. "It's okay, that's what they're for."

"That's not what you told me," Jessica said with a pout.

"I told you that *after* you gobbled up two cookies," Lily reminded her.

Jessica giggled and resumed her cookie decorating.

"So who does she remind you of?" Lily asked again.

Richard shrugged. "Just someone I used to know. It's not important."

"Can I ask you something?" Lily asked.

"Sure, what?"

"Why aren't you spending Christmas with your family?"

Richard stood up. "Do you mind if I pour myself a glass of milk?"

"Help yourself. The glasses are up there." Lily pointed to one of the overhead cabinets.

"I don't have any family," Richard explained as he poured himself a glass of milk.

"No one?"

"My parents were killed in a boating accident about three years ago."

"I'm so sorry. No brothers or sisters?"

Richard shook his head. "It's just me. Like Danielle."

"What do you mean?"

"She's alone too. You mentioned last night her husband was killed last year, and she said something about losing her parents when she was in college."

"I suppose that's one reason Danielle wanted to stay open for the holidays—having people around to spend Christmas with instead of being alone."

"Christmas was never a big deal for me." Richard shrugged.

"Christmas was always a pretty big deal in my family. I don't think my mother was thrilled I decided not to come home for Christmas." Lily sighed.

"We don't have a home anymore," Jessica told them as she doused gold sprinkles over a frosted cookie.

"What do you mean?" Lily asked.

Jessica looked up from the cookie. "We don't have a home anymore. At least I don't think we do."

"I thought you and your mom lived in Arizona," Lily said.

Jessica shrugged. "Before we left, we had to put everything in our car. Mom said after Christmas we'd find someplace new to live."

"Where is your car?" Richard asked.

"At the airport. Back where we used to live." Jessica set her now decorated cookie on the platter and grabbed another one to frost.

"Did you live in a house?" Richard asked.

Jessica shook her head. "Mom called it an apartment. We moved in there after Daddy died. I don't care about moving. I didn't like it anyway. Mr. Beaumont's kids were mean."

"Who is Mr. Beaumont?" Lily asked.

"He's the one who told Mommy we couldn't live there anymore."

"Did you live with Mr. Beaumont and his kids?" Richard asked. Lily felt compelled to change the direction of the conversation, yet Jessica answered before she could say anything.

"No. They lived in an apartment downstairs with Mrs. Beaumont."

"He was your landlord?" Richard asked.

Jessica shrugged.

Richard stared at Jessica. "What about all your furniture?"

"I don't know. I don't think we could take it because it wasn't ours. Mom used to tell me I had to be careful with the furniture, or we'd lose our deposit."

"Let me get this straight," Richard said, sounding slightly annoyed. "You moved out of your apartment, stored all of your belongings in your car, and then went on vacation?"

"This really is none of our business," Lily said under her breath.

TWELVE

Patricia was back downstairs within the hour. Jessica had finished decorating cookies and was once again looking under the Christmas tree, trying to coax Max from his napping spot under the branches. The moment Patricia walked into the living room, Chris tossed the magazine to the coffee table and stood up.

Standing akimbo, Chris glanced around the room. "Who wants to join me for a walk along the beach?" he asked.

Patricia frowned. "Isn't it cold?"

"Nothing a jacket can't cure." Chris grinned. "Certainly, you didn't come all this way to stay inside the entire time? I understand Frederickport has some beautiful beaches."

Richard glanced at his watch. "Where's Danielle?"

Lily, who sat in a chair next to Anna, glanced up from the book she was reading. "She hasn't come back yet."

"Then I suppose I'll join you. Let me go grab my coat." Richard started for the door.

Chris looked at Patricia. "What about you and Jessica? A little fresh air will do you both some good."

"Oh, can we, Mom?" Jessica jumped up from the floor.

"Fine. But go run up to our room. Grab our jackets. And your gloves and hat. I put them in the top dresser drawer."

"I don't need a hat," Jessica protested.

"If you want to go for a walk on the beach, you do." Patricia pointed to the door.

With a sigh, Jessica raced from the room and headed upstairs.

"I think I'll go too." Anna looked over at Lily. "Are you coming with us, Lily?"

Lily shook her head. "No, I told Danielle I'd stay here until she comes back. Go, have fun. Come back with a good appetite; Danielle has a delicious dinner planned."

CHRIS AND ANNA trailed behind Richard and Patricia as they strolled down the boardwalk, heading toward the pier. Jessica ran ahead of the adults, periodically stopping and looking back, careful not to get too far ahead. It was decided they'd stay on the boardwalk when Richard realized sand would get in his shoes, and Patricia decided it was too cold for Jessica to remove her sneakers and walk on the beach.

"He's not with us," Chris whispered to Anna.

Anna glanced behind her and then looked at Chris. "I assume you're referring to Walt Marlow's ghost?"

Chris nodded. "He's been hanging out in the living room all afternoon, watching and listening."

"What is he, some type of ghost spy?" Anna asked under her breath.

"He suspects there's something going on between you and me."

Anna scowled. "Why? We haven't really said anything around him."

"I think he picked up on something, the way we look at each other, maybe."

"Nosey little spirit. He needs to mind his own business."

"Fortunately for me, he has a habit of thinking out loud, so it's easier to get a handle on him. Doesn't seem particularly threatening. I don't think he has any powers."

Still walking alongside Chris, trailing far enough behind Richard and Patricia that they couldn't hear their conversation, she asked, "Why do you say that?"

"For one thing, when I insulted him, he didn't retaliate."

"What do you mean insulted him?"

"I said something about him being nerdy."

Anna laughed. "You do realize the term nerdy was not in use when Walt Marlow was alive? If he's been confined to Marlow House since his death, which I suspect he has, I doubt he knows what that even means."

"Perhaps. But I also called him effeminate." Chris grinned.

"Do you think it's wise to provoke him?"

Chris shrugged. "I have to have some fun."

"No, you have to focus on what you came here to do," Anna reminded him.

"And you, *Anna*, are entirely too bossy."

"I thought you said I was a nag?"

"That too. Which is why I'm here. Anything to get you out of my life."

RICHARD BURIED his hands deep in his jacket's pockets, seeking warmth. He walked alongside Patricia as they headed toward the pier. He watched Jessica, who skipped ahead of them, zigzagging her way down the boardwalk, periodically stopping to investigate some treasure in the nearby sand—such as a feather, rock, or shell.

"Your daughter, she reminds me of someone," Richard told Patricia, his gaze fastened on the young girl.

"Oh really?" Patricia glanced at Richard for a moment and then looked at her daughter.

"It's driving me crazy."

Patricia frowned. "Why is that?"

"I just can't put my finger on it. Have you ever done that before? Seen someone who reminds you of someone else but can't remember who?"

Patricia shrugged. "I suppose. Occasionally, I see someone on television who looks familiar but can't place him."

"It's not just the way she looks—it's a feeling."

"I don't think I understand."

"I can't explain." Richard shook his head. "It'll come to me."

They walked in silence for a few more minutes when Richard said, "Jessica told me you moved out of your apartment before you came up here."

Patricia frowned. "She told you that? When?"

"For the record, I didn't initiate the conversation. You can ask

Lily. When they were decorating cookies earlier, she blurted out you two didn't have a home anymore. Said something about packing up everything and storing it in your car."

Patricia sighed. "She said that?"

"It isn't true?"

"Unfortunately, it is. I lost my job in November. I had hoped I would have found something by now." Patricia pulled the front of her jacket together and zipped it up.

"Don't stores usually do a lot of hiring for the holidays?"

"Yes, they do. But I didn't have anyone to watch Jessica, and if I paid a sitter, I would end up spending about as much as I made. At least with my old job at the preschool, I had school holidays off to be with Jessica."

"I know it's none of my business, but why did you come up here for Christmas? Wouldn't it have made more sense to spend your money finding a permanent home instead of going on vacation?"

Patricia chuckled. "Yeah, well, you have a point. But you see, coming up to Oregon to spend Christmas wasn't really my idea."

Richard frowned. "I don't understand?"

"I won this Christmas holiday—for Jessica and myself. So I figured what the heck? I needed someplace to stay for Christmas, and I couldn't afford to even buy a tree this year, so here I am. The prize included round-trip airline tickets, a rental car, a little cash to cover expenses and the gift tax, and supposedly there will be some gifts delivered for Jessica on Christmas. When I go home after New Year's, I'll have to find a new place for Jessica and myself."

"I didn't realize Marlow House had given away a holiday vacation."

Patricia shook her head. "I don't think they did. Danielle claims she knew nothing about it. And when I asked her about the charity sponsoring the prize, she said she had never heard of them before. But she did say someone had paid for our room at Marlow House— through New Year's."

After a moment of silence, Richard said, "I'm sorry about your job."

"Thanks. But we'll get by. Although, I have to admit, since my husband was killed, it's been pretty overwhelming, being the person solely responsible for my daughter's well-being."

"Don't you have any family?"

"No. I wasn't much older than Jessica when I lost my mother. She was pretty much it."

"And your father?"

"He died a few years before Mom. I suppose one of my greatest fears is history repeating itself."

"How so?"

"After my father was killed, there was only Mom. When she died —well, there was no family to take me in."

"What did you do?"

"I went into the foster care system. I was too old to be adopted —although, if I'm honest, part of that was my fault."

"How in the world could it be your fault? You just said you weren't much older than Jessica. You were just a child."

Patricia laughed bitterly. "Oh, I had some major issues. I did not want to be adopted. I had other things on my mind."

"Other things?"

Patricia smiled ruefully. Staring ahead at her daughter, who continued to run and skip her way to the pier, Patricia wiped the corners of her eyes, preventing any unshed tears from escaping. "That's all in the past."

Forcing a smile, she looked at Richard and said, "So tell me about your family. Why did you come to Marlow House for Christmas?"

"My parents died a few years ago."

"I'm so sorry. Do you have any brothers or sisters?"

Richard shook his head. "There was only room for one child in my parents' life."

"Does this mean you were spoiled?" Patricia grinned.

"I suppose I was. Never wanted for anything."

"It must be hard on you, with them gone now and having to spend Christmas with strangers."

"My family wasn't big on Christmas. Oh, we celebrated it, but it was never about family."

"Christmas was a big thing when I was growing up. Even after my father died. That was one of the many things I missed when I went into foster care. Christmases with my family. Which is why when I got married and had Jessica, I tried so hard to make Christmas special, like it was when Mom was still alive."

"And now you have to spend it with strangers. I'm sorry."

Patricia shrugged. "I'm grateful we aren't spending it in our car

—seriously. And Marlow House is beautiful. I love the way Danielle has it decorated. So far, Jessica hasn't complained about not having her own tree. She seems fine with sharing the one at Marlow House."

"I think she also enjoyed decorating those cookies today." Richard laughed.

ANNA NODDED toward Richard and Patricia. "Those two seem to be getting along."

"I noticed that. Richard was in the kitchen when Jessica was decorating cookies with Lily."

"I think Patricia looks older than her years," Anna whispered. "That troubles me."

"She's had a rough couple of years," Chris reminded her.

"She's had a rough life."

"Maybe. But it looks like she turned out all right. She seems like a good mother. Jessica appears to be happy and loved. A well-behaved kid."

"What do you think about Richard?" Anna asked.

"He's not particularly talkative. I tried to get him into a conversation earlier, but he didn't say much."

"Doesn't seem to be having a problem talking with Patricia."

"No, no, he doesn't. Maybe he just prefers women."

Anna laughed. "Or perhaps you're better at getting women to talk to you than men."

Chris grinned. "That's a possibility."

"Speaking of women…"

"Were we speaking of women?" Chris asked.

"What do you think about Danielle Boatman?"

"She's not bad to look at."

"Is that all?"

Chris frowned. "Why are you asking?"

"I just thought, well, you two obviously have a lot in common."

"Are you suggesting I have some personal interest in her?"

Anna shrugged. "Maybe. I saw how you were watching her."

"What do you mean *watching her*?" Chris scoffed.

"Just differently than you watch other women—like Lily, Patricia…or me."

THIRTEEN

Danielle was sitting on her bed with the laptop when she heard a knock on her door. She had become accustomed to keeping her bedroom door locked, not just when she was downstairs but also in the evenings when she went to bed. Before she had time to move her laptop to one side and get out of bed, Walt appeared and announced it was Lily at the door.

Settling back in her bed, Danielle looked up at Walt. "Would you mind letting her in?"

In the next moment, Danielle's bedroom door slowly opened. Lily stood at the doorway for a moment and looked around before stepping inside and shutting the door behind her.

Lily approached the bed. "I assume Walt's in here?"

"No, why would you think that?" Danielle asked innocently.

Lily rolled her eyes. "Funny. Then that's a neat trick with the door."

Danielle giggled. "Yeah, he's over there, sitting on the couch."

"Evening, Lily," Walt greeted her, not expecting a reply since Lily could neither see nor hear him.

"That was a great dinner. You outdid yourself." Lily sat on the edge of the bed and looked over at the computer screen. "Whatcha doing?"

"Figured I would do a little online sleuthing. I'm a little curious about a few of our guests."

Lily chuckled. "They all seem nice enough. What are you getting all Nancy Drew about?"

"We haven't had much time to talk since the guests started arriving. Did you know Richard is a member of Earthbound Spirits?"

"Seriously? He doesn't seem the type, although he dresses pretty nice, kind of like those guys who came to talk to me. Is he one of the higher-up muckie mucks?"

Danielle shook her head. "I don't think so. Adam remembered him, and according to Adam, Richard comes from money. Dressed like that back then. He was sort of on the same level as Isabella. But of course, that's been over a year ago, so I suppose he could be."

"What's he doing here?"

"Adam suspects he's here to convert me—because of my money. I guess that group doesn't celebrate Christmas."

"Interesting…I heard Richard singing along with the Christmas carols; he complimented the tree. And this afternoon he even decorated a couple cookies."

Danielle shrugged. "I suppose even nonbelievers—or those who don't celebrate Christmas—could still do those things. Christmas carols aren't necessarily religious, and I have a few Jewish friends who put up trees. And decorating cookies isn't exclusively a Christmas thing."

"True…I don't think I told you, but a while back I looked online to see what I could find on Earthbound Spirits, and I came across something I thought was funny."

"What's that?"

"I can't remember her name—she was a medium—explaining what a ghost is…" Lily glanced over to the sofa. "No offense intended, Walt."

"None taken," Walt countered.

"According to this medium, a ghost is an earthbound spirit."

"That makes sense to me," Danielle said. "But that's not how the group uses the term."

"You're right. I found Earthbound Spirits—Morris's organization—online, and they say we are all spirits trapped in a physical body. I believe he calls it our earthly vessel or something like that. In fact, he denies the existence of ghosts or any spirits like Walt."

"What exactly does that make me?" Walt asked.

"A figment of my imagination," Danielle told him. Walt countered with a scowl.

Lily continued. "According to Morris, spirits exist on three separate planes. They are either here on earth—trapped in a physical body."

"I have a body!" Walt protested.

"I think she means a body other people can see or touch," Danielle explained.

"Danielle's correct, Walt. I assume Walt is arguing he has a body?"

"Yep." Danielle grinned.

Lily continued. "The second plane is where one goes after death —I believe he refers to it as the Terminal. In the Terminal you board for your ultimate destination—which I suppose some would see as heaven. Although, Morris doesn't call it heaven. It's more tangible than that. But that place, that's the third plane—it's where spirits end up after they've learned all their lessons. Yet basically, according to Morris, all one has to do is embrace the belief system of Earthbound Spirits, and when you die, you get a ticket straight to paradise and don't have to return here."

"That's pretty much what I've read too," Danielle said.

"I suppose I'm proof the organization is flawed." Walt chuckled.

"And corrupt. We already know they tried to pass off Isabela's old will as the current one. Not to mention blackmailing Darlene." Danielle turned her attention back to the computer and began searching for information on Richard.

"Richard seems really sweet to me. I hate to think he's tied up with that cult." Lily sighed.

Walt stood up and walked to the bed. "I think the one you need to run a check on is that Chris person."

"With a name like Chris Johnson, I seriously doubt I'll find anything." When Lily flashed Danielle a frown over her statement, Danielle explained, "Walt thinks I should run a check on Chris. I don't think he likes him."

Lily glanced to what appeared to be an empty sofa. "Sorry, Walt. I really like Chris. And it's not just because he's eye candy; he has a great sense of humor and has been really friendly. Haven't you noticed how he goes out of his way to get everyone involved? He initiated the walk this afternoon, and at dinner he kept the conversation going. If you think about it, putting all these strangers together for the holidays can be pretty awkward."

Danielle looked up from the computer. "You have a point, Lily. I rather assumed the guests would simply do their own thing, and the only time they would really see each other would be during the meals. But they seem content to hang out together."

"I know. It's like they're spending the holiday together—not just spending it at the same place," Lily said.

Walt frowned. "I don't see what the difference is."

"Here…I found something!" Danielle interrupted, her attention riveted on the computer.

"What?" Lily leaned closer to the laptop, trying to sneak a peek.

"Oh my goodness, I think I found an article on his parents' death. How sad."

"How did they die?" Lily asked.

"Some sort of boating accident off Dana Point."

"Isn't that where Chris is from?"

"I don't know if he's from there exactly." Danielle clicked the mouse, moving from one webpage to another. "But that's where the boat he was staying on was moored."

"Are you sure the article is about Richard's parents?" Walt asked.

"Yeah, Walt. There's a picture of Richard with them on the webpage. Identifies him as their son." Danielle finished reading the article and resumed her search. "Here are some other pictures of Richard and his parents…at what look like fund-raisers. Wow, his folks really were loaded."

"Richer than you?" Lily teased.

"Oh yeah…makes me look like a pauper. Wonder why he would get involved with a group like Earthbound Spirits."

"Well, we know why they would get involved with him. Same reason they sucked in Isabela," Lily said with disgust.

"Hey…what do you know…" Danielle said.

"What?" Lily scooted up on the bed next to Danielle so she could get a better look at the computer screen.

"It seems Richard is having a birthday in a couple days. Christmas Eve to be exact."

"How do you know that?" Walt asked.

"It's an article—written five years ago—photo of Richard and his parents, Christmas tree in the background. According to the article, he's celebrating his thirtieth birthday."

"That makes him five years older than you," Walt said.

"I guess it does. Although, I think he's a young-looking thirty-five."

"You guess it does what?" Lily asked.

"Walt just pointed out Richard is five years older than me."

"I wonder why he never mentioned his birthday was on Christmas Eve." Lily frowned. "Although he did say Christmas wasn't a big deal in his family. Maybe his parents focused more on his birthday than Christmas."

"Maybe." Danielle sighed. "But there sure are a lot of pictures online of Richard and his parents. Looks like the three were involved with a ton of charity events together. In all the photos he's sandwiched between his parents."

"No mention of a girlfriend…a boyfriend maybe?" Lily asked.

Danielle shook her head. "Not really. Just from the articles, seems like they were a close family. Must have been hard on him when his parents died."

"When we were in the kitchen earlier, he said something like—well, he compared his situation to yours. Like he could relate to you."

"If Adam is right and Richard's main reason for being here is to convert me, perhaps that's why Earthbound Spirits sent him. Because they felt he and I shared a similar personal tragedy."

"You really think they sent him?" Lily asked.

"He did tell me Morris recommended Marlow House. It sure sounds like it to me."

"Has he approached you yet? Said anything about the organization?"

Danielle shook her head. "No, not really. Although, I was gone most of the afternoon, and when I got back, I was preoccupied with getting dinner together. He's been friendly, but not like someone trying to pitch their religion."

"I still think you should look into Chris Johnson. There's something about that man I don't like. And there's something going on between him and Anna," Walt insisted.

Danielle smiled. "Anna is an attractive young woman, Walt. Surely you haven't been dead for so long that you can't guess what that something might be."

"What are you talking about?" Lily asked.

Danielle chuckled. "Walt seems to think there's something nefarious going on between Anna and Chris."

"I don't know about that, but I still think it was a little odd, her just showing up on our doorstep. And the way she's trying to get all chummy with Patricia and Jessica. Something about her sort of bugs me. And Ian feels the same way," Lily told them.

"Patricia is another one I'm curious about. She claims she won a trip here. I'd think an organization would let me know they intended to gift a trip here when they made the reservations. That's just odd," Danielle said.

"Maybe you should be looking up that group. What was it called?" Lily asked.

"Benevolent Charities, and I already did. I couldn't find anything."

"Dani, I forgot to tell you, I think Patricia and Jessica might actually be homeless."

"What do you mean homeless?" Danielle frowned.

"When we were decorating cookies, Jessica blurted out that they didn't have a home anymore. According to her, they moved out right before they left for Oregon and stored all their stuff in their car. And earlier, I overheard Jessica telling her mother she was hungry, and Jessica said something about having to be careful with how they spent their money."

"I know they both had breakfast." Danielle frowned.

"This was at lunchtime."

"I hope you told her she was welcome to make Jessica a sandwich."

"Yes. I ended up making Jessica a grilled cheese sandwich."

"Maybe there is no Benevolent Charities. Maybe one of their friends simply wanted to give her and Jessica a Christmas holiday and did it in the guise of a prize," Danielle suggested.

"That's possible." Lily shrugged.

"Well, let me make one more search on Richard. Although, so far I'm not really learning anything new."

Lily got off the bed and was just about to announce she was going to head off to her room when Danielle blurted out, "Well, this is just damn creepy!"

Lily stood by the bed. "What?"

"I just did a search on Richard, plugging in his full name, date of birth and his parents' names. I just found his grave."

Lily frowned. "Excuse me?"

"Yes. His grave. According to this website, Richard Winston Jr., only son of Richard and Rachel Winston, died when he was six years old."

"Are you saying his parents had another son who died, and they gave Richard his dead brother's name?"

Danielle shook her head. "No, because this child—the dead one—had the same birthday as the Richard here—same month, day, and year."

"Maybe it was a twin brother?" Lily suggested. "Perhaps that site got the names mixed up. And some people actually give their kids the same name, look at George Foreman."

"No." Danielle continued to shake her head. "According to the obituary attached to this website, he was their only child. There is no mention of a twin."

FOURTEEN

When breakfast ended on Monday morning, Danielle's guests began filing out of the dining room. Instead of joining the others, Chris lingered and helped Danielle clear the table.

Holding a stack of dirty dishes, Danielle paused a moment and smiled over at Chris, who was busily rounding up the silverware. "You don't need to help me. You're a guest."

Chris chuckled. "I'm more than happy to help. That was a great breakfast, by the way."

"Thanks, I'm glad you enjoyed it." Danielle grinned and began adding more dirty dishes to her pile.

"So what made you decide to open a bed and breakfast?" Chris asked.

"I figured it was time for a change. I've always loved to cook—bake—and I like meeting new people. When my aunt left me this house, I thought it would make a perfect bed and breakfast."

"Did your aunt live here?" Chris commandeered the heavy stack of dishes Danielle carried, setting the dirty silverware atop the pile. Danielle snatched up as many water glasses as she could carry and led the way into the kitchen.

"No, no one had lived here for almost ninety years. Walt Marlow and his wife were the last ones to live at Marlow House."

Once in the kitchen, Joanne took the dirty dishes from Chris and Danielle. They returned to the dining room to clear the rest of the table.

"I remember reading about that in the brochure, but I wondered if maybe it was the edited version of the house's history."

"Nope." Danielle shrugged. "What you read in the brochure is pretty much everything." In the dining room, they gathered up the last of the dishes and glassware.

"I thought maybe there might be a ghost or two you didn't mention." Chris grinned.

Danielle stopped what she was doing and looked over at Chris, a frown on her face. "Ghosts?"

"This is a big old house. I bet it was pretty spooky when you first moved in. Especially since it was vacant for so long. I imagine some people might…start imagining things. Especially since Walt Marlow was killed in the attic. That sort of thing creeps some people out."

Danielle shrugged. "I never found the house particularly scary. It's just a house."

"I think he's trying to frighten you," Walt said when he appeared a moment later. "Maybe I should show him what it feels like to experience fear."

Danielle flashed a warning glare in Walt's direction.

"Of course," Chris said nonchalantly, "after having a look at Marlow's portrait, I don't see him as much of a threat—even if he decided to stick around and haunt this place."

"Please, Danielle, can't I just give him a little scare?" Walt pleaded.

"No, don't think so," Danielle murmured.

"You don't think so what?" Chris asked with a mischievous grin.

"I don't think Walt Marlow would be much of a threat had he stuck around." Danielle looked up and into Chris's eyes. "Because I think he was probably a very nice and caring man and would never do anything to make me feel uncomfortable."

Chris let out a sigh and glanced over at Walt. "Yeah, you're probably right."

<hr>

LATER THAT MORNING Richard found Danielle in the parlor.

"So this is where you're hiding out," Richard said when he entered the room.

Danielle looked up from where she sat on the sofa, a book in hand. "I decided to sneak off and finish my book."

"Oh, I'm sorry. I didn't mean to intrude." Richard took a step toward the door.

"No, that's okay! So tell me, what do you have planned for today?" Danielle motioned to the empty chair across from her.

"Chris has invited us all out to lunch," Richard told her as he sat down.

"That's nice." Danielle smiled. "Glad to see everyone seems to get along so well."

"I don't think I'll be going…unless…will you be joining us? I'm sure he intends to ask you."

Danielle closed her book. "No, I think I'll stay here. Lily's off in Portland, and I don't really like to leave the house alone when we have guests."

"Isn't Joanne still here?"

"She left. She'll be back an hour or so before dinner," Danielle explained.

"I can stay here, keep you company," Richard offered. "If you don't mind."

"Richard, you seem like a really nice person. I'm just curious, why did you decide to spend Christmas here? You mentioned you belonged to Earthbound Spirits, but I know they don't celebrate Christmas."

Richard perked up. "So you know a little about our beliefs?"

"Yes, a little. I know you don't celebrate Christmas. At first I wondered if you were staying here because you were in Frederickport for some Earthbound Spirits event, but you seem content to hang around here."

"I've enjoyed it at Marlow House." Richard smiled. "And I have nothing against Christmas per se."

"So you're simply here for a holiday—which happened to fall on Christmas?" Danielle asked.

Richard shifted uncomfortably in his seat. "I guess I'm not very good at this."

"Good at what?"

"I suppose I am…well, what you might call a missionary. I've never really done this before."

"Missionary? You mean like one of those people who go out and convert others to their religion?" Danielle tossed her book on the coffee table and leaned back in the sofa, studying Richard.

"Yes.

"And you're here on some…mission."

Richard looked down and nodded.

"So who are you here to help see the light?"

Richard looked up into Danielle's eyes. "You."

Danielle smiled. "That's sort of what I figured."

"You aren't mad?"

"You haven't really done anything yet to make me mad. I assume Peter Morris gave you the assignment to convert me?"

"We don't actually say convert—that sounds like some sort of cult. My job is to help you see the light."

"What happens if you aren't successful? Do you get in trouble or anything?"

"Of course not. It's not like that. No one is twisting members' arms to spread the truth. Mr. Morris just felt you and I had a lot in common, and there might be some connection between us—something that would help me, help you."

"If you discover I'm a hopeless cause—which I am, by the way —will you start working on my other guests? Because frankly, that I couldn't allow."

"Oh no. I've been paired with you—not with anyone else here."

"Paired? You aren't implying…you and I…"

"Oh no!" Richard blushed. "Nothing like that. Absolutely not!"

Danielle chuckled. "Not sure if I should be insulted that you find the idea so horrifying—or relieved—which I am, by the way—relieved."

"I promise I won't be discussing Earthbound Spirits with any of your guests. Frankly, it's personal."

Danielle sat up straighter in her chair. "Since you've leveled with me, I think I owe you a little honesty. Ever since I heard you belonged to Earthbound Spirits and that Morris sent you here, I've been curious. Last night I looked you up online."

"And?"

"Found some pictures of you and your parents. Why didn't you mention your birthday was on Christmas Eve?"

Richard shrugged. "Birthdays were about as important as Christmas in our home."

"Meaning what?"

"We didn't really celebrate either one."

"In the picture there was a Christmas tree in the background—a birthday cake."

"I imagine whatever photos you found online were from some charity event—posted by a third party. I certainly never post pictures online."

"Not a member of Facebook?" Danielle grinned.

"No. I prefer my privacy. And when I say we didn't celebrate Christmas, I didn't mean we didn't have a Christmas tree or that I didn't occasionally have a birthday cake. It was pretty standard for my mother to hire a decorator to deck out the house for every holiday. We never decorated a tree together. And during any Christmas event—typically a fund-raiser—my parents loved to point out I was their best Christmas gift."

"Sounds like you were loved."

"Yes. It does sound that way, doesn't it?"

Danielle was silent for a moment and then asked, "What led you to Earthbound Spirits?"

"After my parents were killed, and I was sorting through everything—trying to get a handle on what I was now dealing with—I found myself asking what's the point of it all? And then I met Peter Morris and, suddenly, it all made sense."

"I think it's fairly common for someone to reach out—often finding religion—in an attempt to have things make sense."

"Did you do that? After your parents died?"

"I suppose, a little."

"Are you happy now, Danielle?"

"Happy? Yes, I think I am."

"But are you content?" he asked.

"Content? I suppose." Danielle shrugged.

"I know you've come into a lot of money with your recent inheritances, but I imagine you're like me and understand all that money can't fill the place in your heart after losing your family—your husband."

"You know about my husband?"

"Yes. Ever since Peter met you, he was concerned, worried about you. He looked into your background—but he only did it out of love."

"Oh…I bet he did."

"You see, it's not about what we find on earth—it's what's waiting for us when we move onto the next plane."

"I suppose that's what most religions teach."

"Yes, but when you discover the truth, you'll realize it's all so easy. You simply need to recognize this life is nothing but a place to learn, and then you can move on."

"What about God?" Danielle asked.

"There is no God." Richard told her.

"And you know that how?" Danielle asked,

"I used to believe there was a God, but he never answered my prayers. When I met Peter, I learned the reason God never answered."

"Because there is no God to answer your prayers?" Danielle asked.

Richard nodded.

"So you're telling me all I have to do is believe there's this cool place—that the only reason I'm here is to learn that lesson—not a lesson of how to treat others or to learn what is truly important in life —just that there's this ultimate place, and then I can die and go there."

"Yes! That's it." Richard smiled.

"So tell me, who exactly created this place? Who put your spirit here in this world? Who decides where you go when you reach the Terminal—back on earth or to this heaven of yours?"

"You know about the Terminal?" Richard asked.

"Yes. I've read a little on Earthbound Spirits and what they believe. So tell me, if there is no God—then who?"

"Why, you, of course. The power is all in you."

Danielle was quiet for a moment and then shook her head. "I'm sorry, Richard, I really don't buy it. Of course, you're entitled to your belief system, I just don't believe in it."

"Maybe I'm not explaining it right. I told you you're my first assignment."

"I'm curious, when you die, what happens to your estate?"

"What does it matter? Nothing on this plane is real. It's dust to me when I die."

"I agree, once you die, your money—any of your material belongings—are of no use to you. But they still exist here, even if you don't. What will happen to your estate?"

"I'm leaving it to Earthbound Spirits, of course."

"And don't you find that…well…doesn't that raise any kind of red flag for you?"

Richard shook his head. "I've seen the damage money can do. I would rather my money—the money my parents left me—make a positive difference in this world."

"And you think leaving it to Earthbound Spirits will do that?"

"Absolutely. That money will help fund Earthbound Spirits while they guide other spirits to the truth."

Danielle shook her head sadly. "I'm sorry, Richard, you can't even begin to imagine how much I disagree with you. If you want to start doing something positive with your money, donate it to good causes while you're still alive. Feed the hungry, educate poor children, save some abandoned dogs from euthanasia—anything but leave it to Earthbound Spirits."

"That's just your opinion. When you die, you'll realize I was right. I'm sorry, Danielle, because I really hoped I could help you."

"No, Richard, it's not my opinion. I know for an absolute fact Earthbound Spirits has it wrong."

"How can you say that?"

"Isn't it true Earthbound Spirits believes there are no such things as ghosts? In fact, the existence of a spirit—one not hindered by a material body—would pretty much negate Peter Morris's teachings."

"Yes, but no one has ever been able to prove the existence of ghosts. It's nothing but folklore and superstition."

Danielle leaned toward Richard. "Here's the thing, Richard—I believe in what are truly earthbound spirits—*ghosts*. I know they're real. I've been seeing them all my life."

FIFTEEN

"You actually told him you believe in ghosts?" Walt asked Danielle later that day after her guests had left together to have lunch in town. Walt sat in the parlor, Sadie by his side, with Danielle sitting on the sofa and Max curled up on her lap.

"I couldn't help myself. He seems like a basically nice guy and sincere, but he's hooked up with that wackadoodle cult."

"Not sure I know what wackadoodle means—but I think I can guess."

"Maybe if I could prove there are ghosts, then that might show Richard that Morris is feeding him a bunch of hooey." Danielle paused a moment and looked at Walt. "You do know what hooey is?"

"Yes. We said hooey back in my day."

"Anyway—if we can show him—"

"We? What do you mean we?"

"You could do something—I don't know, levitate a desk or something. Show Richard ghosts are real."

"Parlor tricks, Danielle? I think not."

"You weren't above parlor tricks with Chief MacDonald!"

"That was different," Walt insisted.

"I don't see how. And what about when you slugged Brian or disarmed Smith?"

"So now you're using the times I tried to help you against me?"

"No…of course not…it's just that…" Danielle sighed and leaned back in the sofa, her right hand absently stroking Max's back.

"You have a good heart, Danielle, and I know you want to help this man. But I don't believe levitating a piece of furniture is going to help him. If anything, he'd probably think you rigged it, and it'll end up doing more harm than good."

"I suppose you're right." Danielle glanced down at Max, who had just lifted his head and now stared at her through golden eyes.

"I have one other question."

Danielle stroked Max's back. "What's that?"

"Why didn't you ask him about the headstone you found with his name on it?"

Danielle's hand paused as she considered Walt's question. Max's head butted her hand, demanding she continue. She started petting Max again and said, "Aside from the fact it was just creepy, I started thinking about it and figured it was probably some spoof site."

"Spoof site?"

"Yeah, like the *Onion*, maybe."

"I have no idea what the *Onion* is."

"Just a website that posts outrageous and fake news."

"Why would someone do that?"

"I suppose people find it amusing. In any case, I figure it had to be something like that."

"Did you check it out, see if it was a—as you call it—spoof site?"

"No…but it has to be. After all, Richard looks pretty good for someone who has supposedly been dead for twenty-nine years. Plus, the cemetery was in Europe."

"I've been dead for much longer than that, and I think I've held up very nicely. If I do say so myself."

BRIAN HENDERSON SAT with Joe at Lucy's Diner, having lunch. The waitress had just brought their meals when Brian asked Joe, "You going to Marlow House for the Christmas Eve open house?"

"I'm planning on it. You?" Joe asked.

Brian picked up his burger. "I still can't believe she invited me."

"Is that a yes or no?"

"I guess I'll go. It might be interesting." Brian took a bite of his burger.

"I'll be spending Christmas evening with my sister and Craig. I really don't want to go over there both nights."

"Some women get more romantic over Christmas."

Joe was just about to take a bite of his sandwich when he paused and frowned at Brian. "Just what is that supposed to mean?"

"Come on, Joe, you still have a thing for the woman. I actually wish you two would go ahead and do something—get it out of your system—and then move on."

"You still don't like her, do you?"

"Honestly? I don't know what I think about Boatman anymore." Brian took another bite of his burger.

"Speak of the devil," Joe said when five customers walked into the diner—two men, two women, and a young girl.

Brian glanced at the newcomers and then looked back to Joe. "What?"

"I think that's who's staying at Marlow House. I recognize one of the guys."

"The way you said that, I thought Boatman just walked in." Brian watched as the party sat down at a table. "So they're all staying at Marlow House? Some sort of family Christmas reunion?"

"I don't think so." Joe leaned forward, lowering his voice. "I ran into Joanne this morning. She told me she had just left Marlow House and was going back this evening. Apparently, Danielle is full up. She even took in someone off the street."

"What do you mean someone off the street?" Brian frowned.

"According to Joanne, some woman just showed up at the door, begged for a room, said she didn't want to be alone for Christmas, so Danielle took her in."

"Is she paying for a room?" Brian asked.

"Yeah. Joanne said the woman paid in cash."

Brian shrugged. "So what's the big deal? That's what Boatman does, she runs an inn, takes people off the street. If the woman paid her, so what?"

Joe leaned back and picked up his sandwich. "Danielle put her in the attic. Joanne thought it was a little odd, and so do I."

"I never understood why Boatman keeps running that place like a hotel. It's not like she needs the money." Brian shook his head.

"That's what I keep telling her. Anyway—the other guests

include two single males. They didn't come with any wife or girlfriend."

Brian glanced over to the table and then back to Joe. "Looks like they're with someone now."

"I think they're all guests from Marlow House. The young blonde, I'm pretty sure she's the one who showed up on the doorstep. At least she fits Joanne's description."

Brian glanced briefly at the blonde and chuckled. "Why don't women like that show up on my doorstep and beg for a room?"

"She's young enough to be your daughter," Joe scolded.

"True. Anyway, I've given up younger women. Nothing but trouble. But now that I think about it, *all* women are trouble."

Brian picked up his water and took a sip. After he set his glass back down, he asked, "Who does the little girl belong to?"

"I'm pretty sure she belongs to the other woman. I met the guy in the jeans. He was kind of a smart aleck."

"When did you meet him?" Brian asked.

"I was dropping off her old iPhone when he was checking in."

BRIAN WAS JUST ABOUT to step out of the men's restroom at Lucy's Diner when he heard what sounded like two people arguing in the hallway—a man and a woman. He paused for a moment, his hand still on the restroom door, listening.

"What in the hell are you doing back there, *Anna?*"

"I hate it when you say my name like that," the woman hissed.

"Can you blame me?" the man countered.

"I don't understand why you're so upset."

"Because I don't know what you're trying to do back there. You shouldn't have come."

"Are you serious? How can you say that?" the woman asked. "You just want me dead and gone."

The man laughed. "Dead would be nice. Gone forever, so I never have to see you again, that would work for me."

"You can be so cruel, Chris!"

"Seriously? After all you've put me through?"

"I didn't have a choice," the woman insisted.

"I suppose not. But sometimes I wonder, maybe I should just kill you. See how that works out."

Abruptly, Brian opened the bathroom door, interrupting the couple's conversation. He was startled to discover they were two of the people who, according to Joe, were staying at Marlow House. One was the man Joe had met, and the other was the young blonde who had reportedly showed up on Boatman's doorstep, begging for a room.

"Is there some problem here?" Brian asked gruffly.

"No...no problem, officer." The woman quickly ducked into the door of the women's restroom.

The man she had been arguing with started to turn around and head back to the dining room when Brian grabbed hold of his wrist. Brian remembered the woman had called the man Chris.

Chris came to a stop and looked down at his wrist, the officer's hand still clutching it.

"Is there some problem, officer?" Chris asked, pulling his hand from Brian's grasp.

"I heard you threatening that woman."

"We were just talking. I didn't threaten her; she knows that."

"You're staying at Marlow House, right?" Brian asked.

"Yes." Chris glared at Brian and rubbed his wrist.

"How long are you staying in town?" Brian asked.

"I really don't see how that's any of your business."

"Everything that goes on in Frederickport is my business. I'm tempted to run you in, do a little background check on you."

"Under what grounds?"

"Threatening someone's life, to start with."

At that moment, the blonde stepped back into the hallway from the women's restroom.

"Anna," Chris called out, "this officer seems to think I threatened your life, and he wants to haul me into the police station."

Anna quickly looped her arm around Chris's and glared at Brian. "That's just plain harassment. You and I were just kidding around, and he was obviously eavesdropping on our private conversation. If he makes you go down to the station, you need to sue for harassment!"

Brian stood in silence for a few minutes, looking from the man to the woman. Shaking his head, he let out a sigh. "Fine, you can go. But stay out of trouble while you're in Frederickport."

"WHAT TOOK YOU SO LONG?" Joe asked when Brian returned to the table. He then added with a laugh, "I was beginning to wonder if you decided to take off and leave me with the check."

"I swear, women never cease to amaze me." Brian pulled out his chair and sat down.

"What are you talking about?"

"I ran into two of Boatman's guests by the restroom. That guy you said you met and the young blonde."

"What happened?"

"I could swear the man was threatening her, but when I called him on it and suggested I might take him down to the station and check him for priors, she jumps in with all this noise about me harassing him, and if I take him in, he'll sue me."

"Not the first time an abused woman sticks up for her abuser." Joe paused and then frowned, glancing over to the table where Danielle's guests had been sitting. He watched as they made their way out the door, the blonde occasionally looking back in their direction.

"What is it?" Brian asked.

"According to Joanne, those two just met. So why would he be threatening her, and why would she be sticking up for him?"

"One thing I'm fairly certain about, those two didn't just meet. There's some history there."

"I should let Danielle know," Joe muttered.

"Didn't you say the blonde just showed up on the doorstep and begged for a room?"

"That's how Joanne described it."

Brian laughed. "It's pretty clear what's going on."

"What?"

"She obviously followed him to Frederickport and knew he was staying at Marlow House. He probably broke up with her before he got here, and she's determined to get him back. Some women just can't take no for an answer. I guess I can understand his frustration." Brian picked up the check from the table and looked at it. Tossing it back to the table, he stood up and pulled his wallet from his pocket.

"So you don't think I need to mention it to Danielle?"

Brian pulled some money from his wallet and threw it on the table with the check. "I suppose you could if you want, but I don't see the point."

SIXTEEN

"Would you mind if we stopped at the arts and craft store?" Anna asked as they got into Chris's rental car. She had pointed out the store earlier that afternoon on the way to the diner.

"Oh, can we?" Jessica asked excitedly. She sat between her mother and Anna in the backseat of the car.

"Jessica, we can't buy anything," Patricia whispered.

"Sure we can stop, and I'll treat," Chris offered.

"You already bought us lunch," Patricia reminded him.

Chris started the engine and headed for the craft store. "Hey, it's Christmas."

When they pulled up in front of the craft store, Richard looked out the window and said, "I'll just wait in the car."

"No, you won't!" Chris said with a laugh. "Us guys have to stick together, and the women already outnumber us! You certainly aren't going to make me go in there alone."

Richard gave a disinterested shrug but got out of the car. He figured Chris had bought his lunch, the least he could do was go along with the group.

They followed Anna around in the store as she picked up three cans of spray paint: gold, green, and silver. She then had Jessica help her pick out miniature Christmas ornaments—tiny silver balls, bells, glittery stars, and other festive miniatures, along with several small bottles of white glue. Chris paid for the purchase and carried the sack out to the car for Anna.

"What are you going to do with all that?" Richard asked when he got into the car.

"You'll see," Anna said cheerfully as she fastened her seat belt. "You're going to help."

"Me?" Richard glanced in the backseat at Anna and frowned.

"Yes. Everyone in this car is going to help—right after dinner. All except Chris; I won't make him if he doesn't want to since he was nice enough to buy us all lunch and pay at the craft store."

On their way back to Marlow House, Chris stopped at a gourmet shop to pick up a few items. He asked the group if there were any other stores they wanted to visit. Since Patricia was on a tight budget and reluctant to spend any money, and Richard had nothing to buy, they didn't stop again.

AFTER DINNER THAT NIGHT, four of the five guests of Marlow House gathered around the kitchen table to do Anna's craft project. They soon learned the project she had in mind involved the old, thick phonebooks Danielle had given Anna. Since there were only four phonebooks, Chris begged out of the project. Richard tried to join him, but Chris's gentle teasing and Jessica's begging convinced Richard to be a good sport and join in the craft project.

He sat at the kitchen table and looked down at the phonebook before him. "What exactly are we doing?"

Anna had left the items they had purchased in the sack, which remained sitting on the kitchen counter. Jessica kept looking over at the sack, anxious to bring out the items from the craft store.

When Anna noticed Jessica's eagerness, she patted the young girl's hand and said, "Not yet, dear. First we each need to make our book into a Christmas tree."

"Christmas tree?" Jessica asked.

"Yes. Haven't you ever made one of these before?" Anna glanced from Jessica to Patricia.

Jessica shook her head. "No."

"First we fold our book into a Christmas tree and staple the covers together. Then in the morning, we can take them outside and paint them. You can make yours green or silver or gold. And when the paint dries, we glue on the ornaments," Anna explained.

"I haven't done one of these since I was a little girl," Patricia said, her voice barely a whisper.

Richard stared down at the phonebook before him. Without waiting for Anna's instructions, he opened the book and folded the first page down so that the top edge of the page rested along the book's inner spine.

"Very good, Richard!" Anna praised.

Jessica looked over to Richard and asked, "You've made one of these before?"

Richard shook his head and then folded the next page. "No. I don't think so."

"WHAT'S THIS?" Danielle asked when Chris handed her a cup of hot cocoa and sat down on the sofa with her.

"We stopped at that gourmet shop on Main Street, and I picked up some of their hot chocolate mix. Lily mentioned something about you liking your chocolate."

"What woman doesn't?" Danielle grinned and then gently blew on the hot cocoa before taking a sip.

Cupping his own mug of hot cocoa between his hands, Chris watched Danielle.

"This is really good. I'd never tried their cocoa before."

"I hope you don't mind. I helped myself to some of your milk in the kitchen and used one of your pans. But I washed it and put it away."

"No problem." Danielle took another sip. "That was pretty sneaky, by the way."

"What do you mean?"

"How you managed to get out of Anna's craft project. I have to say I felt a little sorry for Richard."

"Yeah. I think he could have turned down Anna, but I knew he was going to cave when Jessica jumped in and started begging him to do the project." Chris laughed. "But it will be good for him. Get him into the Christmas spirit."

"I imagine it'll take more than a craft project to get Richard into the Christmas spirit. But I'm glad to see all the guests seem to be getting along so well." Danielle finished the last of her cocoa.

Chris looked over at Danielle's empty mug and smiled. "I take it you liked it?"

"It was delicious."

Chris handed her his full mug and took her empty one.

"No, that's yours," Danielle protested. But she took his full cup.

"Nah, I'm more of a beer guy. You drink it." Chris set the empty mug on the end table.

"He's feeding you chocolate?" Walt said with disgust when he appeared the next moment.

Danielle held the cup out to Chris. "You sure you don't want to drink it? It's really good."

"No, I want you to have it. I always heard the way to a woman's heart is with chocolate." Chris grinned.

"Oh brother!" Walt flopped down in the chair facing them and crossed his legs. With a wave of his hand he summoned a lit cigar and glared at Chris.

"So why did you decide to spend your Christmas here?" Danielle asked.

Chris leaned back in the sofa and looked over at the Christmas tree. Its lights seemed to twinkle.

"I've been living on a boat for the last six months. Owner sold it, so I had to move anyway. Figured I might as well go somewhere for the holidays before I had to look for a new place to live. Found Marlow House online. Looked like an interesting place. Plus, it's close to the ocean. I like being close to the water."

"Ask him what he does for a living," Walt said. "You still haven't found out what he does."

"Didn't you want to spend Christmas with your family?" Danielle asked instead.

Chris shook his head. "There really isn't any family. I've been on my own for a while."

Danielle leaned back on the sofa, the mug cupped between her hands. "There seems to be a lot of that going around."

"What do you mean?" Chris asked.

"I don't have any family—my last family member was killed this summer. I get the idea it's just Patricia and Jessica; Patricia doesn't seem to have anyone. And Richard, I know his parents died a few years back, and he doesn't have any brothers or sisters. As for Anna, well, the fact she wanted to stay here instead of being alone for Christmas makes me think she doesn't have anyone."

"Perhaps that's why everyone seems to be getting along so well. Christmas has always been a time for family, but none of us have that—so here we are," Chris suggested. "We've created our own little family."

"If he gets anymore maudlin, I'm leaving," Walt groaned.

"What about Lily, does she have family?" Chris asked.

"Yes. She comes from a large family; they're close. But she and Ian spent Thanksgiving with them. Ian's sister lives in Portland, and she's going to come here for Christmas. She'll be arriving Christmas Eve."

"Is she staying here?"

"No. She'll stay with her brother across the street."

"Have Ian and Lily been an item long?" Chris asked.

"This palooka knows how to beat his gums," Walt grumbled.

"They started going out after we moved up here in June." Danielle flashed Walt a quick frown.

"I like Ian. Interesting guy. I've read a couple of his books."

"Baloney," Walt muttered. "I'd be surprised if this palooka even knows how to read."

"I confess, I haven't read any of his books. But I've seen a few of his documentaries." Danielle sipped the cocoa.

"I was hoping, maybe, one night I could take you out to dinner. Ian was telling me about a nice little seafood restaurant he takes Lily to."

Walt stood up abruptly. "Is he asking you for a date? You don't date your guests."

"That would be nice…" Danielle glanced over to Walt and back to Chris. "But I'm afraid I'm pretty tied down here. For one thing, I'm responsible for providing dinners."

"And it would be very unprofessional to start going out with your guests," Walt added.

"I was thinking maybe one night after Christmas. I heard you say something about how Joanne prepares dinner a few times a week. Maybe we could go one of those nights."

"Okay…sure. That would be nice." Danielle smiled.

"Is this because you think he's good looking?" Walt asked. "What was it you said he looked like—I know—an underwear model? Danielle, are you forgetting what I told you about looks being deceiving. I don't trust this guy. You don't even know what he does for a living. Although, I suspect he does nothing for a living," Walt ranted.

"Good, then it's a date. By the way, I've been meaning to ask you something—about Walt Marlow."

"Walt Marlow?" Danielle squeaked.

"Yeah, the guy who was killed in the attic—the one whose portrait is in your library."

"Yeah, I know who you mean. I'm just surprised you brought him up."

"Why is that? I can practically feel his presence in this house."

"Umm…me too." Danielle set her now empty mug on the end table. "So what did you want to ask?"

"What did Walt Marlow do for a living? Do you know?"

"Umm…well…his grandfather founded this town; he built ships."

"I know that, but what did Walt Marlow do?" Chris asked.

"Well…I know he inherited his grandfather's estate."

"That's it?" Chris asked. "Did he ever actually do anything aside from spending his granddaddy's fortune?"

SEVENTEEN

Danielle had just crawled into bed when Walt burst into her room and announced, "I didn't just while away my time spending my grandfather's money!"

"I never said you did." Danielle pulled the blankets up over her.

"I just want you to know: I was quite active in charity work."

"Walt, it's okay. Really." Danielle snuggled down under the sheets and blankets.

Standing by the bedside, he scowled at Danielle. "I did not appreciate his implication."

"If I didn't know better, I would swear he was saying that stuff to bug you." Danielle yawned and leaned back on her pillows, folding her hands over the top of the blankets.

"What do you mean?" Walt sat on the side of the bed.

"I can't explain it exactly. But when he says certain stuff, I just get the weirdest feeling he's talking to someone else. And in this case, you. Because it obviously irritates you so much."

"Are you saying he knows I'm in the room?"

"Of course not." Danielle yawned.

"Then what are you saying? He likes to talk to imaginary people?"

Danielle shrugged and scooted farther down in the bedding.

"And you're still willing to go out to dinner with him?"

"What can I say?" Danielle yawned and rolled to her side,

curling up in the fetal position, her back to Walt. "The man looks like an underwear model. I'm weak."

AFTER BREAKFAST ON TUESDAY MORNING, Richard, Anna, Patricia, and Jessica were outdoors in the side yard of Marlow House, spray painting the phonebook Christmas trees they had folded together the night before. Danielle had given them some old newspaper to spread out on the ground, which they had placed the trees on before painting.

Looking down at the now painted trees, Anna said, "I guess you were wrong, Richard, you have made these before."

He glanced over to Anna. "What do you mean?"

"I didn't tell you how to fold the phonebook, but you just started doing it right."

Richard shrugged. "You said we were going to make trees, and I figured that's how to do it."

"I can't wait to decorate mine!" Jessica said excitedly. "Did you ever make these before, Mom?"

"Yes, when I was a little girl. My mother taught me how." Patricia let out a weary sigh, her eyes still on the paper trees they had just painted.

"How come we never made them before?" Jessica asked.

"I'm not sure."

"What was your mother like?" Anna asked.

"Honestly, it's kind of hard to remember."

Anna studied her. "Did she die when you were very young?"

"I was ten. So I guess not that young. Older than Jessica." Patricia reached out and took hold of her daughter's hand.

"My parents were killed three years ago," Richard told them. "Maybe it would have been better had they died when I was young so it wouldn't bother me now."

"Who said it doesn't bother me?" Patricia asked.

"I just meant—well, you said you don't really remember her," he stammered.

Patricia gently squeezed Jessica's hand and looked off into the distance, seeing her memories instead of the surrounding landscape. "Oh, I remember some things. Mostly Christmas."

"Like what?" Anna asked.

"My father was killed by a hit-and-run driver a few years before Mother died. Those last few years were especially rough. He didn't have any insurance, and she had never worked before."

"I'm so sorry," Richard whispered.

"Oh, it was a long time ago." Patricia flashed Richard a sad smile. "Anyway, those last few Christmases we couldn't afford a real Christmas tree. But we would make phonebook trees."

Jessica pulled on her mother's hand. "You mean like these?"

"Yes. Just like these. Mom would cut the buttons off my old clothes to use as decorations. And we'd paint bottle caps and add glitter."

"I considered getting glitter, but I didn't think Danielle would appreciate that," Anna said with a laugh.

"No, I imagine she wouldn't." Patricia grinned.

Richard stared blankly down at the painted trees and said, "First you spray paint the bottle caps gold and then add glitter while the paint's still wet, so it'll stick."

"Yes." Patricia looked up at Richard. "You used to do that too?"

"No, but I just saw it." Richard rubbed the heel of his hand against his forehead.

Jessica reached out with her free hand and tugged on Richard's shirt sleeve. "How did you see it?"

Richard shook his head in confusion. "I don't know. I just saw it. Like when we were at the table last night, and Anna said we were going to make Christmas trees. I just saw hands—small hands—folding a phonebook into a Christmas tree. And when Patricia mentioned the bottle caps, I saw it. They were lined up in a row on newsprint. Someone was spray painting them, and I was—at least I felt it was me, but it was me as a very young boy—was sprinkling gold glitter over the bottle caps as soon as they were painted."

"That's probably a memory from your childhood," Patricia suggested.

"No, impossible." Richard shook his head. "I must have seen it on TV and just forgot."

"How can you be so sure it wasn't a memory from your child-hood?" Anna asked.

"Because my parents would never let me play with glitter—or keep bottle caps to paint." He laughed at the thought.

AFTER DINNER TUESDAY EVENING, Richard found Patricia in the library, reading a book. Jessica was in the living room, playing a board game with Lily and Danielle while Anna and Chris watched them from the sofa.

"I wanted to apologize," Richard told Patricia.

She closed the book and looked up at Richard. "Apologize for what?"

"For that crack I made earlier today about how I wished my parents had died when I was younger." He took a seat next to her. "I didn't mean to imply your loss was any less because it happened when you were young."

"I'm sorry about your parents. It must have been painful for you."

"Yes, but not in the ways you might imagine."

Patricia didn't respond immediately. Finally, she asked, "Were you close to your parents?"

"Close? I suppose I thought I was. How about you? Were you close to your mother?"

Patricia let out a sigh and leaned back. "I said earlier that I really didn't remember Mom, but that's not true. I do remember her. But when I think of Mom, I get so mad at her—and then I feel guilty, especially now—so I prefer to pretend I don't remember her."

"Why do you get mad at her?"

"Because she died, and I ended up in foster care. She didn't protect me."

"How did she die?" His question was almost a whisper.

"Mom had cancer. She got so sick, went so fast. I remember having to stay with the neighbors when she was in the hospital. And then she died and they came for us." Patricia closed her eyes.

"Who came for you?"

Patricia opened her eyes again. "Social services."

"When you told me about bouncing around in the foster care system, you said it was partly your fault because of how you behaved."

"Yes, it was."

"I still don't agree it was your fault. I also understand why you were angry with your mom, because she didn't make any arrangements for you. What I don't understand is why do you feel guilty for that?"

"Because now I understand why my mother didn't make arrangements—for the same reason I haven't for Jessica."

"Why is that?"

"I don't really have anyone. If something happened to me tomorrow, I don't know what would become of Jessica. I haven't made any plans. I think about it all the time."

"Don't you have any family or friends?"

"I don't have any family. And I've been so busy just surviving, I really haven't had the time to make close friends—at least not the kind of friend who I would ask to take Jessica if something happened to me."

After a few moments of silence Richard said, "Maybe the answer is for you to find a husband."

Patricia laughed. "Yeah, well, I really don't have time to go husband hunting these days. And having a little girl just makes things more complicated."

"Jessica seems like a sweet kid. I bet there are a lot of men out there who love kids. Who would love a stepdaughter like Jessica."

"Yeah, well, that's what I'm worried about."

Richard was about to ask her what she meant but then stopped when he realized what she was probably saying. "I suppose that does make things a little more—challenging."

"I just need to be careful."

"How about Chris?" Richard suggested.

"Chris?" Patricia frowned.

"He's a nice guy. Seems to like Jessica—but doesn't seem creepy about it."

Patricia chuckled. "I don't think so. He's a nice guy, but not my type. And a little young for me."

"I'm sure there's someone out there for you."

"Thanks, Richard, but I really don't believe a woman should look to a man to solve her problems. I suppose when I return to Arizona, I should make more of an effort to reach out to my friends, make more time for them. *After* I find us a place to live, of course."

"What will that do?"

"Maybe I'm overlooking a friend who'd be willing to step up to the plate and raise Jessica if something were to happen to me."

"Nothing's going to happen to you."

"I hope not." Patricia let out a weary sigh.

After a few moments of silence Richard said, "My mother

always let men solve her problems. My father, to be precise. If Mother ever had a problem, Dad was always there to solve it. The extremes he would go to were mind-boggling."

"Sounds like he loved her."

"I suppose. If that was love, I don't want any part of it."

"You sound bitter, Richard."

"I suppose I do. I suppose I am."

"Do you want to talk about it?"

Richard considered her offer. After a few moments of silence he said, "Mother married well, never had to think of money. Whatever she wanted she bought. They say money doesn't buy happiness, but my father sure tried to prove that adage wrong."

"Was your mother happy?"

"I don't think so. Maybe. Sometimes. I think it was more about her making herself appear happy. To Mother, life had a certain order, and if that order was maintained, then I suppose she was happy, as happy as she was capable of being."

"Was she a…loving woman?"

Richard laughed. "Loving. No. Not like you are with Jessica. People used to tell me how lucky I was to have the parents I did. My parents were never affectionate exactly—more doting—suffocating. And sometimes—sometimes…"

"Sometimes what?"

"Sometimes, they just resented me. I wouldn't be surprised if that resentment bordered on hate."

EIGHTEEN

On Christmas Eve morning, Danielle surprised the guests of Marlow House by hanging twelve Christmas stockings on the mantel of the living room's massive stone fireplace. It wasn't that the stockings were a surprise, it was that each one had a name embroidered along its top. Five stockings bore the names of Marlow House's current guests: Jessica, Patricia, Anna, Richard, and Chris. Sadie and Max each had one, as did Danielle, Lily, Ian, and Ian's sister, Kelly. And the last stocking was for Walt Marlow.

"Who is Walt?" Jessica asked when she read the names on the stockings.

"He lived here before I did," Danielle explained. "His grandfather built this house."

"Is he coming for Christmas?" Jessica asked.

"No, honey." Patricia laughed. "Mr. Marlow died almost a hundred years ago."

Jessica frowned. "Then why does he have a stocking?"

"Because"—Chris spoke up—"sometimes even when someone is gone, it feels like their spirit is still lingering nearby."

"Is Mr. Marlow still here?" Jessica asked.

Chris winked at Jessica and said, "Who knows, maybe."

"You're going to scare the child," Richard scolded.

"No, I'm not." Chris laughed. "Ghosts are only scary if they were bad people when they were alive."

Jessica's eyes widened. "Is his ghost here?"

"Of course not!" Richard insisted.

"Chris is just teasing, honey." Patricia flashed Chris a reproving frown. "Aren't you, Chris?"

"Sure, I'm just teasing, Jessica." Chris smiled.

"Then why does he have a stocking?" Jessica asked.

"It's sort of an honorary stocking, Jessica," Danielle explained. "Walt Marlow used to live in this house, and well, I suppose in some way Chris is correct in that after people die, sometimes it feels as if their spirit is still here. Not in a spooky scary way, but more of a comforting way."

"Is he the man in the big painting in the library?" Jessica asked.

Danielle smiled at the child. "Yes, he is."

"Then that's okay. He looks nice." Jessica grinned.

Walt, who stood by the Christmas tree watching and listening, said, "Thank you, Jessica. And thank you, Danielle, for the stocking."

"I just have one question," Patricia asked. "Who did you get to embroider all the names? They did a beautiful job."

"It wasn't me," Danielle said with a laugh. "And it wasn't some sweet little grandmother I hired. We have a T-shirt store in town that does silk-screening and embroidering. I had them do it. So basically, a machine."

"That was very thoughtful," Anna said from her place on the sofa.

"Tomorrow morning, we'll find out who in this room was good this past year—and who was naughty," Danielle teased.

"What do you mean?" Jessica asked.

"I think she means," Chris said with a chuckle, "the naughty ones will probably be getting coal in their stockings while the good ones will get nice gifts. But that's up to Santa."

Jessica wrinkled her nose. "I hope I don't get coal."

Anna pointed to the Christmas tree and said, "I see Danielle is still adding decorations to the tree. Are they antiques? They look old."

"I haven't put any more ornaments on the tree." Danielle looked to where Anna pointed and noticed two unfamiliar ornaments. She walked to the tree and removed one, examining it. "It's beautiful. Whose are they?"

"Aren't they yours?" Chris asked.

Danielle shook her head. She removed the second one. "No. I didn't put them here. I assume one of you did."

"Maybe Walt's ghost put them on the tree!" Jessica excitedly suggested.

"I seriously doubt that." Patricia laughed.

Holding the ornaments up for all to see, Danielle said, "Which one of you hung them? You better fess up, or I just might keep them! They're beautiful, but they look like family heirlooms."

The moment Danielle held up the ornaments for her guests to see, both Patricia and Richard cocked their heads, a quizzical expression on each of their faces. Stepping to Danielle, they each reached for an ornament, taking them from her.

"I guess this solves the mystery," Danielle said cheerfully.

Patricia shook her head. "No, but I had one just like this when I was a little girl." She looked over to the one in Richard's hand.

Silently, Richard stared at the ornament, mesmerized.

"We had one like that too," Patricia explained.

"You mean they aren't yours?" Danielle asked.

"No." Patricia handed the ornament back to Danielle. She looked at Richard. "Are they yours?"

Richard shook his head. "We never had ornaments like this. But...but..."

"What?" Danielle asked.

Richard abruptly shoved the ornament back to Danielle. "Nothing. It's nothing. No. They aren't mine."

Fifteen minutes later, Patricia followed Danielle into the kitchen, leaving Jessica in the living room. "Danielle, thank you again for the stockings. It was very sweet. I brought Jessica's from home, I was going to ask if I could hang it, but I won't now."

"If you want to hang her stocking, please do." In the kitchen, Danielle began removing platters from one of the cabinets.

"No. That's fine. But I brought a few gifts for her stocking, so if you don't mind if I put them in the one you hung for her." Patricia leaned against the counter and watched Danielle.

"Sure, as long as you don't mind if I add a few items to the stocking. If everything doesn't fit, she can always have two stockings." Danielle flashed Patricia a grin.

"That was really nice of you. You didn't have to do that." Patricia watched as Danielle stood on her tiptoes, attempting to retrieve a platter from the top shelf. It was just out of her reach.

Stepping next to Danielle, Patricia reached up and grabbed the platter and set it on the counter.

"Thanks." Danielle closed the cabinet doors. "As for the little gifts I got Jessica, it was fun. I don't have any little girls to shop for at Christmastime."

"You've really made this a wonderful Christmas for us."

"I'm glad everyone seems to be getting along so well. I didn't know if the guests would stick to themselves or mingle."

"I've sincerely enjoyed everyone. Chris and Richard have both been such gentlemen, and Anna is sweet."

"Patricia, I have a question for you."

"What?"

"Do you have any idea who added those ornaments to the tree?"

Patricia shook her head. "No. I'd like to know myself. When I saw them, it was like I went back in time to my childhood."

"Well, someone put them on the tree." *I need to ask Walt later if he knows.*

"One thing about this Christmas, it hasn't lacked mystery," Patricia said with a laugh.

Danielle smiled. "I prefer to think of it as Christmas magic."

"Christmas magic…yes, I like that. Speaking of mystery and magic, I couldn't find out anything about the group who gave us this trip. Are you sure you don't know who they are?" Patricia asked.

"No, sorry. Haven't a clue. In fact, I did a little Internet search and came up blank. Couldn't find a thing about the organization."

"When they paid for the trip, how did they pay for it? Was it in the organization's name?"

"No, they made it in your name, which is why I assumed you made the reservation. I had no idea it was made by a third party, not until you contacted me."

"What about the credit card they used? I would assume they used a credit card."

"They used a PayPal account. I'll be honest; I didn't pay much attention to it. I believe Lily took the reservation. But I'm sure it was in your name." Danielle frowned. "I didn't even think to look at my PayPal statement when I was looking up the organization online. I guess my Nancy Drew skills are slipping."

"That's okay. I'm just curious about the organization. I suppose I should just be thankful and not overthink it."

"I understand your curiosity. Heck, if I was you, it would probably drive me nuts."

"There is one more thing."

"Yes?"

"According to the information I received, the prize also includes Christmas gifts, which are supposed to be delivered sometime today."

"Oh, fun!"

"Yeah. I really haven't much for Jessica this year, and I haven't told her about the other prizes, because…well, I just don't know if they're really going to show up."

"Why wouldn't they? So far they came through with what they promised—the room, rental car, and plane tickets."

"I know. But still, I've always believed if something seems too good to be true, it usually is. As much as I've enjoyed this trip, a part of me is a little…nervous. Does that make sense?"

"I think so. But don't worry."

"Oh, I'm not… I'll confess, they were the reason I initially decided to come, because I felt I couldn't pass them up since things had been so tight. But now, I'm just grateful to have this Christmas with Jessica and all the nice people we've met. But if no gifts arrive, I'm still glad I came."

<hr>

AFTER HANGING the Christmas stockings and cleaning up after breakfast, the members of Marlow House—including its guests—began preparing for the Christmas Eve open house. Even Jessica pitched in, helping Lily plate up the Christmas cookies.

Meatballs simmered in one slow cooker and oyster stew in another. Danielle confessed that oyster stew was not her favorite, but it was a recipe her father had made every Christmas Eve, so she felt compelled to include it for tradition's sake.

There were homemade tamales—purchased from a local woman who made them each year—and the customary chips and dip. Homemade cheeseballs, first rolled in diced walnuts and sprinkled with parsley, were arranged in the center of Christmas plates and surrounded by crackers. Sticks of celery, carrots, and zucchini joined cherry tomatoes, cucumber slices, and bell pepper strips on platters, paired with bowls of ranch dressing. There were platters of cookies Danielle had baked, along with platters of sliced bread: pumpkin, zucchini, and banana. Danielle had baked them as well.

Added to the feast was homemade rum cake baked by Ian, and Lily's chocolate fudge. Marie Nichols had sent over her homemade divinity and peanut brittle for the party. Several days before Christmas Eve, Millie Samson had dropped off her famous fruit cake, and much to Lily's surprise, it was really quite delicious.

Chris volunteered to help Ian man the bar, which had been set up in the library. Chris, Ian, and Richard were already on their second cocktail when the first guest arrived, who happened to be Ian's younger sister, Kelly. Upon arriving, she grabbed Ian's house key so she could drop her bags off across the street before returning to the party.

After leaving her suitcases and Christmas packages off at Ian's house, Kelly locked up the front door and glanced at her watch. It was a few minutes past 3:00 p.m. Leaving her car in Ian's driveway, she started to walk across the street when a black Mercedes pulled up in front of Marlow House.

Pausing for a moment on the sidewalk, she watched as a tall man with coal black hair got out of the Mercedes. Had she not seen his car, she would still have suspected he had money, considering the exquisite cut of his suit. The man briefly glanced her way, and she recognized the face: Peter Morris, the founder of Earthbound Spirits. She certainly hadn't expected Morris to be on Danielle's guest list.

Instead of starting across the street and heading for Marlow House, Kelly decided to let Morris go in first.

NINETEEN

Danielle was rushing from the library to the parlor when she heard the doorbell. "I'll get it!" she called out, although she doubted anyone else heard the bell. Everyone but Jessica and Joanne was in the library, laughing and discussing drink recipes, while Chris and Ian tried to outdo each other by creating the most outrageous holiday cocktail. Jessica was in the kitchen with Joanne, helping her set out the food.

Dressed in black leggings, an oversized Christmas sweater just hideous enough to be considered a fashion statement instead of a blunder, and red and green ribbons wound throughout her braided hair, Danielle cheerfully threw open the front door. Her exuberant, "Merry Christmas!" quickly fizzled when she came face-to-face with Peter Morris.

"Mr. Morris…what a surprise," Danielle stammered. Instead of opening the door wider, she clung to its edge as if she was preparing to slam it shut at any moment.

"Afternoon, Ms. Boatman." Peter smiled, showing off his straight white teeth. "I hope I'm not intruding, but I stopped by to see one of my friends, Richard Winston."

"Oh…certainly. Richard mentioned you were friends." Danielle stepped aside and opened the door wider, motioning for him to enter.

Peter sniffed the air. The scent of pine mingled with freshly baked bread and simmering stews filled the hallway. He glanced around, but only he and Danielle stood in the entry, yet he could hear voices coming from the direction of the library, and Christmas carols drifted out from the living room.

"Am I interrupting a party or something?" Peter asked.

"We're having an open house, but the guests—other than those staying here—haven't started arriving yet." Danielle closed the front door and pointed to the parlor. "Why don't you wait in the parlor, and I'll go get Richard for you."

Peter followed Danielle into the cozy room. "I'm so sorry to intrude on you like this."

"That's fine." Danielle forced a smile and ducked out of the room, leaving Peter alone, sitting on the sofa. Alone, if you didn't count Marlow House's resident ghost.

"What are you doing here?" Walt asked.

Peter crossed and recrossed his legs and glanced at his wristwatch.

"I don't believe you're on Danielle's guest list. I know who you are. You're that charlatan who was here before, trying to talk Lily out of suing DCL for their part in her abduction." Walt took a seat across from the sofa and glared at Peter. He waved his hand and a lit cigar appeared. He took a puff.

Peter wrinkled his nose and sniffed the air. Waving his hand in front of his face, he glanced around the room. In the next moment the door opened and a young blonde walked in.

Walt looked over at Anna and watched as she shut the door behind her and walked toward Peter, her face unsmiling.

Peter stood up. "Hello." When Anna did not respond, he frowned, noting her angry glare. "Do we know each other?"

"I know who you are," she spat.

"You seem a little angry. I'm here to see Richard. Are you a guest here?"

"Danielle went to get Richard; he went upstairs to his room. He'll be a few minutes. But I think you should leave before then."

Peter frowned. "I'm afraid I don't understand."

"You're just trying to take advantage of that boy!"

Peter smiled. "Boy? He's practically old enough to be your father."

"That doesn't make him any less naive!"

"I really have no idea who you are or what your problem is, but my business with Richard is none of your concern."

"I'm making it my business! You go, and you leave him alone! Stop filling his head with nonsense!"

Peter started to say something and then paused. After a moment he asked, "Is there something going on between you two?"

Before Anna could answer, Danielle opened the door.

"Richard will be down in a moment. He spilled something on his pants and is changing his clothes," Danielle explained.

Without a word, Anna rushed out the door, pushing by Danielle.

"Who was that young woman?" Peter asked after Anna ran off.

Danielle stepped into the parlor. "She's one of our guests."

"Is she here with anyone?" Peter asked.

"I'm not sure what you mean."

"A husband or boyfriend perhaps?"

Before she considered her words, Danielle asked, "Isn't she just a little young for you?"

Peter chuckled. "No, I wasn't interested in her personally. I just got the impression she and Richard might be…well, intimately involved."

"I don't know anything about that. I really have no idea if anything—romantic—has blossomed. But if it has, it's really none of my business." *Or yours.*

"I'll say one thing about Anna, she showed good sense when it comes to this charlatan," Walt called out.

Until she heard Walt's voice, Danielle hadn't noticed Walt sitting on the chair across from Peter. She glanced at him and then looked at Peter.

"Did Anna say something to make you think she and he were… involved?" Danielle asked.

"She seemed a bit—territorial. But then, I imagine you frequently encounter that yourself."

Danielle frowned. "I don't understand what you mean."

"Men who wish to stake their claim on you—try to keep others away."

"Umm…no, can't say that's really been an issue." Danielle suppressed her grin.

"Are you forgetting Joe?" Walt asked.

"I find that hard to believe, Ms. Boatman. Not only are you quite attractive—if you don't mind me saying so—you're a wealthy young woman. It makes you quite vulnerable to those who wish to take advantage of you."

"Fortunately, that hasn't been an issue."

"Sadly, you may not even be aware it's happening. I'd like you to know if you ever need anything—support, counseling—I'm here for you. And I don't want you to get the wrong idea—I would think of you as a daughter."

"I confess, Mr. Morris, I feel just a little uncomfortable with your organization ever since that issue with Isabella's will."

"I understand. But please believe me, you have my word we sincerely thought the will she'd given us was her most current one. We had no reason to believe the will Stoddard found wasn't a fake."

"I understand Clarence Renton issued both wills—and with him being a member of Earthbound Spirits, I'd assume he would have informed you Stoddard's will was legitimate."

"Danielle, do you really want to get into this with him? I don't trust this man," Walt warned.

"Unfortunately, Clarence was overzealous—which is not uncommon with those who've just discovered the truth. I certainly understand your issues with Clarence; he did some very bad things during his time here. But he had reformed. And I believe in this instance he felt he was doing the right thing, but it was wrong. When we submitted Isabella's will to probate, I sincerely believed Stoddard's will was fake, especially since Darlene told the courts Stoddard claimed the will he found was counterfeit."

"Yes, but Darlene was blackmailed to say that," Danielle reminded him.

"That has never been proven, and it was only a theory based on some unsavory photographs found in Darlene's home. If she was being blackmailed, I had no knowledge of it. And if she was, it could very well have been Christiansen or Haston."

Danielle studied Peter. "And they're both dead now."

"Yes, yes, they are."

"If you'll excuse me, my guests will be arriving soon. Richard should be down any moment."

After Danielle left the parlor, Peter pulled out his cellphone and placed a call while Walt silently listened.

"Yes, I'm at Marlow House now," Peter said into the phone. "I'm waiting on Richard; he's upstairs, supposedly changing his clothes. I don't feel good about this at all…and I think he's gotten personally involved with one of the guests, which might explain why he hasn't called…Boatman? She's hostile toward us. I'm disappointed. Sending Richard here doesn't seem to have done any good. In fact, it may have hurt us if he's gotten involved with this other woman…no…she obviously knows about us, and she definitely is not a friend of Earthbound Spirits…we may have to get rid of her before it's too late."

Peter quickly ended his phone call when Richard walked into the room. "Richard!" Peter cheerfully greeted him, giving him a quick exuberant hug. The moment he hugged Richard, he could feel the younger man tense.

When the two men parted, Peter sat back down on the couch, and to Walt's annoyance, Richard decided to sit on the chair he was using.

"There is another chair!" Walt quickly stood up and moved to the empty seat and sat down.

"You haven't called," Peter said.

"I'm sorry." Richard looked down at his folded hands. They fidgeted nervously in his lap. "I've been pretty busy."

"By Ms. Boatman's attitude toward Earthbound Spirits, I suspect you haven't been spending your time helping her find the truth."

"I did speak to her, but she's not very receptive." Richard looked up from his hands.

"You were supposed to call me, arrange for me to be invited to the open house. As it is, I had to crash the party—certainly not how I like doing these things."

"I'm sorry, Mr. Morris. Sincerely. It's just—well, things have been a little strange for me here."

"Strange? How?"

Richard shook his head. "Old memories. Things I haven't thought about in years."

"We talked about memories, Richard. They are pointless. You need to let them go."

Richard nodded. "Yes, I know that."

"Have you made friends with any of the other guests?"

"Don't tell him, Richard!" Walt cried out. "He's up to no good!"

"Yes, all of them, actually. They're really very nice."

"I met one—a young blonde woman. She came in here while I was waiting for you."

"You must mean Anna," Richard suggested.

"So you two have become close?"

Richard shrugged. "She's nice, maybe a little bossy."

Peter leaned back in the couch and crossed his legs again. "So tell me a little about her."

"Not much to say, really. She just showed up here without a reservation; all the rooms were already taken. So Danielle put her in the attic."

Peter glanced briefly to the ceiling. "The attic?"

"I know, it sounds funny when I say it." Richard laughed. "I get the feeling she doesn't have any family and didn't want to be alone for Christmas. I can understand that."

"Have you forgotten we don't celebrate Christmas? It's nothing but a commercial holiday to generate money for large corporations, and it perpetuates harmful myths—myths which prevent people from discovering the truth."

"Yes, I know that." Richard nodded. "I just meant I can understand how someone—someone who hasn't found the truth—might be extra lonely around Christmas."

"Why did she come here?"

"She told us she saw Danielle's ad promoting an old-fashioned Christmas, and she just knew she had to come."

"Did Ms. Boatman just take her off the street? I told you someone like Ms. Boatman is more vulnerable to these types of people. Which is why we need to help her."

"What do you mean *these types of people*?"

"Those who try to exploit women like Ms. Boatman—play on their sympathy."

Richard shook his head. "No, Anna isn't like that. All I said is that she showed up without a reservation. Not that she was trying to get a room for free. I know Anna paid for her room—paid in cash through New Year's. I heard Danielle tell Lily that."

"You seem rather defensive over this Anna, Richard."

"She's just been very nice, that's all. We've had some fun together."

"Fun?"

"Not with just Anna, the entire group."

"I'm disappointed that you seemed to have forgotten your reason for coming to Marlow House."

TWENTY

Perched atop a stack of boxes in the far corner of the attic, Max watched and waited. With tail swishing and whiskers twitching, his golden eyes focused on the intended target. Before the day was over, he vowed, he would take down the trespassing rodent.

Since Danielle had turned the attic over to a guest, the area had been off-limits for him and Sadie and also for Walt. Yet the woman had left the door ajar when she went downstairs, and that was when he spied the interloper.

At first it was just the flash of a long tail peeking out from the end of the sofa and disappearing. Max saw it when he peered into the open doorway. The moment Max crept into the room, the body attached to the tail dashed from the sofa and ran across the attic floor, diving behind a dresser adjacent to the pile of boxes from which he now perched.

Time ticked away and Max didn't know how long he had been waiting for the rodent to show himself again. Yawning, he decided it was time for a quick nap. The sofa bed the woman had been using was still made out into a bed. Someone had spread a quilted comforter over the mattress and linens. Max thought it looked rather inviting. Leaping down from the boxes, he strolled over to the sofa bed and jumped up onto the mattress.

He could sleep on the pillows piled at the head of the bed, yet the suitcase sitting on the center of the mattress looked more inviting. Persistently nosing the suitcase, Max wedged it open just enough for him to slip inside. He discovered it was empty. There were no clothes to use as a makeshift mattress. Max didn't care. The dark space was a perfect place to nap.

DOWNSTAIRS, the guests had already started arriving. Peter was no longer in the parlor, but had joined Richard in the living room, where the two men mingled with the other guests.

Joe had just arrived and stood with Danielle in the hallway, looking into the living room.

"You invited Peter Morris?" Joe asked.

"Of course I didn't. He's friends with one of my guests, and I couldn't very well toss him out on the curb," Danielle told him.

"Sure you could." Joe made no attempt to walk toward the living room or to the library, where Danielle had told him the bar was set up. "Let me guess, that guy who was checking in the last time I was here, he's pals with Morris."

Danielle rolled her eyes. "Don't be so negative, Joe. It's Christmas."

"You know how I feel about you taking in strangers off the street. You've already had a few who proved to be dangerous."

"I can handle myself, Joe. Anyway, it's not Chris. And I don't think it's so much that Richard and Morris are friends, but Richard is a member of Earthbound Spirits—like Isabella was."

"Richard? I take it that's your guest who invited Morris?"

"Not sure if he invited Morris or if Morris crashed my party. Richard is actually a sweet guy; I just think he's looking for something, and at the moment, he believes Earthbound Spirits is his answer."

Joe shook his head. "I wonder why they're here. I didn't think Christmas was their thing."

"Not to sound full of myself—but I think I'm the reason Morris showed up." Danielle chuckled.

Narrowing his eyes, Joe studied Danielle. "He's trying to recruit you?"

Danielle shrugged. "That's my guess." She added with a dramatic sigh, "Yes, being that I'm a vulnerable naive heiress— prime for the con."

When Joe didn't laugh, Danielle rolled her eyes again and gave his arm a smack with the back of her hand. "I forgot, you actually believe I am a vulnerable naive heiress."

"I just think—"

"Oh, save it, Joe, and go get some spiked eggnog. Lighten up and enjoy Christmas. Don't worry about Morris, I have him handled."

"It's not just Morris or this Richard. I think you have other guests you need to be worried about."

"Gee, which one? Maybe Jessica? I know seven-year-olds can be terrifying."

"That guy who checked in the last time I was here."

"Chris?" Danielle laughed after Joe nodded the affirmative. "Oh, brother, Joe. Chris has been nothing but a gentleman. He's been generous and kind with the other guests—even took them all out for lunch."

"He also threatened to kill one of your other guests." Looking from the hallway into the living room, he didn't see Chris—or the blonde who had been threatened.

Danielle frowned. "What are you talking about?"

"I didn't hear it, but Brian did."

Danielle laughed. "Well, *that* explains it. Brian has been known to jump to the wildest conclusions. But I have to ask, just which guest did Chris supposedly threaten?"

"You have a young blonde woman staying here?"

"Yes, Anna. But I seriously can't imagine in what alternate universe Brian could come to the conclusion that Chris would threaten Anna." *Although...Walt did seem to think there was something between those two.*

"It was in Lucy's Diner on Monday. Brian was coming out of the restroom and overheard them arguing. He said something about wanting her dead. But you would have to ask Brian; I don't know what the exact words were."

"Did Brian say anything to them?"

"Yes, but the woman—Anna, you called her?—she got in Brian's face and defended the man."

"Well, there you have it. Brian obviously misunderstood the conversation."

"But—"

"Go, Joe." Danielle gave Joe a nudge toward the library.

"Lighten up and have some Christmas cheer. I think I heard the doorbell."

"I don't think Anna needs to worry about Chris, but Peter Morris is another matter altogether," Walt said when he appeared in front of Danielle as she turned toward the front door. She caught herself in time and didn't cry out in surprise.

"I hate when you do that!" she hissed under her breath. Walking to the door, Walt by her side, she asked, "And what are you talking about?"

"I overheard a phone conversation Morris had in the parlor. I don't know who he was talking to, but he said they might have to get rid of Anna."

Danielle paused by the front door and glanced at Walt and then looked behind her, toward the open door leading to the living room. She couldn't see in the room, but she could hear the mingling of Christmas carols—streaming through the living room speakers—with the voices of her guests.

"Why would he want to get rid of Anna? Do they know each other?" Danielle asked in a whisper. "Now that you mention it, she was in the parlor with Morris when I went to tell him Richard would be a few minutes."

"He didn't seem to know her, but she knew him. And she told him to stay away from Richard. When he was alone in the parlor, he made a phone call and said they may need to get rid of her. From what I heard, he believes there's something going on between Anna and Richard."

"Funny, Morris asked me about that. Which, of course, you already know, since you were in the room with us." Danielle reached for the front doorknob. She paused a moment.

"I haven't seen anything to indicate something romantic is going on between those two," Walt told her.

"I haven't either. But maybe it has nothing to do with romance." Danielle opened the door. Brian Henderson stood on the front porch, and in his hand he held a bottle of wine

"Merry Christmas." Brian handed Danielle the wine.

Accepting the gift, Danielle opened the door wider. "Merry Christmas, Brian. And thank you. Come on in."

"I thought for a moment there you changed your mind about inviting me," Brian said with a chuckle. Once inside the house, he started to remove his jacket.

Danielle closed the door. "Why do you say that?"

"Took you a while to answer the door. Figured you looked out the window and thought, *Damn, he actually showed up.*"

Danielle laughed and took his jacket from him. "Nah, it's Christmas. All is forgiven—or at least there's a truce until New Year's." Danielle walked over to the nearby coat rack and hung Brian's jacket on a hook.

"I guess the chief won't be coming," Brian said. "He's off for a few days."

"I heard. He took the boys to Portland so they could see their grandparents."

"Yeah, his late wife's family." Brian glanced around. "I thought I saw Joe's car."

"He's here. I made him go to the library and get a drink. He needs to lighten up."

"What did he do now?" Brian chuckled.

"Got on my case again about running a B and B. I guess you ran into a couple of my guests in town, and there was a bit of a misunderstanding."

"Joe told you?"

"Didn't you know he would?"

"Actually, when he asked if he should say anything to you, I said something like, *I don't see the point.*"

"Well…thanks, I think." Danielle lifted her hand with the bottle of wine and pointed down the hall. "We have a bar set up in the library; you'll find hot food in the kitchen, other goodies throughout. Go mingle." The doorbell rang again.

EN ROUTE TO THE LIBRARY, Brian came to an abrupt halt when a little girl darted out from the kitchen, carrying a platter of cookies. She slammed into him, spilling the cookies onto the floor. By her startled expression and the tears now pooling in her brown eyes, he expected she might start crying at any moment.

He dropped to his knees and quickly began snatching up the cookies off the floor and setting them back on the platter.

"I'm sorry! I ruined them!" The little girl held tight onto the platter and looked down at Brian, who knelt before her, picking up the remaining cookies.

"Nah, they're fine. Haven't you ever heard of the five-second rule?" Brian asked as he dropped the last cookie back on the platter and stood up. He smiled down at the little girl.

"Five-second rule?" she asked with a frown.

"Yeah. As long as you pick it up before five seconds, you can still eat it."

She shook her head. "If they fell on the floor, no one will want them now."

"Who says?" Brian grabbed a cookie and shoved it in his mouth. He made growling sounds as he quickly chewed and swallowed it.

The little girl giggled.

"See, it didn't hurt me…" Brian then grabbed hold of his throat and pretended to choke and swoon.

The little girl started to laugh.

"Here, Jessica, let me take those," Joanne said as she stepped out of the kitchen.

Jessica handed Joanne the platter. "I'm sorry."

Joanne ruffled the top of Jessica's head and said, "Hey, don't worry. We have plenty of cookies. Danielle's been baking for days. I'll just bag these up for Brian, and he can take them home with him." Joanne flashed Brian a smile and wink.

"I'd like that." Brian grinned. "Merry Christmas, Joanne. So Danielle did all the baking?"

"Yes, she's quite a good baker—and cook. Must say I'm impressed. Glad to see you made it."

"And who is this young lady?" Brian glanced down at Jessica.

"Brian, this is Jessica. Jessica, this is Officer Henderson. He's one of our local police officers."

"You can call me Brian, Jessica. I saw you the other day at the diner with your friends."

"We've been having so much fun since we got here! We went to the craft store after we went out to lunch."

"You did? Did you buy anything?" Brian asked.

"Chris bought us stuff to make phonebook Christmas trees, but Anna picked it all out. Anna said he didn't have to make them with us because he paid for everything."

"So this Chris and Anna, they're married? Boyfriend and girlfriend?"

Jessica giggled. "No, silly."

TWENTY-ONE

"Why were you asking Jessica about Chris and Anna?" Joanne asked when Brian followed her back into the kitchen. Jessica had already run off, looking for her mother.

"I ran into them the other day when they were at the diner. They seemed to be having a disagreement. Just wondered what was up with them."

Joanne carried the platter of cookies over to the counter and set them down. "That surprises me. All the guests have been getting along. If I didn't know better, I'd think they've been friends for years."

Brian lifted the lids off the slow cookers to see what was inside. "So what's this about one of them showing up without a reservation and taking a room in the attic?"

"That's Anna. I'm surprised someone her age is so content just hanging out with the other guests. She even had them doing a craft project together."

"What are the other guests like?" Brian grabbed a clean spoon from the counter and dipped it in the slow cooker with the oyster stew.

"You met Jessica. She's here with her mother. From what I understand, they won their trip here." Joanne picked the cookies up from the platter.

"Danielle is giving away trips?" Brian blew on the spoonful of oyster stew before sampling it.

"No. According to Patricia, she won a Christmas holiday for her and Jessica. Danielle knew nothing about it. But it appears to be legit, because Danielle was paid for the room." Joanne tossed the cookies into the trash can.

"Odd Danielle didn't know about it." Brian dropped the spoon in the sink.

"I'm happy for them. They seem to be enjoying themselves."

MARIE NICHOLS ARRIVED at the open house just as Peter Morris stepped out the front door to leave. Holding onto her grandson's arm with one hand and a cane in the other, she made her way up Marlow House's front walkway. She paused when she saw Peter walking her way. Lifting her cane, she asked in a loud voice, "What is he doing here?"

"Grandmother, please, it's Christmas," Adam said in a hushed voice.

"I know what time of year it is. I'm not daft. But he doesn't believe in Christmas; why is he here?"

"Good evening, folks," Peter said politely as he walked past Marie and Adam, making his way to the street.

Marie stubbornly refused to budge. She stood and watched as Peter got into his car and drove off. "I can't believe Danielle would invite him."

"I doubt she did. And, Grandma, just because someone's religion doesn't acknowledge Christmas doesn't mean they don't attend Christmas parties. I've been to a few of your Christmas gatherings where you've invited your Jewish friends—and they attended."

"That's different," Marie spat, turning to the house. "Jewish is a real religion."

"I believe it's called Judaism," Adam corrected.

"Are you being obstinate?"

"PETER MORRIS, he's a friend of Richard's?" Chris asked. He

stood in the corner of the living room with Danielle, sipping brandy-laced eggnog.

When Marie had arrived two hours earlier, she spared no time letting everyone within hearing distance know what she thought of Peter Morris and Earthbound Spirits. Richard did not defend Morris or the organization. He made no comment and silently listened to the elderly woman's rant. He had since retreated to the parlor with Patricia. Marie and Adam were now in the library, where Adam was chatting with Ian at the bar, and Marie was visiting with Millie Samson and several other people she knew.

"I don't know if *friend* is really the correct term. Do you know anything about Earthbound Spirits?" Danielle asked.

"I've read a little bit about them. I noticed Richard didn't speak up when your friend—Marie, is that her name?"

"Yes."

"When Marie let us all know what she thought of the—cult—as she called it. If Richard hadn't introduced me to the man when he was here, I wouldn't have known they knew each other. Well, at least not if I walked in when Marie was giving her opinion." Chris sipped his eggnog.

"He did look a little embarrassed," Danielle said.

"Why wouldn't you necessarily call him Richard's friend?" Chris asked.

"Richard's a member of Earthbound Spirits. I don't think he's high up in the group—but Morris is its founder."

"Richard has never once mentioned Earthbound Spirits to me," Chris told her.

"Hmm, that's kind of interesting. I sort of assumed someone who is a member of a group like that—well, that they would want to talk about it. He did mention it to me. To be honest, I have a feeling Morris showed up tonight thinking I might be a likely recruit."

"You, in Earthbound Spirits?" Chris chuckled. "Like that would ever happen."

Danielle smiled. "Thanks, I think. So why don't you think I'd be a likely member?"

"You just seem far too savvy to fall prey to something like that. While I like Richard—what I know about him—he comes off a little insecure, searching for something in spite of his money."

"How do you know he has money?" Danielle asked.

Chris arched his brows. "Have you looked at that guy's shoes? They probably cost more than what I pay for my shoes—in a lifetime."

Danielle glanced down at Chris's feet. "Oh, your shoes don't look *that* cheap."

Chris laughed. "Thanks a lot!"

Danielle grinned. "So what did Morris say to you? Did he give you the recruitment speech?"

"Not at all. In fact, he never mentioned Earthbound Spirits. But he did ask a lot of questions."

"About what?"

"Me. What I did, where I lived. Came off as one of those people who are genuinely interested in you. That can be very seductive for some people."

"Are you saying he really wasn't interested in getting to know you?"

Chris chuckled. "Oh, he wanted to get to know me—or should I say, my net worth. But once he figured out I was some drifter who'd spent the last six months living on someone else's sailboat and wasn't sure where I was going next, he cut the conversation short and moved on."

"Doesn't really surprise me."

"He wasn't the only one asking me questions tonight." Chris set his empty glass on a side table. "Your friend Joe was giving me the third degree earlier. But I guess that's what cops do."

"Oh…" Danielle cringed. "I'm sorry about that."

"No problem. But I'll give you the heads-up, that guy he was with—also a cop…"

"You mean Brian?"

Chris nodded. "I think that's his name. I ran into him at the diner the other day, and he overheard me and Anna talking and got the wrong impression and—"

"Yeah, Joe mentioned that to me."

"He really did misunderstand. We were in the hallway, and he was behind the door, standing in the men's bathroom. Not really sure what he thought he heard, but he got in my face."

"Yeah, well, Brian has a tendency to do that. Did he say anything to you tonight?"

"No, but he did a lot of glaring. I didn't notice him talking to Anna either—she got a little feisty with him when he confronted me in the diner. But I did see him sitting with Patricia for a long time tonight. And then that cowboy came in. Your friend Brian seemed a little annoyed with the competition."

"Oh, you must mean Will Wayne. Yes, Patricia is from Arizona. She recognized him. He was something of a celebrity in the Phoenix area. Had a big car dealership; his ads were always on TV."

"I assume he was in the ads?"

"Yes. He was known as Billy Bob Wayne. I'm glad he was able to stop by tonight, if even for a while. His daughter was in Earthbound Spirits—Isabella Strickland. Her uncle's the one who had Lily, the man you read about."

"Yeah, I sort of figured that by what was said in there."

"So tell me, Chris, what are your plans for after the New Year?"

"You mean when I leave here?"

Danielle nodded.

"I haven't gotten that far. Just trying to enjoy my time here. Get into the Christmas spirit. What about you; how's it been spending this Christmas with a bunch of strangers? I know Marlow House just opened this past summer."

"To be honest, it's gone a lot better than I had hoped. I sort of figured my holiday guests would be comprised of a few couples— who would have minimal contact with each other aside from the meals. And even then, I gave a two-hour window for meals, so everyone could have eaten at different times—which hasn't been the case. It's been fun. It's felt like Christmas."

"Yes, yes, it has." Chris smiled. "I've enjoyed all the different Christmas cookies. When I was a kid, my mom used to do this thing —I think she called it a cookie exchange."

Danielle's smile broadened. "We used to do that. Get about six friends together. Each of us would make six dozen cookies. We'd take our cookies to the exchange and return home with six different kinds of cookies, a dozen each." Then she added with a laugh, "Minus whatever we ate at the exchange."

"In my case it was more like twenty of Mother's friends."

"Wow! That's a lot of cookies!" Danielle laughed.

"I'd say you've almost done that—and by yourself."

"Not quite twenty." Danielle grinned. "I remember one year someone brought store-bought cookies—were people mad!"

"Isn't this fascinating. You're discussing *cookies*," Walt said when he appeared, standing between Danielle and Chris.

Trying to ignore Walt, Danielle asked, "You mentioned your parents are gone too?"

"They've been gone for three years now," Chris explained.

"Any brothers or sisters?"

"I have a sister. She and her husband moved to London two years before our parents were killed. That's where my brother-in-law's from. I'm happy for her, but it makes it a little difficult to get together for the holidays."

"Did you meet Ian's sister? She was here for a while, but went back over to Ian's, said she was exhausted, but she'll be here in the morning."

"Ian's sister seems like a nice girl," Walt chimed in. "She and Chris would make a nice couple. You should seat them together at the dinner table for tomorrow night. Too bad you didn't hang any mistletoe. You never know, a gentle nudge under the mistletoe for those two and Ian might have a new brother-in-law."

"Yes, I did. Ian introduced us. She seems like a nice girl. Maybe you should seat her next to Richard tomorrow night at the dinner table. I think they would make a cute couple." Chris smiled. "You don't happen to have any mistletoe, do you? Nothing like a little Christmas romance to spice things up."

Momentarily speechless, Danielle stared blankly at Chris. She blinked her eyes. Finally, she asked, "Have you ever felt that maybe you're a little…umm…clairvoyant, maybe?"

Suppressing a grin, Chris asked, "Clairvoyant, what do you mean?"

"Oh, I don't know…like you start humming a song, and then in the next minute it comes on the radio. Or a friend starts talking about something, and it's something you were just thinking about. Stuff like that."

"You're thinking of Hunter, aren't you?" Walt asked. "How he heard me say Marvin. Of course, he got everything else wrong."

Chris shook his head. "No…what made you think of that?"

"Oh…I don't know. Sometimes the goofiest, off-the-wall stuff just pops into my head. Never mind. It's nothing."

JESSICA WAS TUCKED into bed for the night, and the open house guests—except for Ian and those staying at Marlow House—had all gone home, when the packages arrived. They weren't brought by a carrier Danielle recognized—it wasn't FedEx or the United Parcel Service. The man delivering the packages dropped them on the front doorstep, rang the bell, and returned to his van. Danielle managed to catch a glimpse of the van as it drove off.

Chris and Ian helped Danielle bring the gifts inside and set them under the Christmas tree. There were twelve packages in all—each one wrapped in festive Christmas paper and adorned with silk bows and silver bells. Half of the packages were addressed to Jessica and half to Patricia.

Patricia stood by the fireplace, her right hand wiping away any escaping tears. "I've never won anything before."

"I think it's all very exciting!" Anna exclaimed. "I can't wait until morning to see what you and Jessica got!"

TWENTY-TWO

Max hated storms. Lightning streaking across the window and lighting up the night sky terrified him. Fortunately, he had discovered a comfy dark retreat sheltering him from night terrors. Peeking his head out of the suitcase, he looked around. It was morning.

Climbing out of the bag, he stretched out on the bed and yawned. He wondered if the rat was still in the room. Outside, the rain continued to fall.

THE SCENE REMINDED Danielle of one from her childhood. No one had bothered to get dressed yet, aside from putting on their robes and slippers. Ian and Kelly were still across the street, yet Danielle did not expect them to be over until later in the morning. Everyone but Jessica had stopped by the kitchen to grab a cup of coffee to take to the living room with them.

Danielle entered the living room, carrying a tray laden with cinnamon rolls, slices of pumpkin bread, and banana muffins. She set the tray on the coffee table in front of the sofa, where Anna and Patricia sat. They watched Jessica excitedly opening her stocking gifts from her place on the floor by the Christmas tree.

Lily sat on the floor next to Jessica, enjoying watching the young girl's excitement. In the chairs across from the sofa, Chris and Richard leisurely enjoyed their morning coffee.

"Those look good," Chris noted after Danielle set the tray down.

"Help yourself." A clap of thunder rang out. Danielle glanced to the window. "I guess I should be grateful the storm started after everyone went home last night."

"It's one hell of a storm out there." Chris stood up briefly and snatched a cinnamon roll off the tray and then sat back down on the chair. "I sure wouldn't want to be out in it."

Instead of finding a place to sit, Danielle picked up the Christmas stockings lined up along the wall. They were no longer hanging empty on the mantel, but sitting on the floor, each one stuffed to its brim. She began handing them to whosever name was embroidered on the particular stocking.

"What's this?" Richard asked when Danielle handed him one.

Danielle shrugged. "Ask Santa. He must have shown up last night in spite of the storm."

"You filled our stockings?" Anna asked when Danielle handed her one.

"Don't be silly." Danielle glanced over at Jessica, who was too busy opening her stocking gifts to pay attention to what the adults were saying. "It had to have been Santa."

"Oh…of course." Anna blushed.

"If you see Santa," Patricia said when Danielle handed her a stocking. "Please let him know how much we appreciate all he's done."

"I will." Danielle grinned.

Danielle wasn't surprised to discover her stocking had also been filled. She glanced over at Lily, who flashed her a smile

"Lily," Danielle said, lifting her stocking, "if you see Santa before I do, tell him thanks. It was really sweet of him."

"From what I heard, it was a tough call for Santa. You almost got coal," Lily teased.

"He probably heard about all the times you were arrested this past summer," Walt said when he appeared a moment later.

Unwrapping one of her small packages from the stocking, Danielle grinned over at Walt.

"Merry Christmas, Danielle. You've really outdone yourself," Walt told her. "You've created a beautiful Christmas for everyone."

Instead of opening the gifts from the stocking on his lap, Chris glanced over to the remaining stockings lined up along the wall. "Is there something in the stocking for Walt Marlow?"

Walt looked to his stocking. "You got me something?"

Not waiting for Danielle's reply, Chris set his stocking on the floor by his feet and stood up.

"Oh, it's nothing…umm…more a private joke between me and Lily," Danielle lied.

"Can I look? After all, Walt isn't here to open it." Chris picked up the stocking off the floor.

"Yeah, please do," Lily called out. "I'm kinda curious myself."

Chris dipped his hand in the stocking and pulled out a wrapped gift. He was about to open it when he looked over at Walt and noted the serious expression on his face. *Don't be a jerk, Chris. This gift is not about you,* Chris told himself. He returned the small wrapped package to the stocking.

"What's in it?" Walt asked. "Do you have any idea how long it's been since I got a Christmas gift?"

Setting Walt's stocking back on the ground, Chris glanced over to Walt, who for a moment—reminded him of Jessica. Not Jessica exactly, just her excitement over the unexpected gifts.

"Have him open it," Walt told Danielle.

"Open it, Chris. Let's pretend Walt's here," Danielle said.

"That would be kind of scary," Richard teased.

Chris nodded and then picked up the stocking and removed the gift. After setting the stocking back on the floor, he carefully unwrapped the package. Inside he found a book. It was obviously old, yet in pristine condition.

"Is this a first edition?" Chris opened the book. "It's signed."

"I thought it would be nice in the library," Danielle said quickly.

Walt smiled. "Thank you, Danielle. I love it."

"Can I see?" Richard asked. A moment later, Chris handed him the book.

Reverently, Richard turned the pages. He came to the middle of the book and frowned. "What's this?" He pulled out a slip of paper stuck between two of the book's pages. "It looks like a handwritten…gift certificate?" He looked up at Danielle, a puzzled expression on his face. "You also got Walt Marlow a subscription to Netflix?"

THE RAT SHOWED HIMSELF, but then thunder rattled the attic and Max decided the rodent could wait. Jumping down off the bed, Max strolled out of the room and headed downstairs.

When he reached the living room, there were boxes everywhere, strewn across the floor. Jessica was holding up clothes for the others to see, and everyone was talking. He didn't see Sadie—or Ian—so he figured they were still across the street.

Just as Max was about to investigate the empty boxes, Danielle scooped him up and kissed his head. "Max! I wondered where you were!" He started to purr, and she set him back on the floor in front of a Christmas stocking.

"Merry Christmas, Max. This is for you." Danielle slipped her hand inside the stocking and then Max heard something squeak. His ears twitched. She pulled opened the top of the stocking for him to look inside. There was something green and purple sticking out. It looked interesting. He pressed his nose inside and began to investigate.

EVERYONE HAD FINALLY GOTTEN DRESSED. They had opened all the gifts, eaten breakfast, and picked up all the empty boxes, wrapping paper, and ribbon. Lily and Ian had gone for a ride with Kelly to show her around town. It had stopped storming, but by the clouds in the sky, it looked like there would be more rain before the day ended.

In the kitchen, Jessica sat at the table, painting, using a paint by number set she had received for Christmas. The gift was from Richard. He had purchased it at the craft store when no one was looking.

In the living room, Danielle sat with her other guests while flames flickered in the nearby stone fireplace.

"I couldn't say it with Jessica here, but thank you for the stocking, Danielle," Richard told her. He reached down and petted Sadie, who slept by his feet. "And everyone, I really didn't expect gifts. It's been a few years since I've exchanged gifts with anyone... and well...frankly...Christmas was never much with my parents.

Oh, I got presents, don't get me wrong. But it's been a long time since I ever felt…well, the Christmas spirit. Thank you."

"Yes, thank you," Chris agreed. "I had some great Christmases with my parents. Since they've been gone, well, basically it's just been another day. This has been nice."

"I agree." Anna nodded. "Thank you for the stocking gifts, Danielle. A very generous Santa."

Danielle blushed. "It was fun to do."

"You all don't know how grateful I am for this Christmas. After I lost my job, I thought this was going to be the worst Christmas of my life. Jessica has had such a good time here. You've all been so nice to her," Patricia told them.

"She's a good kid," Richard said. "And that's pretty amazing, how you won the holiday here, not to mention some pretty nice gifts."

"You know, I'm really grateful for those gifts—the clothes, gift cards, and the computer. We didn't have a computer, and Jessica was growing out of her clothes. And I will certainly put all those gift cards to good use, especially the ones for the grocery store! But in all honesty, if the prize was just for the trip, I'd still be thrilled. At first, I wasn't going to come. I needed to find a new place to live. But I couldn't afford to pass up the gifts. Yet now…well, it's been a wonderful Christmas. The gifts were frosting on the cake, but frankly, it's the cake not the frosting that means the most to me."

"If you ever find out who sponsors Benevolent Charities, I'd love to know," Danielle said.

Patricia nodded.

"Patricia, you mentioned you don't have any family," Chris said.

"No. It's just me and Jessica. My husband and I were both in foster care—that's where we met. Neither of us had family."

"No brothers—sisters?" Chris asked.

Patricia didn't respond immediately. Instead, she looked over at the Christmas tree. Finally, she said, "I have a brother. Somewhere."

"What do you mean somewhere?" Chris asked.

"I had a younger brother. He was six when Mom died. They didn't keep us together."

"That's terrible. Have you ever tried to find him?" Richard asked.

"Yes, a number of years ago. I learned he was adopted, the

records sealed. I really didn't have the resources to look for him. And if I found him, would he even remember me?"

"What do you remember about him?" Chris asked.

Patricia smiled softly. "I remember he was a sweet boy. Shy. It was hard on him when our father died. He might have been young at the time, but those two were so close. And when Mom died—he was devastated. Refused to talk."

"Did they try to keep you together?" Danielle asked.

Patricia shook her head. "No. I was pretty angry at the time—acting out. Defiant. I was furious when they separated us. You see, after our father died, Mom had to get a job. After school, we stayed at a neighbor's, but my brother had never come out of his shell after losing Dad. So he clung to me. I was really the only one he would talk to other than Mom." Tears filled Patricia's eyes. "Technically, the neighbor was his afterschool babysitter, but I was the one who took care of him."

"Why didn't they keep you together?" Danielle asked. "I don't understand why they would separate siblings like that."

Patricia wiped away her tears. "I always figured it was my fault. I overheard one of the caseworkers saying something about how I would never get adopted out because of my age and my attitude, and that my brother's only chance of finding a real family was to get away from me so they could help him. I guess they figured I was my brother's problem—not the fact he had lost both his parents in a relatively short time."

"It wasn't your fault!" Anna fumed. "Those idiot caseworkers! You were a good loving sister who was just a child and needed help."

"I agree with Anna," Richard said.

"What was your brother's name?" Danielle asked.

"Robert James, but we called him Bobby." Patricia glanced back to the Christmas tree. "And yesterday was his birthday. Mom called him her Christmas baby."

TWENTY-THREE

The flashes of lightning outside the bedroom window did not wake Danielle, but the rumble of thunder that followed did. Sitting up in her bed, she sleepily rubbed her eyes and looked toward the window. She saw Walt lounging leisurely on her sofa.

Yawning, she asked, "How long have you been there?"

An unlit cigar appeared in Walt's right hand. He fidgeted with it a moment before it disappeared. "Not long."

Danielle yawned again and stretched, making no effort to get out of bed. Just as she turned to look at the time on the alarm clock, its radio started blaring jazz music.

"Good grief!" Danielle leaned over and slammed her hand against the off button. "Jazz music first thing in the morning is not happening! Who turned my channel?" When she glanced at Walt, she had her answer. "I knew it was a bad idea to put my old clock radio on the nightstand!"

Walt shrugged. "Joanne got here a few minutes ago."

Danielle leaned back on her pillows. "She's probably starting breakfast. I guess I should get up."

"I think you cooked enough yesterday. Why don't you rest and let her take care of it?"

"If you thought I should sleep in, why did you have my alarm clock blaring jazz this early?"

"Sorry. I didn't realize I had actually set the alarm."

Another clap of thunder shook the room. Both Danielle and Walt looked briefly to the window.

"Has it been storming all night?" Danielle asked.

"Yes. I don't remember the last time we had a storm quite like this."

"Where did you spend last night?"

"In the parlor, since you've taken away my attic."

"I'm sorry, Walt. I just felt sorry for Anna, and she's turned out to be a nice person—not some crazy lady like you thought when she first showed up."

"I know." Walt gave Danielle a smile. "You were right, it is Christmas. People shouldn't be alone at Christmas."

"Technically, it's the day after Christmas." Danielle grinned.

"No, Christmas doesn't officially end until January 5," Walt reminded her.

"True…the Twelve Days of Christmas."

"I wanted to thank you again for the Christmas gifts. The book's extraordinary, and I enjoyed the other gift too."

"Enjoyed, does that mean you've been watching Netflix?"

"Yes, I spent most of the evening watching television."

"I just hope none of the guests heard you."

Walt shook his head. "No. I had Max stand guard in the hallway. If anyone had started down the stairs or had Chris opened his bedroom door, Max would let me know."

"Lucky someone didn't trip on Max in the hall."

"No one came downstairs, and Chris only came out of the room once during the night."

"Did he come into the parlor? See the television on?"

"No." Walt shook his head. "I assume he went into the kitchen to get something to drink. He didn't walk in the direction of the parlor."

"That's good." Danielle let out a sigh and then said, "I think Marlow House's first B and B Christmas holiday has gone well so far, don't you?"

"Extremely well. Your guests certainly seem to be enjoying themselves."

"Yes. But I thought that was so sad when Patricia told us last night about her brother."

"Do you think Richard is right, she might be able to use Facebook to find him?"

"It's a shot. I know other people have found missing family members and friends by making posts to share. Now that she has a computer, she'll be able to search if that's what she wants to do."

"You don't think she wants to find him?" Walt asked.

"Not that exactly. I just sort of got the feeling she's accepted the fact he's gone from her life…oh, and another thing…has nothing to do with Patricia's brother, but I just thought of it when you mentioned Richard…remember how Morris was quizzing me about Anna and Richard?"

"He was also asking Richard about Anna," Walt reminded her.

"Maybe Morris was onto something."

"What do you mean?"

"Last night, when I got up to use the bathroom, I thought I heard something, so I looked out my bedroom door, and guess who I saw coming down the stairs from the attic?"

"Richard?"

Danielle nodded.

"What time was that?"

"I don't know, it was late. I didn't think to check the time. It was after everyone went to bed."

"Hmm…interesting."

Danielle tossed her blanket and top sheet to the side. "I guess I better get up and see if Joanne needs any help getting breakfast on."

IN THE KITCHEN twenty minutes later, Danielle found Joanne shredding potatoes for hash browns.

"Good morning," Danielle cheerfully greeted as she poured herself a cup of coffee. "Did you have a nice Christmas?"

"Yes, I did. And thank you for the gift. I love it. It was very sweet of you."

"I just appreciate all you do around here." Danielle sipped her coffee and took a seat at the kitchen table.

Joanne glanced around the room. "I have to say I'm impressed with how everything looks this morning. I would've never have guessed you prepared a Christmas dinner in here last night. I thought you were going to leave me the dishes to clean up this morning."

"When Lily and I started to clear away the dishes, everyone just pitched in. It felt a little like I was back home, when everyone would help clean up."

"Even the men?" Joanne chuckled. "In our family they fall asleep on the floor or couch after Christmas dinner and the women end up in the kitchen for the rest of the evening. Of course, I don't really mind that. Gives us all a time to visit without the men underfoot."

Danielle shrugged. "My dad was pretty good about helping in the kitchen. So was my uncle Carl. Last night, Chris ended up washing all the pots and pans while I dried and put them away."

WHEN DANIELLE WALKED BACK into the hallway twenty minutes later, she found Lily hurrying to the front door.

"Morning, Lily, you certainly aren't going outside in this weather." Danielle followed Lily.

"Hardly. Ian just called. He and Kelly are coming over in a few minutes, and I promised to have the front door unlocked so they don't have to stand in the rain and wait for someone to answer the door."

"He has a key," Danielle reminded her.

"I don't think he wants to be fumbling around with the lock in this weather." Lily unlocked the front door.

"I guess I don't blame them."

"Hey, guess who I saw sneaking down from the attic last night," Lily smirked.

Danielle grinned. "Richard?"

Lily laughed. "No, not Richard. That's funny."

"Why funny?"

"I can't see Richard and Anna together. Of course, I really can't see Chris and Anna together, either."

Danielle frowned. "Chris and Anna?"

"Yeah, that's who I saw sneaking down from the attic last night. Chris."

"Chris? What time?"

Lily shrugged and shook her head. "I don't know. It was late. After everyone went to bed. I didn't check the time. I don't think he saw me."

"That's really weird."

"I agree. Chris and Anna? Who woulda thunk it?"

"That's not what I mean, Lily. I saw Richard coming down from the attic last night too."

"Really? What time?"

"I don't know. It was late. I didn't check the time either."

The front door flew open. Laughing, Ian and Kelly raced inside with Sadie and slammed the door shut behind them. Rain dripped from their umbrella. Sadie immediately shook off the water and went to find Walt, her tail wagging.

"We had to share my umbrella." Kelly laughed. "It seems my brother is too cool to own one."

"What self-respecting Portlander owns an umbrella?" Ian slipped out of his wet jacket and hung it on the coat rack.

"For one thing, you're not a Portlander," Kelly countered.

"No, but you are. And you should be ashamed."

"Yeah, well, you weren't too proud to crowd under it when we came across the street." Kelly lifted the umbrella up. "You want me to put this outside?"

"Nah, just hang it in the bathroom," Danielle suggested.

"SHOULDN'T WE WAIT FOR ANNA?" Patricia asked after they all sat down at the dining room table to eat breakfast. Almost everyone was there—Lily, Danielle, Ian, Chris, Richard, Patricia, Kelly, and Jessica—everyone but Joanne, who was in the kitchen, and Anna, who hadn't yet come downstairs for the morning.

"She's probably sleeping in," Richard suggested.

"I don't know how she can sleep with all that thunder—especially with her in the attic. It must be loud up there," Patricia said.

Danielle picked up a platter of hash browns and handed it to Richard. "I think we should go ahead and eat before this gets cold. She'll come down when she's ready."

ANNA DID NOT COME down for breakfast. Lunchtime approached, and still she had not joined the group. No longer in the dining room, they gathered in the room with the Christmas tree. Ian, Lily, Kelly, and Patricia played Mexican Train at the small table in the room while Danielle and Chris chatted. Richard sat on the floor with Jessica, playing Go Fish. Walt lounged on a chair in the corner, Sadie by his feet, while Max lurked under the branches of the Christmas tree, periodically batting at a hanging ornament.

Danielle stood up from her place on the sofa. "I think I'll go check on Anna, make sure she's not sick or something."

Patricia looked up from the game. "That's probably a good idea. I would've thought she'd be down by now. It's almost eleven."

"When I was younger, I could sleep until noon—of course, that was after being up all night," Lily said with a chuckle. Danielle looked over at Lily and they exchanged glances, each of them thinking of what they had seen Christmas night.

Walt stood up. "I'll go with you. I'd like to see what she's done to my attic."

"I'm sure your attic is just fine," Danielle said after they left the living room and started up the stairs. "But there is something funny; remember how I told you I saw Richard coming out of Anna's room late last night?"

"Yes."

"Apparently, when Lily got up last night to use the bathroom, she saw Chris coming down the stairs from the attic."

Walt arched his brows. "Really?"

Danielle nodded. "I don't know why they were up there. But I don't think there's anything—well, romantic—going on. I never noticed her flirting with either of them. She didn't seem interested in them that way."

"You can tell when a woman is interested?"

"I think so."

"What about the men?" Walt asked. "Maybe they were returning downstairs after being rejected."

"You think they went up there for some late night booty call?"

"Not really sure what a booty call is. But perhaps they were pursuing her."

"I certainly never noticed anything going on between them."

Walt shrugged. "She is an attractive young woman. A little pushy, in my opinion, but good looking. Although, by the way Chris has been behaving, I thought his interests lie elsewhere."

They reached the second-floor landing. Still holding onto the handrail, Danielle paused a moment and looked at Walt. "Interested in who?"

"You, of course."

Danielle perked up. "Really?"

Walt scowled. "Are you seriously interested in Chris after he's been lurking around in the attic with Anna?"

Danielle continued to the attic stairwell. "Who said I was interested?"

"Oh, please." Walt rolled his eyes. "Maybe Anna hasn't been flirting with Richard and Chris, but you certainly have."

Danielle stopped and looked at Walt. "I have not been flirting with Richard!"

Walt arched his brows again. "And Chris?"

Danielle shrugged. "Well, maybe a little. But you're right, if he has something going on with Anna, I'm not really interested. I don't need that kind of drama in my life."

"Or that kind of man."

"True." Now on the stairs leading to the attic, Danielle paused again and looked at Walt. With a mischievous grin, she added, "But that doesn't mean I still can't look."

Walt let out a sigh and shook his head. Danielle laughed and started back up the attic stairs, Walt by her side.

When they reached the attic door, Danielle started to knock, but noticed the door was not shut all the way. "Anna?" Danielle called out. When there was no answer, she knocked on the door and called out Anna's name again. "Anna? Are you all right? Anna?" There was no sound inside the room.

She pushed the door open and called out again, "Anna, it's Danielle. We were worried…" Danielle stepped into the attic—there was no Anna. She glanced around.

"She's not in here," Walt said, walking into the room.

"She must be in the bathroom."

"Danielle, if you're talking about the bathroom on the second floor, the door was wide open when we walked by. No one was in it."

"Then I guess she must have gone downstairs and we missed her. She's probably in the kitchen with Joanne, getting something to eat."

"Is that blood?" Walt asked.

"Blood?" Danielle walked over to where Walt stood and looked down at the small white throw rug on the floor.

Danielle frowned. "It sure looks like blood."

TWENTY-FOUR

"Joanne, have you seen Anna?" Danielle asked when she walked into the kitchen a few minutes later.

Joanne looked up from the sink full of dirty pots and pans. "Anna? No. I haven't seen her all morning."

"She has to be around here someplace," Danielle mumbled as she left the kitchen and headed for the library. When she finally returned to the living room, there was still no sign of Anna.

"Is Anna feeling okay?" Patricia asked when Danielle walked into the room.

Danielle frowned. "She hasn't been in here?"

Lily turned to face Danielle. "No. We thought you were going to the attic to check on her."

"I did. She wasn't in the attic. I figured she was probably in the bathroom, but she wasn't in there either."

"Danielle, we didn't check all the guest bedrooms," Walt said. "I'm going to see if she's in someone's room." Walt disappeared.

"When she wasn't upstairs, I figured she probably came down to the kitchen for something to eat; I must've missed her. But Joanne hasn't seen her either. And I looked in all the other rooms on the bottom floor…" She glanced at Chris. "Except for the room Chris is staying in, but I don't think she's in there."

"She isn't," Walt said as he appeared a moment later. "She's in none of the bedrooms. I even checked the basement. She's not in the house."

"You don't think she left, do you? I thought she was staying for another week," Patricia asked.

"Her suitcase is sitting on the bed. But she doesn't seem to be in the house."

Richard stood up. "I can't believe she'd go out in this weather."

"Anna didn't leave, did she?" Jessica asked.

"We don't know, honey," Patricia said.

"She has to be here somewhere," Ian insisted. "I agree with Richard, she wouldn't go out in this weather, and if her suitcase is still sitting on the bed, then I doubt she left."

"I need to use the bathroom," Danielle said abruptly, looking at Walt. "I'll be right back."

"Did you want to talk to me?" Walt asked.

Chris watched as Danielle gave a silent nod and turned toward the door. Walt followed her out of the room.

"Something about this creeps me out," Danielle whispered as she went into the downstairs bathroom with Walt, closing the door behind her.

"What do you mean?"

"The blood on the rug, for one thing. But I didn't want to say anything about it with Jessica in there."

"She probably just cut her foot on something," Walt suggested.

"I'm sure you're right. But seeing the blood there…" Danielle shivered.

"What do you want to do?" Walt asked.

"I'm not sure…if it weren't for this weather, I wouldn't be so concerned. Do you think she went out when we were having breakfast?"

Walt shook his head. "I don't see how she could have passed by the dining room without someone seeing her."

"Then she must've slipped out last night, but why? And where did she go?"

"If she'd gone down those stairs last night—I would've known. Max was standing guard all night."

"So you're saying she's somewhere upstairs? What, hiding from us?" Danielle frowned.

"I suppose she could've slipped by without me noticing. Maybe

Max fell asleep on the job—he does sleep a lot. What do you want to do?"

"I know you've already checked the house, but before we start looking around outside, we need to check the house again. I can't very well tell everyone you already did that."

Walt glanced at the closed door. "It wouldn't hurt to go through the house again."

"But I don't want them to see the rug—especially Jessica. It might freak her out. I was thinking maybe you could go upstairs and move it somewhere."

"You want me to hide it?"

"Just for now. Like you said, she probably cut her foot. I seriously don't think anyone's been stabbed in the attic."

A knock came at the bathroom door. "Dani, you okay?" It was Lily.

"I'll go move the rug. You arrange the search party." Walt vanished.

THEY SEARCHED ALL the rooms of Marlow House, even the basement. There was still no Anna. When they returned to the living room, Ian announced he was going to check the grounds. Perhaps Anna had stepped outside for some reason, maybe to watch the lightning, and then tripped and fell. Richard and Chris joined him on the search. When they returned fifteen minutes later, all the men were drenched, and still no Anna.

"Jessica, would you please go into the kitchen and get us a plate of cookies? Joanne can help you," Lily asked.

"I think you need to call the police," Lily said after Jessica darted from the room.

"The police? Why?" Chris asked.

Lily looked at him. "To begin with, Anna's missing."

"As far as we know, she left the house a few minutes before Danielle checked on her. So she hasn't been missing for even an hour. The police aren't going to do anything," Chris insisted.

"If she went out in this storm, she could be in trouble. I can't imagine anyone intentionally staying outside in this weather."

"Maybe whoever dropped her off picked her up last night," Chris suggested.

Danielle shook her head. "No, Chris, her suitcase is still here."

Patricia pointed to the opened packages shoved under the tree. "And her presents are still here. She wouldn't leave without them."

Danielle looked at Lily. "What are you thinking?"

"Anna's not here. She obviously went out last night for some reason. And if her things are still here, I have to believe she intended to come back. But this weather…"

DANIELLE SAT in the parlor with Joe and Brian. She wished the chief wasn't out of town for Christmas—she would rather be dealing with him.

"So one of your guests has gone missing?" Brian asked as he opened his notebook.

"Yes. Anna, Anna Williams. I believe you met her at the open house. She's the young blonde, early twenties. If it wasn't for this storm, I wouldn't have called you. I would've just assumed she had walked down to the beach or something. But she's been missing all morning, and if she's out there somewhere, hurt…in this weather…"

"Why would someone want to hurt Anna?" Brian asked.

Joe held a stainless steel travel mug in one hand. Waiting for Danielle's reply, he took a sip of his now cold coffee.

"I'm not saying anyone hurt her," Danielle said impatiently. "I just meant if she took a walk down to the beach and maybe tripped, sprained her ankle, got stuck in the storm. Something like that."

"What do you know about Anna?" Brian asked. "Is she someone who likes to walk around in thunderstorms?"

"I really don't know her that well. She checked in on Saturday."

"Is her car still here?" Joe asked.

"She doesn't have a car. Well, at least not here. Someone dropped her off."

"Who?" Brian asked.

Danielle shrugged. "I have no idea."

"Do you know how to contact her family—any of her friends?" Joe asked.

"No. All I have is her name. She told me she'd been living in Portland, but nothing specific."

"Do you know what she does for a living?" Joe asked.

Danielle shook her head. "No. We never talked about it."

"When was the last time you saw her?" Brian asked.

Danielle considered the question for a moment. "Umm…a little after midnight. She said goodnight before heading up to the attic. I was just going into my bedroom. We all stayed up pretty late last night."

"It's been storming nonstop since before midnight last night. Why would Anna go outside?" Joe asked.

"I have no idea. That's why I decided to call the police and file a missing persons report."

"Do you know if anyone else saw her after she went upstairs?" Brian asked.

Danielle shifted nervously in her chair.

"You have to tell them, Danielle. You have no choice," Walt told her.

"Well, I don't know if they actually saw Anna or not…but I saw Richard coming down from the attic sometime after midnight. And according to Lily, when she got up to use the bathroom, she saw Chris coming down the attic stairs."

"What time was this?" Joe asked.

Danielle shook her head. "I have no idea. I asked Lily what time she saw Chris, and she didn't remember. Just that it was after we all went to bed."

"Can we look at where she was staying?" Brian asked.

Danielle nodded and stood up. Brian and Joe followed Danielle out of the parlor and to the stairs. In the living room, Lily, Ian, and Kelly waited anxiously with the rest of Marlow House's guests.

Walt was already in the attic when Danielle arrived with the two police officers.

"You've fixed it up nice up here," Joe noted as he glanced around. He walked to the bed and looked at the suitcase sitting on the center of the mattress.

"I never really intended to rent this room out, but Anna was so insistent, and I hated the idea of her being alone for Christmas," Danielle explained.

Joe opened the suitcase and looked inside. "It's empty. I assume she put her things in a closet or something?"

Danielle walked to an antique oak chifforobe next to the window. "I told her she could put her things in here."

Brian walked to the chifforobe and opened its closet. It was empty. "Why would she take her things and leave her suitcase?"

"Maybe she put her things in the drawers," Danielle suggested.

"No! Don't have them look in there! I put the rug in the top drawer!" Walt called out.

Brian reached for the top drawer, but it was stuck. He tugged on the handle, but the drawer stubbornly refused to budge.

"That drawer always sticks," Danielle lied. "I doubt she put anything in it."

Brian abandoned the top drawer and reached for the one below it. It opened. "It's empty."

A clap of thunder momentarily distracted Walt. He looked to the window. In that instant, Brian tried the top drawer again, giving it a quick jerk. It flew open, almost falling out of the cabinet.

"What's this?" Brian pulled the stained rug from the drawer and looked at it.

"Is that blood?" Joe asked. He and Brian looked to Danielle.

"Have you ever seen this before?" Brian asked.

"Yeah…it's my throw rug."

Brian handed the rug to Joe while asking, "Where do you normally keep it?"

Danielle pointed to where the rug had been before Walt had moved it. "On the floor by the bed."

"Do you know what the blood's from?" Brian asked.

Danielle shook her head.

"Where was the rug the last time you saw it?" Joe asked.

Danielle pointed back to the space on the floor.

"I'm assuming it didn't have blood on it the last time you saw it?" Joe asked.

"It didn't," Danielle lied. She watched as Joe touched his finger to the red stain.

He paused and looked up. "This is still wet."

Danielle's eyes widened. She looked at his finger, now red tipped. "What?"

"Whatever this is—blood or something that looks like blood—it's still wet. Whoever put this rug in the drawer couldn't have done it that long ago," Joe said.

"How many suitcases did Anna arrive with?" Brian asked.

"Just the one on the bed."

"I'm assuming she brought clothes, cosmetics with her." Brian glanced around the room. "None of which appear to be here."

"She didn't wear the same outfit every day, so she obviously had clothes in her suitcase," Danielle said.

"How long was she supposed to stay for?" Joe asked.

"Until after the New Year. She already paid, in cash." Danielle glanced from Joe to Brian. "She also left the things we got her for Christmas."

"You got her a Christmas present?" Joe asked.

Danielle nodded. "I got stockings for all the guests and filled them. And they ended up exchanging gifts. Little things—but I can't imagine Anna would leave hers behind."

"It looks like she decided to leave, but for some reason left her suitcase behind," Brian said.

"And the rug?" Joe asked.

"Maybe she cut herself, got blood on the rug. Looks like she left in a hurry. Probably shoved the rug in the drawer because she didn't want to clean it," Brian suggested. "If Anna put the rug there, then it means she hasn't been gone that long."

Danielle shook her head. "Strange. Maybe she did leave. But why leave her suitcase?"

"Who knows why people do things," Brian said with a sigh. "But it looks to me like she simply decided to move on. You said someone dropped her off. Maybe that someone picked her up last night. Maybe she decided she didn't like her suitcase anymore and shoved her stuff in a sack. Who knows?"

"Of course, someone else might have put this rug in the drawer," Joe suggested.

"What are you thinking?" Brian asked.

"Maybe we should talk to one of the guests, Chris Johnson."

Danielle frowned. "Chris?"

"You did say Lily saw him coming from her room last night, and I heard him threatening Anna at the diner," Brian told her.

Danielle didn't respond immediately. Finally, she said, "I know you think Chris threatened her. And even if he did, which I'm not convinced was the case, he wasn't the only one who had an issue with Anna."

"Who else had a problem with Anna? Richard? You mentioned you saw him leaving the attic last night," Brian asked.

Danielle looked up into Brian's eyes. "Peter Morris, of Earthbound Spirits."

TWENTY-FIVE

"What does Morris have to do with your missing guest? Did they know each other?" Joe asked.

"No, I don't think so. But Richard's a member of Earthbound Spirits; in fact, he was a friend of Isabella," Danielle explained. "When Morris was here on Christmas Eve, he started grilling me about Anna—asking me if she and Richard were involved."

"Are they?" Joe asked.

"Aside from seeing him come down from the attic last night, I never noticed anything between them—between any of the guests, in fact—other than friendship. But you need to understand, Earthbound Spirits preys on people like Isabella and Richard—vulnerable, young, wealthy people who have no family—"

"Like you?" Joe said, his expression somber.

Narrowing her eyes, Danielle glared at Joe. "I said vulnerable, Joe. I'm fairly certain one reason Morris stopped in here the other night was an attempt to get close to me—intending to exploit me like he did with Isabella and Richard. But I'm not interested in what he's peddling. So no, not like me."

"And what does this have to do with Anna's disappearance?" Brian asked.

"I'm not saying it has anything to do with it. I'm just suggesting if you're looking for people who might have wanted to hurt Anna— or make her disappear—I would put Morris on top of the list. From what I understand, Anna didn't like Earthbound Spirits, and she told Morris so."

"How do you know that?" Brian asked.

"Anna told me," Danielle lied. *I can't very well tell them Walt overheard her ripping into Morris.*

"So she didn't like Earthbound Spirits, so what?" Joe asked. "I don't like them either."

"If Morris thought you were getting chummy with Richard and afraid you might be able to influence him, then maybe he'd want to get rid of you too. After all, members of Earthbound Spirits typically leave their estates to the organization. Look at Renton. Even Isabella was going to until she had a change of heart," Danielle explained.

Brian scribbled some notes into his book while Joe silently considered what Danielle had said. When Brian finished writing, he said, "The fact is, there's really no sign of foul play here. Chances are Anna decided it was time to move on. Who knows, maybe she's the type who enjoys drama—what woman doesn't?"

Danielle arched her brows. "Drama?"

"You know, the attention, the mystery." Brian closed his notebook. He glanced down at the rug. "As for the blood, maybe she cut herself. But we can't really go accusing Earthbound Spirits of anything based solely on the fact she didn't like them."

"I never implied anything nefarious happened," Danielle said with annoyance. "I simply wanted you to be aware she had basically vanished, in case some unidentified woman shows up in the hospital or something. I'm worried about her."

"If something nefarious happened to her, I'd be more apt to look at your Chris Johnson," Brian told her. "I don't care what anyone says, he was threatening her. And he's staying at Marlow House, not Morris."

Joe glanced down at the stained rug. "Would you mind if I took it?"

Danielle shrugged. "I guess it's okay."

"While we're here, we should probably talk to your guests. Maybe we can figure out where Anna went," Joe said. "Brian's probably right, but we might as well talk to everyone while we're here."

"Okay." Danielle glanced over to Walt and then looked back at

Joe and Brian. "They're probably still in the living room. You want to talk to them there?"

Joe shook his head. "I'd rather we talk to them individually. One of them may have seen something they'd feel uncomfortable talking about around the others. Can we do it in the parlor?"

BRIAN AND JOE talked to Lily first. Other than verifying Danielle's story about seeing Chris coming down the attic stairs, she provided no other clues to help them determine where Anna might have gone. They then spoke to Jessica, followed by Ian, and then Kelly. None of the three were able to shed any new light on where the missing woman could be.

While Brian and Joe questioned each person, Walt sat on the edge of the parlor desk, watching and listening. After Kelly left the room, it was Patricia's turn. She took a seat on the sofa and faced Joe and Brian.

"Danielle's concerned something may have happened to Anna. If she went outside for some reason in this storm, she could have gotten hurt and needs help," Joe explained. "Or maybe whoever dropped her off picked her up last night, and she went home."

"How can I help?" Patricia asked.

"If we knew a little more about Anna, we could call her family or one of her friends. Maybe they've heard from her. If Anna doesn't show up for the rest of the week, we really won't know if she's a missing person or just decided to go home," Brian explained.

"I'm sorry, I have no idea how to contact her family."

"Do you know where she lives?" Joe asked.

"Anna was friendly; she was always asking us questions about our families—our lives. She seemed genuinely interested in everyone. But she really didn't talk about herself. The only thing I really know about her is that she once lived in Portland. Whenever I would ask her specific questions, especially about her family, she would change the subject."

"How did she get along with the other guests?" Joe asked.

"Chris and Richard? Fine. We all get along."

"Did you ever notice anything going on between her and either of them?" Brian asked.

Patricia frowned. "What do you mean?"

"Something more than friendship," Joe suggested.

Patricia shook her head. "No, not at all."

"So she treated them the same, didn't seem to prefer one over the other?" Brian asked.

Patricia considered the question a moment before answering. "It isn't that she shows a preference for one over the other, she just treats them differently."

"In what way?" Joe asked.

"Anna's much younger than I am. I'm probably old enough to be her mother—if I had her as a teenager, that is." Patricia smiled. "But she's a very self-confident young woman. A dominant type. I never felt any of us intimidated her."

"Why should she feel intimidated?" Brian asked.

"I'm not saying she should feel intimidated. I just meant, being a young woman, coming to a place where you don't know anyone, I could see how that might be intimidating. Even though she was here by herself, she was never shy. She initiated conversation with all of us. Reminded me a little of a cruise director, you know, wanting to make sure everyone was having a good time." Patricia smiled.

"How did you mean she treated the men different?" Brian asked.

"Anna treated Chris…well, more like a colleague. I noticed she was a little more bossy with Richard. Maybe bossy isn't the right word. Domineering maybe? Liked to give him advice. She liked to give me advice too. Which I always found fairly amusing, considering her age. But I never noticed her do that with Chris."

"Did you feel either Chris or Richard was romantically interested in her?" Joe asked.

"No."

"Did she argue with either of them?" Brian asked.

"No. I don't recall any tension between any of them. Why is this important? Do you think Chris or Richard did something to Anna?"

"We're just trying to understand all the players," Brian explained.

"Do you know anything about Earthbound Spirits?" Joe asked.

"Who?" Patricia frowned.

"Did you meet Richard's friend Peter Morris at the open house?"

"You mean the older gentleman with the dark hair?"

Joe nodded. "Yes."

"Richard introduced him to me, but I didn't really talk to him. Why?"

"He's the founder of Earthbound Spirits. You never heard of the organization before?" Brian asked.

"No, I don't think so."

RICHARD SAT on the parlor sofa, where Patricia had been sitting ten minutes earlier.

"We understand you were probably the last one to see Anna last night."

Richard fidgeted nervously. "Me?"

"You went up to the attic last night, didn't you? After everyone went to bed?"

"I…I went up the stairs, but I didn't go into the attic…I didn't see Anna."

"Why did you go up there?" Brian asked.

"I wanted to talk to Anna about something. It was stupid of me. When I got up the stairs, I realized if I knocked on her bedroom door in the middle of the night, she might get the wrong impression. So I came back downstairs. Figured I'd talk to her today."

"What did you want to talk to her about?" Joe asked.

"I wanted to ask her about something she said."

"What was that?" Brian asked.

"Private things."

"What do you mean private things?" Brian pressed.

Richard stared down at his hands; they fidgeted nervously on his lap. "She told me things that had happened to me. But they didn't."

Brian frowned. "I'm not following you."

Richard looked up at Brian. "She reminded me of things that happened when I was a child. But those things never really happened to me."

"Are you saying she made up stories about you?" Brian asked.

Richard shook his head. "Not exactly. They were dreams I had. She knew."

"WELL, THAT WAS WEIRD," Brian said after Richard left the room.

"Just a little," Joe agreed.

"I think we're wasting our time. If this woman can see into dreams, maybe she's down on the beach doing some pagan rain dance." Brian shut his notebook and started to stand up.

Danielle popped her head in the parlor and asked, "You want me to send Chris in now?"

"Give us five minutes, and then send him in," Joe told her.

When Danielle left and closed the door, Brian asked, "Why? We're wasting our time."

"You heard Johnson threaten her. There's blood on the rug. Do you really think she's out walking in the rain?" Joe asked.

"So what do you want to do?" Brian asked.

"I want to find out more about Johnson. I don't trust him." Joe picked up his travel mug and wiped the outside of it with his shirttail until it shined. Gingerly holding the mug by its rim, he set it on the end table next to the sofa.

"Are you doing what I think you are?"

"Hey, I learned the trick from you." Joe grinned.

***

"WE UNDERSTAND you were the last one to see Anna last night," Joe told Chris, who sat on the parlor sofa.

"How do you figure that?"

"You were seen coming down the attic stairs last night after everyone went to bed," Joe explained.

Chris shrugged. "So?"

"Why were you up there?" Joe asked.

"Just talking."

"Was it common for you to go up into Anna's room at night when everyone was asleep?" Brian asked.

"If you're trying to insinuate there's something going on between Anna and me, you're way off base. We were talking, that was it. Purely platonic."

"What were you talking about?" Joe asked.

"Nothing particular."

"Did she mention anything about leaving or going anywhere?" Joe asked.

Chris stared at Joe for a moment. Finally, he shook his head. "No. But I got the feeling she was the type of person who does things impulsively. So I suppose it wouldn't be unreasonable to imagine she'd just take off if the mood suited her."

Joe started to cough. He glanced around and then looked over at the end table next to Chris. He coughed again and pointed to his stainless steel mug. "Could you please hand me my water."

Ten minutes later, after they told Chris he could go, Brian and Joe stood alone in the parlor. Walt watched as Joe gingerly held the rim of the stainless steel travel mug. Joe looked at Brian and said, "Let's get out of here."

TWENTY-SIX

Danielle closed the front door after Joe and Brian said their goodbyes and headed down the front walk toward their car. She turned away from the door and came face-to-face with the remaining occupants of Marlow House.

"Well? What are they going to do?" Lily asked.

"I don't think anything. Chris was right; this really isn't a missing persons case. She hasn't been gone that long, and Anna is an adult; she has the right to take off if she wants. But they said they'll keep an eye out for her in case she's stranded in the storm."

Lily scowled. "That's it?"

"I'm sure she's fine," Chris chimed in.

Danielle shrugged. "It's past noon; why don't you all go into the kitchen and have some lunch. There're plenty of leftovers. Joanne can help. I need to make a couple phone calls. I'll be out in a minute. Who knows, maybe Anna will be back before you finish lunch."

DANIELLE STEPPED into the parlor and closed its door. Turning around, she faced Walt.

"I probably shouldn't have called the police or let Joe take the rug."

"Why do you say that?"

"If the blood was still wet, then it must have been a recent cut. I think if anyone was in the attic this morning playing slasher, we would've heard it."

Walt chuckled. "I don't know about you, but I never considered the blood on the rug was from anything other than a cut on the foot or something like that."

"I know, but Joe took the rug, and you know how when he or Brian get involved in something like this, everything gets twisted. And more often than not, it means I get arrested."

"I don't think they're going to arrest you for anything."

"Maybe not. But I wish I hadn't called them. I keep thinking I want to move past all the misunderstandings of the last six months, and then something like this happens. Maybe I'm just paranoid."

"Where do you think Anna is?" Walt asked.

"Not sure. Maybe she did just leave and for some reason didn't take her suitcase with her. I'm assuming the blood on the rug is hers, so she must have left sometime this morning, since it's still wet. Probably when we were all in the dining room eating breakfast."

"I still don't see how she could've gone by the dining room without being seen."

"Did you hear anything interesting?"

"I saw something interesting." Walt waved his hand and a lit cigar appeared. He took a puff, exhaled, and then proceeded to tell Danielle about Joe's unusual treatment of his stainless steel drinking cup.

BRIAN WALKED into Joe's office late that afternoon and found Joe sitting at his desk, staring at his computer monitor.

"Anything interesting?" Brian asked, taking a seat at one of the two chairs in front of Joe's desk.

"Did you just get back?" Joe asked.

"Yeah. I dropped by Marlow House again. Curious to see if the missing guest showed up."

Joe looked up from his computer and stared across the desk at Brian. "Did she?"

Brian leaned back in the chair. Stretching, he crossed his ankles. "No. When I got to Marlow House, the only one there was

Joanne and Jessica. Joanne told me that when it stopped raining, they all took off to go look for Anna. They hadn't gotten back yet."

Joe leaned forward, resting his elbows on the desk. "In answer to your question, did I find anything interesting. Yes. It seems Chris Johnson is not Chris Johnson."

Brian sat up straight and leaned forward. "Really? Who is he? Does he have a record? Outstanding warrants?"

"His real name is Chris Glandon. No outstanding warrants. The only prior was disorderly conduct when he was in college. Charges were dropped. Aside from that, nothing. Not even a single traffic violation."

"So why is he going by a fake name?"

"I tried to find something on Anna Williams, see if there was some connection between her and Glandon. I couldn't find anything on her, so I decided to look at the other guests. Started with Winston, because he was also seen coming down from the attic last night. That's when I found a connection."

"Between Winston and Williams?"

Joe shook his head. "No, between Winston and Glandon." He then went on to explain the connection between the two men.

"Do you think this has anything to do with Williams's disappearance?" Brian asked after he heard all that Joe had learned.

Joe shrugged. "I don't know. But both men were seen coming down from her room late last night after everyone went to bed. Danielle told us about Morris's concerns regarding Williams and Winston. Maybe he was onto something, and those two were getting closer than casual friends. And you overheard the conversation between Glandon and Williams. Were they ex-lovers? Is this some love triangle gone bad?"

"Even with this connection, we don't really have anything. Hell, we don't even know if Anna Williams is Anna Williams. Maybe she's like Glandon and using an alias."

Joe stood up. "Let's grab something to eat and then head back over to Marlow House. Hopefully they'll be back from their walk. Who knows, maybe Anna will be with them."

"What do you want to do?" Brian stood up.

"I'm going to let them know what I found out."

"Them?"

"Yes. I want to see what sort of excuse Glandon comes up with for using an alias. I'm curious to see how Winston will react. And if nothing else, I want Danielle to know who's staying under her roof."

BY THE TIME Brian and Joe returned to Marlow House, it was already dark outside, and it had started to rain again. They found everyone in the living room except for Jessica, who was in the parlor with Sadie and Max, watching a Disney movie.

Danielle answered the door and led Brian and Joe into the living room. A fire blazed in the massive stone hearth. The room's only other illumination came from the Christmas tree's flickering lights and several flameless candles strategically placed around the room.

The moment the officers entered the living room, Lily stood up and asked, "Did you find out anything?"

"No, not about Anna," Joe said as he fiddled with the baseball cap in his hand. "But after I returned to the station and looked into a few things, I discovered one of you was not exactly truthful, and I was hoping that person could offer some explanation."

"What are you talking about?" Danielle asked.

Joe looked at Chris. "Chris, I think you have a few things to explain."

"This has to be about the fingerprints Joe lifted from Chris." Walt spoke up from the corner. Both Danielle and Chris briefly glanced Walt's way.

Chris took a deep breath and smiled at Joe. Leaning back in the chair, he studied the sergeant. "I can't imagine what you're talking about unless it's the fact I prefer to be called by my mother's maiden name than my father's surname. But that's not a crime, so I'm not sure what the problem is."

"Your name is not Chris Johnson?" Lily asked.

"Technically speaking, my first name is Christopher. But I go by the nickname Chris. So I suppose you could say I also use a nickname for my surname."

"Why?" Lily asked. "I know why Ian uses two names, but why do you?"

"I'd like to hear the answer to that question," Joe said.

Chris glared at Joe. "Frankly, it really is none of your business."

"Mr. Winston, do you know what Chris Johnson's real name is?" Brian asked.

Richard shook his head. "No, why should I?"

"It's Glandon."

"Glandon?" Richard repeated.

"His parents were Heath and Margaret Glandon," Joe explained.

It took a moment for the names to register with Richard. When it finally did, his eyes widened and he turned and stared at Chris.

"Your parents…they were killed in the same boating accident as my parents."

Chris nodded the affirmative.

"Oh my god, that's horrible," Patricia cried out. "Does this mean your parents were friends?"

"The boat they were on belonged to their attorney—who was also the Winstons' attorney. They knew each other socially, but I wouldn't call them friends exactly," Chris explained.

"Why didn't you say anything?" Richard asked.

"I didn't see the point." Chris shrugged. "It's Christmas, sharing stories and comparing notes on our parents' tragic death isn't really the best way to instill the holiday spirit."

"So you two have never met before?" Patricia asked.

"On a few occasions," Chris explained. "Nothing more than a casual introduction. Until this week, we'd never had a real conversation."

Richard frowned. "If we met before, I can't believe I wouldn't have recognized you."

Chris smiled. "Back then, I was sporting a beard and I wore my hair longer. And you would have known me as Chris Glandon."

"Is that why you used Johnson instead of Glandon, so Richard wouldn't recognize you?" Danielle asked.

Chris looked at Danielle. "That would mean I knew Richard was also staying at Marlow House. I made my reservation before I ever saw Richard here. And like I said, I typically use my mother's maiden name when I meet new people."

"Why is that?" Joe asked. "Do you have something to hide?"

"You tell me, Sergeant Morelli. You're the one who seems to know all my deep dark secrets."

"Joe, how did you figure out Chris's real name?" Ian asked.

"I suspect it was that stainless steel cup he asked me to hand him," Chris told Ian.

"You took his fingerprints, why?" Ian asked.

"Danielle did call us here this morning regarding her missing guest. Who, by the way, still has not shown up. Yet she left her suitcase and other belongings behind," Joe reminded them. "We're just trying to determine if there was possibly foul play. Mr. Glandon happens to be not only the last person who saw Anna before she disappeared, he threatened her life just days before the disappearance."

"Threatened her life?" Patricia looked anxiously from Joe to Chris.

"I didn't threaten her life, Patricia." Chris sighed. "Officer Henderson overheard a private conversation between Anna and myself and misunderstood. This was right before we left the diner in town. You were with us that day—when we went out to lunch and shopping. Did you notice any animosity between Anna and myself?"

Patricia shook her head. "No, not at all."

"And from what I understand, the suitcase is empty." Chris continued. "Maybe there's something wrong with it? Did you check it? Maybe it has a broken latch; the handle is loose. Maybe it has a funny smell. If she decided she was ready to leave and felt something was wrong with the suitcase, maybe she used a sack. I'm sure she could've found one in the kitchen easy enough. As for the gifts she left behind, perhaps she simply forgot them."

"So you're saying you believe Ms. Williams decided to leave early and not tell anyone?" Brian asked.

"It's entirely within the realm of possibility." Chris leaned back in the chair.

"You still didn't explain why you're using a fake name," Joe said.

"And I told you it really is none of your business," Chris countered.

Ian began to chuckle. All heads turned in his direction.

Kelly frowned. "What's so funny?"

"I just figured out who Chris is." Ian looked at Joe again and shook his head. "Think, Joe, if you were him, would you go around introducing yourself as Chris Glandon?" Ian laughed again.

Unsmiling, Joe stared at Ian. "I don't know where you're going with this."

"Exactly where did you get your information on Chris?" Ian asked. "If it was on the Internet, you obviously didn't read much. What happened, did you just pull up the story on his parents' death, figured out the connection between him and Richard, and stopped there?"

Chris let out a weary sigh and leaned back in his chair, closing his eyes. When he opened them again, he found the entire room staring in his direction.

"I've always wanted to do a story on you," Ian said. "I've sent inquiries to your attorney. You're a difficult man to track down."

Chris smiled at Ian. "Yeah, I got your inquiries. Not big on interviews. No hard feelings?"

Ian chuckled. "And to think I spent Christmas with you and didn't even know." Ian laughed again.

Kelly's eyes widened. She looked from her brother to Chris and back to her brother. "Oh my god…Chris Glandon. *Glandon.*"

Ian chuckled and looked at Kelly. "A little slow on the uptake, sis. But yeah. Chris Glandon."

TWENTY-SEVEN

"They call Chris one of the most elusive—yet generous—philanthropists," Ian explained. He flashed Chris an apologetic smile and said, "Sorry. But they already know your real name now. All they need to do is go online and do a thorough Google search."

Kelly looked at Chris. "In all the online photographs I've seen of you, you always had the beard."

"These days I tend to avoid getting a current photograph taken. Makes life easier."

"I imagine. People always wanting something from you. While you're trying to figure out where you want to give your money," Ian said.

"I remember now…" Richard looked at Chris. "You're the one who's been giving massive amounts of money away to charities ever since your parents were killed."

"Well, hell," Walt grumbled, slumping down in a chair. He tossed his lit cigar into the air. It vanished. "I was rather hoping to find out he was a mass murderer. At the very least, a con man who took advantage of sweet little old ladies."

"Wait a minute…are you saying Chris is rich or something?" Lily asked.

"Put it this way, Danielle is considered below poverty level compared to Chris." Ian chuckled.

"I don't consider using my mother's maiden name a lie. But I did lie about one thing, and I'd like to come clean now."

Walt sat up in the chair and grinned. "I hope it's good. Something unforgivable."

"I don't have a sister. In fact, I don't have any siblings," Chris explained.

"Why would you lie about that?" Danielle asked.

"Chris Glandon is an only child. By taking an imaginary sibling, I put more distance between him and me."

"We'll be going now," Brian said abruptly. "If Anna shows up, let us know."

***

"I HAVE A QUESTION FOR YOU," Brian asked when he and Joe got into the squad car.

"What's that?"

"I don't believe you missed the online articles about how Glandon likes to give away his money." Brian buckled his seat belt.

"I read a few. But as far as I'm concerned, that really doesn't explain why he likes to go around using an alias. He has a direct connection to Richard and chose to keep that a secret. Why didn't he just tell us when we were interviewing him?"

"Sounds like this guy is loaded."

Joe buckled his seat belt. "So? We both know rich people are capable of doing evil things. You more than anyone should realize that."

Brian let out a sigh. "Yeah, well, I have a feeling the chief isn't going to be thrilled with us when he gets back in town. He's gotten pretty tight with Boatman."

"This time, Danielle called us. There is no way she can say we harassed her." Joe put the key into the ignition and turned on the engine.

"I know. But if Chris Glandon feels we've harassed him, he has enough money to make the chief's life miserable. And if the chief is miserable…"

"Won't happen," Joe said as he pulled away from the curb. "You forget, Glandon doesn't like attention. Of course, if he does make a fuss, we'll know he was lying."

"Lying, how?"

"If Ian's right, then Glandon won't want to do anything to draw public attention to himself. But if he was using Johnson because he didn't want Richard to recognize him, well, that cat's now out of the bag. So no reason not to retaliate against us if that's what he wants to do."

"Hell, I hope Ian was right."

"But if Ian is wrong—I don't care how much money the guy supposedly has. As long as he's in town, I'm keeping an eye on him."

DANIELLE SAT across the kitchen table from Chris. She had cut them each a slice of pumpkin pie. Chris had almost finished his while she toyed with her piece, breaking off tiny bites with her fork. They weren't alone. Walt sat on the chair between them. It was late and everyone else in the house had gone to bed.

"Chris, I would like you to tell me the truth about Anna."

Chris looked across the table into Danielle's dark eyes.

"Did you have anything to do with her disappearance?"

In a clear, unwavering voice he said, "No."

"Do you know where she went?"

He took a deep breath. "No."

"Do you think she's coming back?"

"I doubt it."

"What about what Brian claimed, that you threatened her."

"I admit Officer Henderson heard something. And I suppose it sounded bad. But he misunderstood. It was a private conversation between Anna and me, and honestly, I was not threatening her. Not really."

"Not really?"

"I made a joke. I suppose you might call it a private joke between me and Anna. But Henderson took it completely wrong. And even he'll admit Anna told him he misunderstood."

"Did you and Anna…I mean…were you…"

"Are you trying to ask me if Anna and I were in some sort of intimate relationship?"

"It's really none of my business," Danielle backpedaled.

"I agree; it's none of your business. I'll answer your question anyway. No. Anna and I have never been—will never be—in that type of personal relationship. Never. Ever."

Danielle couldn't help but smile. "You seem pretty adamant about that."

"Put it this way, even without the age difference, there's a massive personality difference."

"Did you know Anna before you came to Marlow House?"

Chris stood up and grabbed his empty plate. "Enough with the questions." He walked to the counter and rinsed his plate in the sink.

"How about if the question isn't about Anna?"

"Maybe. Try me." Chris left his plate in the sink and sat back down at the table.

"Is it true, do you like to give away your money?"

Chris shrugged. "My parents were billionaires back when rich people were still millionaires. When they died, they left everything to their only child, me. My needs are pretty simple, and no one person needs that much money."

"How long have you been going by Johnson?"

"Since about a year after my parents died. While I try to keep my donations anonymous, that doesn't always work out. People were appearing out of thin air—literally—needing me to help them."

"Out of thin air…literally?" Danielle chuckled.

"You would be surprised," Chris said with a snort. "Anyway, I decided if I wanted to maintain some sense of normalcy, I needed to go back to flying under the radar. Using Mom's maiden name was a start. Even if the press figured out my alias, tracking down Chris Johnson was going to be a hell of a lot more difficult than Chris Glandon."

"What do you mean going back to flying under the radar? I always thought children from families like that were always in the spotlight."

Chris shook his head. "My parents were private people. They did a good job sheltering me. I suspect one reason the spotlight started shining in my direction was my parents' death. The boating accident received a fair amount of press at the time. And then there was the issue with the will."

"The will? Your parents'?"

Chris nodded. "My father's two brothers. Mom and Dad left everything to me; my uncles were not happy. I was more than willing to give them something. After all, I had far more than I needed, and I felt bad they hadn't been mentioned in the will. Of course, when the lawsuit started, I realized why Dad didn't leave his brothers anything. They wanted it all—every last billion."

"Wow. They didn't get anything, did they?"

Chris shook his head. "No. I always thought it was karma at its finest. Had they never brought the lawsuit, I would have given them something. Of course, now I know whatever I would have offered would never have been enough."

"Why would they ever imagine they were entitled to your parents' money instead of their son?"

Chris smiled up at Danielle. "Because I'm adopted."

"So?" Danielle frowned. "You're still as much their kid as if you were their biological child."

Chris reached across the table and covered Danielle's hand with his. He gave it a squeeze and then let go. "Thank you, Danielle. Some people don't get that."

Danielle shrugged. "So have you always known you were adopted?"

"Yes. I spent my first six years in foster care. So not exactly a secret." Chris grinned.

"Wow, your parents adopted an older child, I'm impressed. Seems most people want babies, and with your parents' money..."

"My folks were good people. Mom couldn't have kids, and they initially intended to adopt a baby. At the time, she was doing some charity work for older children trapped in the foster care system. She heard my story and asked to meet me. When we did, I suppose you might say we fell in love."

"Why didn't they adopt any other children?"

"Not sure, really."

"Your father was okay with adopting an older child?"

"As far as I know. He was never anything but loving and supportive with me. I learned later how opposed my uncles were to the adoption. Of course, now I know why."

"Can I ask you a question?" Danielle asked.

"Sure."

"Are you behind Benevolent Charities?"

He said nothing.

"I take that as a yes."

Chris let out a sigh.

"I have to wonder, why here? Why did you send Patricia and Jessica to Marlow House?" Danielle set her fork down on the table and studied Chris. "Oh my god, you're him!"

Chris stared across the table at Danielle, noting her wide-eyed expression. "Him who?"

"Patricia's brother!"

Chris let out a short laugh and shook his head. "No, Danielle."

"That's why you brought Patricia here."

Chris shook his head again. "No. And I never said I was behind Benevolent Charities. You just jumped to that conclusion."

Danielle studied Chris for a few more moments. "Are you sure?"

"Is there any family resemblance between me and Patricia… even a little?"

After a few moments of silently studying Chris, Danielle let out a sigh. "No. Not really…Okay, one last question. Why were you living on someone else's sailboat?"

"Because he told me I could."

"Who told you?"

"The guy who owned the boat, of course. Who wouldn't want to live right on the ocean in a free sailboat?"

"Sounds like you can afford to live anywhere you want."

"I didn't want to live anywhere else at the time. Anyway, I understand you don't have to run this place as a B and B and cook for other people. You've got plenty of money to do something else."

Danielle smiled. "Touché. You got me with that one."

"Damn, I'm starting to like him," Walt grumbled and then disappeared.

TWENTY-EIGHT

Cleve heard a crashing sound and then felt the wall shake. Instead of knocking on the office door, he barged in and found Peter standing some six feet from the now broken wall mirror. Shards of glittering mirror glass littered the floor. In the center of the debris sat the apparent missile, a bronze bust, its eyes staring up at the ceiling.

"Is everything okay?" Cleve asked as he walked into the room and glanced around.

Returning to his desk, Peter sat down and said, "I hate Christmas."

Careful not to step on the broken glass, Cleve walked over to the mess and picked up the bronze bust, setting it back on its stand.

"What happened?" Cleve asked as he grabbed a piece of cardboard from the trash can and began pushing the pieces of mirror into a pile.

"I threw the damn thing," Peter snapped. With his fingertips he massaged his temples.

"I can see that. Why did you throw it? What happened?" Kneeling down at the pile, Cleve scooped up the debris and dumped it in the trash can.

Peter leaned back in his chair and closed his eyes. "It seems Emily Peterson decided to ignore my advice and accepted her sister's invitation for Christmas. The two have reconciled." Opening his eyes, Peter sat up, leaned across his desk, and picked up an already open envelope. He tossed it to the floor by Cleve.

Throwing the cardboard in the trash with the broken pieces of mirror he had cleaned up, Cleve grabbed the envelope and stood up. "What's this?"

"It's a notice from Emily's attorney. The donation she promised to deliver by the first of the year has been cancelled. Plus, her will has been changed. Her dear sister is back in, and we're out."

Cleve pulled the papers from the envelope and looked at them. Taking a seat in a chair by Peter's desk, he studied the papers for a moment before tucking them back into the envelope. "That was quick. It's only been two days since Christmas."

"I suspect her estranged sister had this lined up long before she begged Emily to come for Christmas."

Cleve looked at the outside of the envelope again before tossing it back onto Peter's desk. "Who delivered it? There's no postmark."

"A courier dropped it off a little while ago."

"I'm sorry, Peter. But I feel worse for Emily. She's taken a giant step backwards. And that donation—we needed it."

"Yes, we did. The money coming in from Renton's estate won't even cover half of what she'd promised."

"She's not a young woman." Cleve sighed. "With the health issues she's been having this past year…"

"I doubt she makes it another two years. And when she dies, it'll be that greedy sister of hers who inherits the ten million dollars, not Earthbound Spirits."

"I'm sorry. I wish I could help in some way."

"There's nothing we can do about that now. But I'm also worried about Richard. I haven't heard from him since I saw him on Christmas Eve. I'm afraid sending him to Marlow House was a very bad idea. Now that I think about it, I should have sent someone like you."

"Me?"

"Someone who is firm in their belief—who isn't swayed by insecurities or sentimentalities. You're a true believer, Cleve, which is why you're such a treasure to Earthbound Spirits."

Blushing, Cleve glanced down. "Thank you, sir."

"I'm serious. I don't know what I'd do without you." Peter abruptly stood.

"Thank you." Cleve looked up at Peter and watched as he

started to pace the room. "And you don't have to worry about Anna Williams influencing Richard. She's no longer a threat."

Peter stopped pacing a moment and looked at Cleve. His lips curled into a satisfied smile. "So she's gone?"

Cleve nodded. "Rumor has it she just up and left on Christmas night."

"I wonder what Richard thinks about this. Hopefully the boy won't do anything foolish and try to find her." Peter resumed his pacing.

"I spoke to one of my contacts at the police department." Cleve turned around in his seat so he could watch Peter.

Hands on hips, Peter paused again and faced Cleve. "Police? Why are they involved? Certainly they have no reason to suspect foul play."

"Apparently, Danielle Boatman called them because Anna left a week early without telling anyone. She had already paid for her room. But for now, the police aren't considering this a missing person—"

"Why would they?" Peter punctuated his point with a wave of his hand. "Anna Williams is an adult. She's free to come and go as she wishes."

"They found blood in her room."

Peter frowned. "Blood where?"

"Fresh blood. It was on a rug they found shoved into a cabinet in her room. From what I was told, they probably won't test it since they don't suspect foul play."

Peter returned to his office chair. The two men sat in silence for several moments.

"Even with Anna gone, I don't feel good about this," Peter said.

"I told you she won't be a problem."

"But Richard hasn't called. While he's made Earthbound Spirits his beneficiary, he still hasn't come forward with a significant dona-tion. I feel we could lose him at any time."

"What do you want to do?"

"I think perhaps it's time to call him home before he lets the truth slip away."

"Isn't there some other way?" Cleve pleaded.

"It's for his own good, you know that."

"Give me a couple hours. Time to find out what's going on with Richard, see if he's straying from the truth. Please."

"Fine. You have until tomorrow morning. But if you discover he's wavering—even the smallest amount—call him home."

"You want me to do it?"

"I trust you above anyone else, Cleve. You've never shirked your duties before. If it must be done, do it."

PATRICIA SAT across from Richard in a booth at the Pier Café. He stared into his cup of coffee, absently stirring it with a spoon.

Richard shook his head and let out a weary sigh. "I can't understand why Anna would just leave like that. She didn't say anything to any of us."

"It's weird. I just hope everything is okay with her."

"I wish I had knocked on her door that night." Richard removed his spoon and set it on the table. "Maybe she would have said something to me about leaving."

"What do you mean?"

Richard looked up into Patricia's eyes. "Christmas night, she said some things to me that...well...were strange. I kept thinking about what she said, couldn't sleep, so I decided to ask her about them. Everyone had already gone to bed. I went up to the attic, stood at the door to her room, debated with myself about knocking, and then decided to talk to her in the morning. I started worrying she might get the wrong impression, me coming to her room so late at night. I wasn't thinking straight. But now...now I wonder if I should've just gone ahead and knocked."

"What did she say?"

"Remember when you mentioned your brother's birthday was on Christmas Eve?"

"Sure, what about it?" Patricia picked up her ham sandwich and took a bite.

"She said something like *don't you think it's a strange coincidence you and Patricia's brother share a birthday?*"

Patricia set her sandwich back on her plate and frowned. "Your birthday's not on Christmas Eve, is it?"

Richard nodded.

"Why didn't you say anything to anyone about it being your birthday?" Patricia asked.

Richard shrugged. "I didn't see the point. I don't celebrate my birthday anymore." He broke off a piece of his tuna sandwich and popped it in his mouth.

"Why not?"

"I just don't." He broke off another piece of sandwich.

"So how did she know?"

"I know Danielle knew, but when I asked her about it later, she said she never said anything to Anna about it. But that's not all."

"What else?"

"Do you remember those two ornaments on the Christmas tree, the ones Danielle said weren't hers?"

"Sure. How could I forget? We had two just like that when I was a kid. Brought back memories."

"They looked so familiar to me."

"Maybe you had the same ornaments when you were a kid."

Richard shook his head. "No. We never had those types of ornaments. Ours were imported from Germany—trust me, we never had anything like that."

Patricia shrugged. "You probably saw them somewhere, in a store or on someone else's tree."

"That's the thing, I know exactly where I've seen that ornament."

Patricia set her half-eaten sandwich down on her plate. "Where?"

"A recurring dream I've had all my life."

Patricia frowned. "A dream?"

"Yes. In the dream I'm a small boy and I'm sitting on a man's shoulder. In the dream, he's my father, but he looks nothing like my real father. He's lifting me up to a Christmas tree so I can hang the ornament."

"And what does it have to do with Anna?"

"After Christmas dinner, Anna and I returned to the living room. We were alone for a few minutes. She took the ornament off the tree—the one that looks like the ornament from my dream. She showed it to me and asked me if I remembered how I used to sit on my father's shoulders to hang it on the Christmas tree."

"I guess that's a little strange, but maybe she just meant ornaments in general. A lot of fathers lift their children up on their shoulders or help them to hang ornaments on high branches."

"But why did she show me that ornament?"

"If you'll remember, you seemed fascinated with it when

someone first pointed it out. I suspect Anna was just making conversation, suggesting something she figured probably happened when you were a kid. I think she tried a little too hard to make conversation sometimes. She seemed to go out of her way to stir up old childhood memories."

"What do you mean?"

"If you think about it, when did Anna ever really share anything about her life? Whenever any of us would ask her a question, she would turn it around and ask us something. I think it was her way of making friends—showing an interest in our lives. I know she did it with me."

"But it wasn't just that. She knew about the dream I had about Jessica."

Patricia frowned. "You've been dreaming about my daughter?"

"No, not Jessica exactly, someone she reminds me of," Richard explained.

"I don't understand."

"The dream about the ornament—me as a child on the man's shoulders—I have that one maybe once a year, normally around Christmas time. I had it a few weeks before I came here. But I have another recurring dream, this one I have maybe three or four times a year. I've had it for as long as I can remember. When I was younger, I had it more frequently."

"What was it about?"

"I'm a small child in the dream, and I'm holding the hand of a little girl. She's helping me. I feel safe. And she looks just like Jessica —except she's blonde. When I first saw Jessica, I knew there was something familiar about her. Of course, she has jet black hair and brown eyes, and the little girl in my dreams is a fair blonde with blue eyes. It didn't dawn on me why Jessica looked so familiar—that she resembled the girl in my dreams—until Anna mentioned it."

"You told Anna about your dream?"

Richard shook his head. "On Christmas morning, when I was watching Jessica open her packages, I mentioned to Anna that Jessica reminded me of someone, but I just couldn't figure out who it was. She smiled and said, 'Jessica looks just like the little girl you dream about, except she has dark hair.'"

"Can I ask you a question, Richard?"

"Sure."

Patricia studied Richard. "What year were you born?"

Richard and Patricia failed to notice Cleve Monchique, who sat in the booth behind them. Slumped down in his seat, wearing a wool cap pulled down to his eyebrows, and bundled up in a bulky jacket, Cleve appeared to be reading the newspaper while drinking his coffee.

TWENTY-NINE

Ignoring the persistent cries of the man and woman, he raced toward the ocean. Sand kicked up from beneath his paws. They continued to call his name, but he kept running. He stopped when he reached a massive pile of seaweed. By the time the man and woman reached his side, he was already frantically tugging on the tangled mass.

The man, now out of breath, shouted, "Bear, get out of there!" The black Labrador retriever ignored his command. With a mouthful of seaweed, the dog shook his head and pawed at the salty heap of sea foliage.

The woman looked down at the dog. They stood just a few feet from the water's edge. She was about to grab his collar and drag him from the seaweed when she noticed a bloated foot sticking out from beneath the pile.

CHIEF MACDONALD STOOD on the beach, talking to Brian Henderson. Some ten feet away were the responders, processing the scene. One was the coroner, who knelt by the bloated body of a woman. There wasn't much left of her face. The coroner suspected it had been scraped off by a fall onto the rocks, turning it into a pulpy mass of fish food.

The couple who found the dead woman stood some twenty feet away, with their dog, Bear, who was now on a leash. They huddled together, shaken by the experience, talking to Sergeant Joe Morelli.

"They're staying in a rental down the beach," Brian told the chief. "They were taking a walk; the dog found the body."

"Any idea who it is?" The chief glanced up to the sky. Only a few lingering clouds remained. According to the weather report, it was supposed to be sunny through New Year's.

"Hard to tell, but I'm afraid who it might be."

"You think it's Danielle's missing guest?" the chief asked.

"About the right size. Same color hair. Not much left of her face. Appears to be wearing some sort of nightgown. It's possible Anna Williams was wearing a nightgown when she went missing."

MacDonald looked over to the body. "If it is Anna Williams, how did she get from the attic of Marlow House to the ocean without anyone seeing her? And in the middle of a storm."

"If it is her, and if she left Marlow House willingly, why did she go out in her nightgown?" Brian countered.

"Do you know what room Glandon is staying in?" MacDonald asked.

"The downstairs bedroom."

"If Williams really did follow him here, like you suspect, maybe she came downstairs for a late night booty call," MacDonald suggested.

"We know he went up to her room; Lily saw him. And he admitted being there. He said it was just to talk."

"Maybe it was more than a talk." MacDonald rested his hands on his hips, looking from the body to Brian. "If she followed him here and was trying to rekindle their romance, maybe she was becoming a nuisance, so he slipped up to her room to tell her it was over. But she didn't want to take no for an answer, so she came downstairs in her nightgown, trying to convince him. Maybe they argued; he hit her. Things went too far, and he had to get rid of the body, so he dragged it outside in the storm, put it into his car, and then drove somewhere and dumped the body over a cliff."

"If Glandon killed her, he has the resources to disappear the moment he realizes we're onto him."

The chief sighed. "Let's not jump too far ahead. We need to ID our Jane Doe first."

CLEVE HAD HEARD ENOUGH. Pulling cash from his pocket, he threw enough bills on the table to cover his tab and a tip. Tugging the top of his jacket collar up to his chin, he slid off the booth bench, leaving the newspaper on the table. Hastily making his way to the exit, he kept his head down.

Once outside, he picked up his pace, hurriedly walking along the boardwalk to where he had parked his vehicle. When he was a good distance from the café, he pulled off the knit cap he had been wearing and tossed it into a trash can along the way.

Before coming to Pier Café he had stopped at Marlow House, asking to see if he could speak to Richard. According to Boatman, Richard had gone with another guest to Pier Café for lunch.

The idea came to Cleve when he was returning to his car after talking to Danielle. According to her, Richard and the other guest were first dropping Lily and Jessica off at the theater to watch *The Penguins of Madagascar*. After they dropped the two off at the show, they were heading to Pier Café, and Danielle told Cleve he could probably catch Richard there, or he could try calling him on his cellphone.

Before going to the café, Cleve had stopped at the camping store and picked up the first coat he found that was one size larger than his normal size. He then grabbed a nondescript knit cap. After making his purchases, he made his way to the diner. The best he hoped to do was to observe Richard and try to get a general feel for what was going on with him. The Richard he knew tended to be reserved, awkward, and somewhat insecure, despite his money. Cleve never imagined he would secure a seat behind Richard, enabling him to clearly overhear his conversation.

When Cleve reached his car, he pulled his cellphone out of his pocket and accessed a file stored on the phone. Reading through the document, he let out a curse and called Peter.

"If you're calling for more time, don't bother asking. I refuse to watch another member slip away," Peter said when he answered his phone.

Looking out to the ocean, Cleve held the cellphone by his ear. "I'm not calling for that. You were right."

"You found out something?"

"We shouldn't have worried about Anna. It was the other woman staying at Marlow House, the one with the little girl."

"He's gotten involved with her?"

"Not that way." Cleve pressed the heel of his free hand against his forehead. He was getting a headache.

"In what way?" Peter asked.

"Her name is Patricia," Cleve told him.

"Yes, I remember. I met her at the open house. So?"

"Think a minute, Peter. Patricia—Richard's Patricia."

Peter didn't respond immediately. After a few moments of silence, he said, "That's impossible."

"I don't think so. I have a horrible feeling about this."

"Have you seen them together?" Peter asked. "When he introduced me to her at the open house, there was nothing to suggest anything more than the most casual of relationships. A new acquaintance—nothing more."

"They're friendly—and if she is who I think she is—"

"Call him home," Peter snapped.

"I knew you were going to say that. But I may not be able to do it quick enough. And if he's already turned his back on the truth, what's the point?"

Peter did not respond. After a few moments of silence, he said in a stern voice, "Just do it."

"I will, sir. But it may take time."

"As you pointed out, Cleve, we do not have time. I trust you to take care of the matter, and do it in such a way it does not come back to hurt Earthbound Spirits. Do you understand?"

"Yes, sir," Cleve choked out.

"Come now, Cleve," Peter said, his voice no longer stern, but gentle and soothing. "The worst that can happen is the best that can happen. You know that."

Cleve sighed. "Yes, I do. But I'm also a little afraid…anxious."

Peter laughed. "I envy you, Cleve, having this chance. Of course, don't be selfish, and if you discover there's no reason for you to go home, stay and continue in your service. It's our duty. We must lead as many to the truth as possible before we move on."

When Cleve said goodbye a few minutes later, he felt better than he had when he had initially placed the call. Getting into his vehicle, he started for home. He had driven not quite a mile when he noticed the police cars and ambulance parked along the road next to the beach. Curious, he pulled over and parked his vehicle. Getting out of his car, he walked toward the beach, stopping on the boardwalk. He looked out toward the ocean.

A crowd had gathered on the beach, surrounding a number of police officers and other responders. Stepping onto the sand, he walked toward the first group of people.

"What's going on?" he asked one of them.

"They found a body. It washed up on shore. A woman," one of the people said.

"Do they know who it is?" Cleve asked.

"No. I heard there's not much left of her face," another person told him. "But I overheard two of the officers talking, and they think it's a woman that went missing from Marlow House on Christmas night."

"They said that?" Cleve asked.

"Yeah. I don't think they meant for me to hear. I asked another cop about it, and he said they have no idea who she is and probably won't know until they run fingerprints."

"I heard she's wearing a nightgown," another one said.

Cleve turned from the group and made his way back to his car. Once inside his vehicle, he made a second call to Peter Morris.

THIRTY

W hen Danielle opened her window on Sunday morning and looked outside, she was relieved to see the sun shining and only a smattering of white puffy clouds in the sky.

There was no reason to rush downstairs and prepare breakfast. The previous night, Chris had offered to take everyone for Sunday brunch at Pearl Cove. They wanted her to join them, but all Danielle wanted to do was sleep in on Sunday and spend a lazy morning drinking coffee while reading her Sunday paper. She didn't mention she also wanted some quiet time with Walt, where they could chat and discuss the strange events of Christmas week.

The night before, she had convinced Ian to leave Sadie with her while he and his sister joined the group for brunch. In no hurry to dress, she slipped a robe on over her pajama bottoms and T-shirt and stepped from her room.

She found Sadie curled up by her door in the hallway, waiting for her. The dog jumped up, wagging her tail. Following Danielle out of the bedroom was Max, who strolled panther-like behind her. As Danielle headed down the hallway, Sadie leaned over to Max and nipped his tail. Max responded with a hiss and swatted the dog's nose. Unaffected by the swat and hiss, Sadie let out a bark and charged down the stairs, rushing past Danielle.

Danielle's first stop was to turn on the coffee pot. Once the coffee started brewing, she headed for the front door. She stepped out on her porch to pick up the Sunday morning newspaper when she came face to face with Chief MacDonald. "Hey, Chief, you're back!"

"Morning, Danielle."

Sadie charged outside, heading straight for the chief. Butt wiggling, tail wagging, she enthusiastically greeted him. After receiving several hearty pats, the golden retriever turned and ran back into the house, her tail still wagging.

The chief leaned down, picked up the newspaper, and handed it to Danielle.

"Thanks. When did you get back?" Danielle stepped back into the house.

"Yesterday morning." He followed her inside.

"So tell me about your Christmas." Danielle shut the front door.

"This isn't really a social call; you think we can talk alone? Maybe in the parlor?"

"Sure. But they're all gone, anyway." Danielle tossed the newspaper onto the entry table and led the way into the parlor.

They found Sadie and Max already in the room. Max sat on the windowsill, looking outside, his tail swishing back and forth, while Sadie stood behind him, trying to grab the tip of his tail in her mouth. Each time she made an unsuccessful grab, the tail twitched again. Danielle suspected the cat was enjoying the game.

"Where're your guests? I heard you have a full house." He tossed his hat onto a chair and sat down.

"They heard about Pearl Cove's Sunday Brunch, so they all went. Joanne even went with them."

"Why didn't you go?"

Walt appeared in the room. "Ahh, the chief's here." He took a seat on the sofa.

Upon seeing Walt, Sadie let out a bark and turned from Max. Charging for the sofa, she jumped up on Walt. The ghost's lap disappeared under the golden retriever.

Danielle glanced briefly at the pair, rolled her eyes, and then looked over to the chief. "I kinda wanted some quiet time, especially with everything that's been going on. I suppose Joe and Brian told you about my guest who vanished in the middle of the night on Christmas."

"Yes, that's one reason I'm here."

Danielle took a seat on the sofa next to Walt and Sadie. "Did you find out anything about her?"

"I'm not sure. I hate to be the one to tell you this, but a woman's body washed up on the beach yesterday morning."

Danielle's left hand gripped the sofa's arm. "Oh my god, not Anna!"

"We don't know."

Danielle frowned. "What do you mean?"

"She's about the right size, right age. Blonde."

"Joe and Brian know what she looks like; couldn't they make an identification?" Danielle asked.

The chief shook his head. "It looks like she fell from quite a distance, face down, on some ragged rocks. Ripped her up pretty badly."

"Oh no…" Danielle leaned back in the sofa and closed her eyes. She felt ill.

"How in the hell did that happen?" Walt asked. "One minute she's in my attic and the next she's in the ocean?"

Danielle opened her eyes again and looked across at the chief. "What about fingerprints?"

"There's nothing in our database. We ran them, but she's not there. I was hoping you might know what her nightgown looked like."

"Her nightgown? Why?"

"That's what our Jane Doe was wearing, a nightgown. I have a picture of it on my phone." The chief started to reach for his cellphone.

"Don't bother, Chief. I never saw her in a nightgown. She might have one, but I never saw it. On Christmas morning she came downstairs in a robe, with pajama bottoms."

"Do you know if anyone might have seen her in a nightgown on Christmas night?"

Danielle considered the question a moment. "I suppose you could ask. But the only one I know who ever went up into her room was Chris, one of the other guests. It was late Christmas night, the night she disappeared. He could've seen what she had on."

"Where's Chris now?"

"He's with everyone else, having brunch at Pearl Cove. I don't expect them back for a couple hours."

"We're having the blood tested from your rug, hopefully that might help identify her," he told her. "I have to assume the blood belongs to Williams. Maybe she had a cut and it got on the rug."

"That's sort of what I thought too."

"Plus, I can't imagine the killer would leave such an obvious clue behind. But we'll have to wait for the results of the test."

"Killer? You're saying this was murder?"

"Who would want to murder Anna?" Walt asked.

"According to the coroner, she has defensive wounds."

"Do you think she was dead before or after she went into the ocean?" Danielle asked.

"The coroner says before."

Danielle folded her arms across her chest and leaned back on the sofa. "If it was Anna, what do you think happened? Did she sneak out and meet someone in the storm…wearing her nightgown?"

"Or maybe she came downstairs in her nightgown and something happened here, and whoever killed her took her to one of the cliffs and pushed her in the ocean, assuming the body would wash out to sea," the chief suggested.

"Someone here? Are you saying one of my guests might be a killer?"

"According to Brian, your guest Chris Glandon, who goes by the alias Chris Johnson, threatened Ms. Williams days before Christmas. It's possible they were in a relationship, Glandon tried to break it off, she followed him here, they argued at the diner, she went to his room Christmas night, and they fought there."

Danielle turned to Walt. "Did you hear any fighting coming from Chris's room on Christmas night?"

"Walt is here?" the chief asked.

"Yes."

"I didn't smell any cigar smoke." MacDonald scratched his head.

"I thought you knew the lack of smoke doesn't mean he isn't in the room." Danielle sounded annoyed.

"No, Danielle. At one time I would've delighted in helping the chief put Chris away, but he's starting to grow on me." Walt waved his hand, summoning a lit cigar.

"I smell it now," the chief mumbled.

"Chief, I bought Walt a subscription to Netflix and on—"

"A ghost watches Netflix?" MacDonald interrupted.

"You know he hates that word," Danielle chided.

"Fine, a spirit watches Netflix? Seriously?"

"Why is that so strange?" Danielle asked.

"I thought it was a very thoughtful gift." Walt puffed his cigar.

Danielle smiled. "Thank you, Walt." She turned her attention back to the chief. "Anyway, Walt spent Christmas night in the parlor, watching television. After Anna checked in, the attic was basically off-limits for him."

"Why?" the chief asked.

"I think guests deserve privacy. And don't you think it would be a little creepy, Walt lurking around in one of my female guests' rooms?"

"I do not lurk," Walt told her.

Danielle sighed. "You know what I mean, Walt."

"Are you telling me he was downstairs all night? He didn't see anything suspicious going on?"

Danielle glanced at Walt. He shook his head. She looked back at the chief. "Nothing. He had left the door slightly open, had the television on low. Max was playing guard in the hallway."

"Max? Your cat?"

"Yeah. Letting Walt know if Chris was coming out of his room —which he only did once. I assume that was when he went upstairs to talk to Anna. But he returned to his room alone and shut the door."

"How are you so certain of that?" the chief asked.

"Max told Walt, of course."

"You forget one thing, Danielle," the chief reminded her.

"What's that?"

"Anna obviously came downstairs sometime, because she's gone. What does Max say about that?"

Danielle let out a heavy sigh and leaned back in the sofa. "I don't know. That one has me stumped. The only thing we can figure out, Max fell asleep and she got by him. But had Chris had some sort of fight with Anna in his room, not only would Max have heard it—Walt would have too."

"You seem very certain this Chris guy is innocent of any wrongdoing."

"Yes, you do, Danielle." Walt studied her. "And I suspect it isn't just because Max and I were downstairs all evening."

Danielle silently considered the series of events before responding. After a moment, she said, "You're forgetting Anna's clothes."

"Her clothes?"

"When Anna left, she took everything with her that she brought—except for the suitcase. I'm not sure why she left it behind, but she didn't leave anything else."

"I understood she left the gifts she received behind," the chief reminded her.

"True, but you're missing my point. If she snuck down here like you suggest, to see Chris, and then they got into some fight, then that would mean he went back up to her room afterwards and gathered up all her clothes to make it look like she left. But if he did that, why leave the suitcase behind? That doesn't make any sense. It just raises more questions."

The chief stood up. "It's all a theory at this point. But if that blood on the rug matches the woman we found yesterday, everyone in Marlow House will be coming under closer scrutiny."

"If it's Anna, I don't believe she was killed here." Danielle stood up.

"How can you be so certain of that? If she was in Glandon's room with the door shut, it's possible something happened without Walt hearing."

"Ahh, but you're forgetting one crucial fact." Danielle grinned.

"What's that?"

"Anna's spirit. A murdered person's spirit is not going to just disappear without making some commotion."

"I thought you said you can't always see or hear a spirit. So if she made a commotion, you might not know," MacDonald said.

"True, but Walt would."

"Walt?"

"Certainly. While I can't necessarily see or hear every spirit that passes my way—or at least I don't think I can, an assumption I made because I never saw my parents or Lucas—that's not true for spirits. You put a bunch of spirits in a room, and they can see each other—just like if you put a bunch of living people in a room, they can see each other."

"Not true for blind people," Walt pointed out.

Danielle glared at Walt. "You know what I mean."

Walt shrugged and took a puff off his cigar.

"And there's also the matter of the blood," Danielle added.

"What about it?" MacDonald asked.

"If it was Anna's, it was still wet when Joe found it. In your scenario, this would have all gone down before we got up in the morning, and I would assume by the time Joe found the rug, the blood would have been dry."

"Not necessarily," MacDonald disagreed. "With all the rain we've been having, I imagine it's rather damp in the attic. Quite possible for the blood to still be wet hours later."

THIRTY-ONE

"It was a great brunch, you should've come with us," Lily told Danielle when she returned later Sunday afternoon. Danielle stood in the kitchen, making herself a sandwich.

"Glad you liked it. Did everyone come back?" Danielle piled turkey on a slice of bread.

Lily leaned against the counter and watched Danielle build her sandwich. "Joanne went home, and Kelly left for Portland."

"Yeah, Kelly mentioned she was going to head back to Portland after the brunch. We already said goodbye." Danielle set her sandwich on a plate and cut it in half. Before carrying it to the table, she put the lid back on the jar of mayonnaise and returned it to the refrigerator.

"I put a movie on for Jessica in the parlor."

"Where's everyone else?"

"In the living room." Lily followed Danielle to the table and took a seat across from her. "They had this amazing lobster quiche."

"A woman's body washed up on the beach." Danielle took a bite of her sandwich.

"What?"

Danielle nodded, finished chewing her bite, and then swallowed. "The chief stopped by. He said an unidentified woman washed up on the beach yesterday, and he thinks it might be Anna."

"Oh no!" Lily's eyes darted to the doorway.

"I don't want to talk about this around Jessica."

Lily shook her head. "Of course not. But why hasn't there been an identification made—umm—we don't have to go down there and do it, do we?"

"No. Joe or Brian could have made an ID, but the woman's face —I guess it's pretty messed up. She must have fallen on the rocks. It's impossible to tell what she looks like." Danielle set her partially eaten sandwich back on the plate.

"Oh, poor Anna."

"That's assuming it's Anna, which I'm not. The woman was wearing a nightgown. I don't believe anyone forced Anna out of this house. And if she decided to leave in the middle of the night in a storm and take her clothes with her, I would think she'd first put her clothes on. She wouldn't go out in a nightgown. That doesn't make sense to me."

"If they can't tell by her face, what about fingerprints?"

"They already ran them, but the woman isn't in the system. I guess they plan to have the blood on the rug tested."

"To see if it matches the woman they found?"

"Yeah."

"When are you going to tell everyone?"

"You said they're all in the living room?" Danielle picked her sandwich up.

"Yes."

"After I eat my lunch, I'll come tell them. Might as well do it before they hear about it on the radio or before Jessica finishes her movie."

WHEN DANIELLE WALKED into the living room fifteen minutes later, she found Patricia sitting on the sofa with her MacBook on her lap. It was one of the gifts she had received from Benevolent Charities. Lily sat next to her, helping Patricia hook up to Danielle's Wi-Fi.

Danielle glanced around the room; she didn't see Chris.

"Missed you at brunch. We're going to help Patricia find her brother," Ian called out. He sat on one of the chairs facing the sofa. Richard sat on the other chair.

"Really?" Danielle walked toward the sofa and looked down at the computer. "How are you going to do that?"

"Ian said he'd help her search on the Internet," Chris said when he entered the room.

Danielle glanced behind her, looking at Chris, who had just come in from the hallway. She assumed he was either returning from his bedroom or the bathroom off the foyer. She flashed Chris a smile and then looked back to Patricia.

"I've never been good at computers," Patricia told her.

"I see they're all gathered together. Are you going to tell them about the woman?" Walt asked Danielle when he appeared in the room.

"You're doing great so far." Lily glanced up at Danielle, her expression questioning.

Danielle looked at Walt and then at Lily. She shook her head and whispered, "Later." Looking over at Patricia, she asked in a clearer voice, "So what's this about finding your brother?"

"Christmas has stirred so many memories for me this year," Patricia explained. Smiling over at Richard, she added, "And I think a lot of it is Richard."

"Richard? What do you mean?" Danielle sat on one arm of the sofa.

"In so many ways, he reminds me of my brother. I have to admit, I got this crazy idea that maybe…well, maybe Richard is my brother."

Danielle glanced over to Richard, who fidgeted nervously in his chair. She thought he looked embarrassed.

"How so?" Danielle asked.

Patricia shrugged. "Little things. Some things he said, strange coincidences. And then I found out he and my brother share the same birthday. Not just the day, but the year."

"Does this mean your birthday was on Christmas Eve?" Lily asked Richard. She already knew the answer, since she'd been with Danielle when uncovering information on him.

Richard nodded. "Yes."

"Patricia isn't kidding." Ian chuckled. "Last night she confided in me that she thought he might be her brother, so I did a quick Internet search on Richard this morning."

Surprised at the announcement, Richard and Lily turned abruptly to Ian.

"You never told me that," Lily said.

"Well, he isn't my brother." Patricia sighed. She looked at Richard and smiled. "I suppose I always knew you really weren't. After all, in the fairytale the princess—or prince in this case—is raised as a pauper and discovers he's really a prince. Not the other way around."

"I'm curious, what did you find online?" Chris asked. He sat on the floor by the Christmas tree.

"That proved Richard isn't Patricia's long-lost brother?" Ian asked.

Chris nodded. "Yeah."

"It didn't take me long. First article I found was an extensive interview with Richard's father. Discussed the birth of their only child on Christmas Eve; included pictures of him and his wife bringing Richard home from the hospital. Discussed their time living abroad, returning to the States."

"I have to admit I was disappointed." Patricia laughed.

"Look on the bright side," Ian said. "You found a new friend in Richard, and if we're lucky, we'll track down your lost brother."

"You don't know how much this means to me," Patricia told them. "I really appreciate your help."

"First we need to—" Ian began.

Richard stood up abruptly and blurted, "I can't do this."

Wide-eyed, Patricia looked at Richard. "I—I'm sorry if I made you uncomfortable, all this talk about how you remind me of my brother—I know you have your own family—"

"No, no, I don't." Richard shook his head and began to pace the room.

"What is it?" Chris asked.

Richard stopped pacing and looked at Patricia. "I think I'm your brother."

The room went silent. Everyone stared at Richard.

After a few moments of silence, Ian said, "That's impossible. I found your birth information."

Richard shook his head. "No. You found the other Richard. The real one."

"I don't understand," Patricia muttered.

Standing in the middle of the room, Richard looked around. They continued to stare at him. He took a deep breath. "I always knew there was something different, that something was wrong. I had memories, but my parents told me I needed to forget, that it was all a dream."

"Richard, perhaps it would be better if you started at the beginning," Chris suggested.

Looking down at Chris, Richard nodded and then returned to his chair. "After my parents died, I found papers in their safe. My adoption papers—and the other Richard's death certificate."

"Other Richard?" Lily asked.

"I learned that the people I knew as my parents—Richard and Rachael Winston—had another son. Richard Jr., who coincidentally was born on the same day as I was. They were living in Europe when he drowned in a swimming pool—he was six years old."

"Are you saying you aren't their biological son?" Patricia asked.

Richard nodded. "I'm not sure how—but they learned of a little boy in the foster care system, one who was up for adoption—who happened to be born on the exact day their son had been born. My mother—my adopted mother—saw it as a sign. She had to have me, and if Rachael Winston wanted something, Richard Winston got it for her."

Danielle and Lily exchanged glances. They were both thinking of the grave website Danielle had found on the first Richard Winston.

"Oh my god, are you Bobby?" Patricia whispered.

Richard looked at her. "I'm not sure, but I think so."

"How old were you when they adopted you?" Danielle asked.

"Six," Richard told her.

Patricia frowned. "If you're Bobby, that would mean they adopted you right after our mother died."

"I'm not saying the adoption was finalized when I was six, but according to the papers, that's how old I was when I went to live with them. So yes, it would have been the same year, if I'm your brother."

"Six isn't that young," Danielle said. "I was six in the first grade, and I remember my teacher, my best friend from that year and even a field trip I took. Wouldn't you remember?"

"I...I think I did. My parents told me I had vivid dreams. Over the years, I came to accept the belief that those things I thought were memories were nothing more than dreams. And in later years they told me a little girl I insisted on remembering was nothing more than my childhood imaginary friend."

"Imaginary friend?" Lily asked.

Richard looked Patricia in the eyes and said, "Yes. My imaginary friend. Her name was Patricia."

"And they never discussed your adoption?" Ian asked.

"No. I never knew. In fact, my mother used to talk about when she was pregnant with me. She would show me pictures of her when she was pregnant. I have baby pictures. But they're not me. I remember once I dated this girl and my mother brought out the family photo album and showed her some pictures. The girl made a comment about how much I had changed from when I was a toddler to school age, even joking about how I looked like a different child."

"What did your mother say?" Lily asked.

"She was furious. Hated that girl after that. I never really thought much about it. I just figured the girl offended my mother. It wasn't long after that we stopped seeing each other."

"What about your parents' friends, family? Wouldn't they have said something?" Danielle asked.

"The first Richard died when they were living in Europe. From what I can tell, they got me within a week after returning to the States. Quite frankly, I think they led their friends here to believe I was their biological child."

"That's how our parents knew each other." Chris spoke up. Everyone in the room looked at him. "The boating accident that killed our parents—that boat was owned by their attorney—their adoption attorney."

"You're adopted too?" Patricia asked.

Chris nodded. "Yes, although it sounds like my situation was much happier than Richard's. For one thing, I didn't have to compete with my parents' dead child. And I never doubted my parents loved me."

THIRTY-TWO

The inevitable happened. Patricia and Richard hugged. Of the two, which one started crying first wasn't clear. Even Lily and Danielle found themselves wiping away tears, and while tears weren't slipping down Ian's cheeks, they were in his eyes. Chris was the only one of the six with dry eyes, yet Walt—who was sitting back observing the scene—thought Chris wore a supreme expression of relief, and Walt couldn't figure out why.

"Even if the DNA test proves we aren't brother and sister, that this is just some bizarre coincidence, we have to stay friends, please," Patricia begged.

Richard laughed. "The way my memories have been flooding back this week, I would be surprised if the DNA proves we aren't, but yes. And even if we aren't, I still want to help you and Jessica, be there for you."

"Help?" Patricia frowned.

"I can buy you a house...and..."

Patricia grabbed Richard's arm. "This isn't about money. I don't expect you to buy us anything, even if the DNA tests proves our hunch is correct. I just want my brother back."

Richard shook his head and laughed, giving Patricia another hug.

"This is all very touching," Walt said as he stood up. "But this sentimentality—it's draining." Walt disappeared.

WHEN THE DOORBELL RANG, Danielle was reminded of what she meant to discuss with everyone—before Patricia and Richard's startling revelation. She was fairly certain who was at the door—Chief MacDonald. Her initial intention was to let everyone know about the body that had washed up on shore before he arrived. Now, she didn't want to say anything, because Richard and Patricia were so excited about finding each other. That was, of course, if they really were siblings.

She excused herself and went to answer the front door. As she suspected, it was the chief.

"Afternoon, Danielle, I assume they've all returned?" Wearing his uniform and cap with the department insignia, MacDonald stood on the doorstep.

"Yes, Chief. Have you gotten the blood test results back yet?"

"No. I doubt we'll have that until tomorrow. Are you going to let me come in, or do you plan to make me stand on the porch all afternoon?"

"Chief," Danielle whispered, stepping outside and partially closing the door behind her, "this really is a bad time. And Jessica, she's the young girl staying here, is in the parlor watching a movie. I really don't want her to know anything yet—or at all. She really liked Anna, and if the woman you found isn't Anna, I see no reason to upset her."

"I guess this means you are going to make me stand on the porch all afternoon."

"Please, Chief, can we do this tomorrow…after you get the blood test results?"

"Why don't you want me to come in? Who are you protecting?" He tried to look over her shoulder.

"This has nothing to do with Anna or the body that washed up, I promise," she whispered.

The chief stared at her.

"Chief, you don't even know if the woman is Anna. So why don't you wait until the results of the blood test are in before upsetting all my guests."

"Danielle, what's going on?"

She let out a sigh and glanced over her shoulder and then looked back at the chief. In a rush she said, "If you must know, two of my guests—Patricia and Richard—who just happened to come here for Christmas and didn't know each other before this week, or at least didn't realize they knew each other—just discovered they may be each other's long lost sibling and at the moment the emotions are very high, and springing this on them right now—especially when we really don't know if that woman is Anna—just does not seem like the right thing to do." When she finished, she took a deep breath and added, "Please, Chief, can we wait until tomorrow after the test results?"

MacDonald blinked several times and asked, "You're serious?"

"About what? Wanting to wait until tomorrow or about Patricia and Richard maybe being siblings?"

"Both, I guess."

Danielle nodded. "Very serious."

After a moment he said, "Fine. But tomorrow, when the test results come in, I expect you all to come into the station. We'll talk there."

Danielle nodded. "Okay, deal. I'll make sure everyone is there."

WALT STOOD in the attic and looked around. The sleeper sofa was still pulled out, made into a bed. No one had moved Anna's suitcase from the center of the mattress. He wondered if Danielle expected Anna to return. She might, providing she wasn't the woman who had washed up on shore the day before.

Walking to the window, Walt was about to adjust the spotting scope when he heard small feet race across the wood floor and then a thumping sound, as if whoever was running had just hit the wall. Looking in the direction of the sound, he spied a flash of dark fur disappear under the bed.

Hands on hips, Walt turned from the window and looked down at the mattress. Assuming the cat was hiding under the bed, he asked, "Max, what are you doing?"

White-tipped ears popped up in the narrow opening where the head of the mattress butted up to the sofa's backrest. After a moment, the rest of the head pushed its way through. Max blinked and stared at Walt.

"You're going to get stuck in there," Walt warned. "What do you mean we have rats?...You what?"

WALT FOUND Danielle in the living room. They were all still discussing Richard and Patricia's possible connection, and now Patricia was recounting stories of their youth, in hopes Richard would recall some of the events.

"Danielle," Walt interrupted, ignoring the story Patricia was currently telling, "I need to talk to you about the blood in the attic. Please meet me in the library." Walt then disappeared.

A few minutes later, when there was a break in the conversation, Danielle excused herself, making up a story about a phone call she forgot to make. When she got to the library, she found Walt sitting on the sofa, waiting for her, a lit cigar in his hand. She entered the room and closed the door behind her.

"What about the blood?" She sat next to Walt on the sofa.

"I'm afraid I have to be the one to tell you this…" Walt casually took a puff off his cigar and then blew out a smoke ring. It lazily drifted to the ceiling and disappeared. "Someone was murdered in the attic."

"Murdered?"

Walt turned to Danielle and nodded. "Yes, a poor rat. The killer is Max; he confessed."

"We have rats?"

"Had. As I mentioned, Max killed it."

"What does this have to do with the blood?"

"Isn't that obvious?" Walt flicked an ash off his cigar. It vanished as it hit the floor. "The blood on the rug was from the rat."

"While I remember a few gruesome body parts licked clean and left for me to find when I had a cat as a kid, I don't remember ever finding blood."

Walt shrugged. "Apparently he just wanted to play with the poor little guy for a while. Didn't realize how sharp his teeth were. Must have hit an artery or something. It happened on the white throw rug. He took what was left of the poor creature outside. He's currently on patrol in the attic in case there are more."

Danielle glanced up at the ceiling. "While I'm relieved to know the blood wasn't from someone being killed in the attic, I'm not thrilled to hear we may have rats. Plus, I wish the blood was Anna's."

"Why?"

"I was hoping it would prove the woman they found wasn't her."

"I'm sure they'll be able to eventually ID the woman."

"I suppose you're right. There're also dental records, DNA…"

Walt stood up. "I just thought you should know."

"Where are you going?"

"Back to the attic to keep an eye on Max. Is Sadie still in the parlor with Jessica?"

"I think so."

Walt waved his hand and disappeared with his cigar.

Instead of rushing back to the library, Danielle let out a sigh and leaned back in the sofa, staring at the fireplace. Contemplating if she should light a fire in the library hearth or return to the living room, her thoughts were abruptly interrupted when a blonde woman stepped out of the fireplace.

Wearing a blue floral nightgown, the woman looked around the room, a frown plastered on her face. "Where is he?" she demanded.

Danielle sat up straight on the sofa, her eyes focused on the apparition. "Who?" Danielle found herself asking.

"The cop, of course. I followed him here. Where did he go?" The woman walked farther into the room and looked around.

"Chief MacDonald?" Danielle asked.

Exasperated, the woman flopped down on a chair and propped her bare feet on a table. "I don't know what his name is. Just a cop, that's all I know."

"Who are you?" Danielle asked.

The woman stared at Danielle a moment before answering, "I'm Beatrice Montgomery, if it's any of your business." The woman glanced around again. "Where am I?"

"You're at Marlow House."

"Marlow House?" The woman scowled. "Never heard of it."

"Why do you want Chief MacDonald?"

"I never said I wanted Chief MacDonald. I want the cop I was following."

"Chief MacDonald is the cop who was just here."

Beatrice shrugged. "Maybe that's his name, I don't know. He wouldn't talk to me. Rude. He ignored me at the beach, none of them would answer my questions. I followed him back to the police station. I even went to his house. Lord, he has some wild little boys! One of them told me to leave and threw a toy truck at me!"

"One of his sons saw you?"

"What kind of question is that?" Beatrice shook her head in disgust.

"Maybe you should tell me why you want to talk to the chief...I mean, the cop."

"I want him to arrest my husband, Herbert."

"Umm...what did Herbert do?"

"He pushed me off that cliff, that's what that jerk did! And then just drove off in the motor home. This is the last time Herbert pulls something like this on me. I want a divorce!"

"Can you tell me what happened exactly?"

Beatrice let out a sigh and leaned back. "I wanted to take a cruise, but Herbert got this bright idea to rent a motor home and travel up the Oregon coast. Who travels up the Oregon coast in December? What was he thinking? I wanted somewhere tropical and warm."

"Where were you staying?"

"Staying? Why, anywhere that wouldn't charge us a camping fee. Cheap jerk. We ended up on some pull-out along the highway for Christmas. Sure, it had a great view, but the wind starts howling and the rain keeps falling, and the thunder and lightning! I told Herbert I wanted to move, that I didn't want to be washed away in some tsunami."

"So what happened?" Danielle asked.

"We started arguing—*again*—and he says, I'll show you a tsunami, and he grabs me by the wrist and starts to jerk me outside. I don't want to go outside! It's raining, and I only have my night-gown on. But we start fighting, and the next thing I know we're outside in the rain, yelling at each other, and that jerk pushes me off the cliff!"

Before Danielle could respond, the door to the library opened and Chris walked in.

"Hey, Danielle, I wanted to ask you..." Chris stopped talking and looked at the blonde woman. "Oh, I'm sorry. I didn't realize you had company."

Beatrice's eyes widened and she broke into a smile. Sitting up straight in the chair, she crossed her legs, attempting a flattering pose, and said, "Well, hello, cutie. Who are you?"

Danielle glanced frantically from Beatrice to Chris and then asked, "You can see her?"

THIRTY-THREE

"What kind of question is that?" Beatrice asked, flashing Danielle a dirty look before turning her smile back to Chris.

Frowning in confusion, Chris looked from Danielle to the stranger. It was then he noticed the blonde wasn't wearing a dress—she wore a nightgown. A woman wearing just a nightgown, sitting in the library of Marlow House wouldn't be so unusual if she happened to be staying at the B and B, he thought.

"Are you a new guest?" The moment he asked the question, he realized how idiotic it was. All of the guestrooms were occupied, and he didn't think Danielle was about to rent out Anna's room. After all, she had paid through New Year's, and technically it was still hers, even if she wasn't coming back. As for the blonde's attire, he couldn't imagine a potential guest would just show up wearing a nightgown. However, it was Danielle's question—*you can see her?*—that gave him a sickening feeling.

"Guest? Goodness no!" Beatrice laughed. "But...if you're staying here, I might seriously consider checking in." She winked at Chris, recrossed her legs and wiggled the toes of her top foot.

Walt took that moment to re-enter the room. He seemed as surprised to find the nightgown-clad blonde as Danielle was to discover Chris could see Beatrice.

"My goodness, the good-looking men just seem to pop out of the woodwork around here!" Beatrice gleefully exclaimed.

Walt walked to the blonde and took note of her floral night-gown. He then looked at Danielle. "I take it she's the blonde who washed up on shore yesterday?"

"What are you talking about?" Beatrice shrieked.

Walt shrugged. "I guess the chief won't be arresting Chris now."

"What do you mean arrest me?" Chris blurted.

Walt's and Danielle's eyes riveted on Chris.

"You can see him too?" Danielle shrieked.

Chris let out a sigh and sat down on the empty chair. "Pretending is getting too damn exhausting. Yes, I can see Walt. I can also see the blonde. Who is she, by the way, and what is this about me not getting arrested?"

"What are you people talking about?" Beatrice shouted and then disappeared.

"I wonder if she's coming back?" Chris murmured, looking at the now empty chair. When no one responded, he glanced over to Walt and Danielle, who continued to stare at him, their expressions blank.

Chris let out another sigh and leaned back in his chair. He looked from Walt to Danielle. "Yes, I can see Walt. What's the big deal?"

"And you never said anything?" Danielle could feel her face turning red.

Chris shrugged. "Oh, come on, you know how it is. You tell people you can see ghosts and they start looking at you like they want to lock you up."

"But you could've said something to me," Danielle fumed. "Because I obviously could see Walt."

Walt tapped a finger against his chin and studied Chris for a moment. "Does this mean Chris could hear everything I said to you when he was in the room with us?"

Chris flashed Walt a smile and nodded.

"Even when I discussed what Danielle and Lily thought of your looks?"

Chris's grin broadened.

Danielle let out an embarrassed gasp and grabbed the sofa pillow sitting next to her. "Why, you rat!" she shouted just before standing up and slamming the pillow against Chris. Using his arms to shield himself from her blows, he tried to dodged the assault. She continued to smack him with the pillow.

Danielle didn't stop swinging her weapon because she was hurting Chris, but because she heard him laughing. Enraged, she threw the pillow against the fireplace. It fell to the floor and she sat back on the sofa, angrily crossing her arms over her chest.

"Oh, come on, Danielle," Chris cooed, "don't be angry with me. I didn't mean any harm."

"I could just slug you," Danielle fumed, glaring at Chris.

"Yeah, I know. You just did." He chuckled.

"Perhaps Danielle didn't do any damage just now, but you may not be so lucky with me," Walt warned in a stern voice.

Chris looked over at Walt and rolled his eyes. "Yeah, right. If you think jumping in my face and yelling boo is going to shake me up, you'd have better luck smacking me with a pillow, if you actually could."

Walt raised his brows. "Oh really?" The chair Chris sat on began to rise up into the air.

"Oh crap," Chris muttered, his hands now gripping the chair's arms. He looked down and then up. His head was almost touching the ceiling.

"Oh, put him down, Walt. And don't break anything," Danielle said with disgust.

Slowly, the chair lowered back toward the floor. Just as it was about two feet from touching back down, it tipped forward suddenly, dropping Chris face-first onto the library floor. He landed with a loud thumping sound before letting out a grunt.

Danielle cringed. "Ouch. I bet that hurt."

Chris groaned and pulled himself up off the floor. Rubbing his face, he said, "Okay, I deserved that. I confess, I misjudged Walt's abilities. I hadn't seen him do anything, and I just assumed—"

"Assumed what?" Walt asked.

Chris glanced at the chair he had been sitting on a moment earlier. It sat quietly in its original place. "Can I sit down? Or will you send me across the room?"

"Go ahead. Just be warned." Walt smiled smugly and sat on the sofa next to Danielle. They faced Chris.

Feeling calmer now, Danielle asked, "When did you first realize you could see spirits?"

Chris shrugged. "For as long as I can remember. My mother told me I had a vivid imagination, that I would probably be a writer someday. She encouraged me to tell her about my *imaginary friends*, yet she suggested I keep it our secret."

"When did you realize they were more than just your imagination?" Danielle asked.

"I suppose when I was about ten and went to my first funeral and the guest of honor decided to sit next to me and chat."

"Was it someone you knew very well?"

"It was a neighbor. Nice enough guy. I was a bit freaked, but after that things started to make sense. How about you?"

Danielle told Chris about seeing her grandmother and of the neighbor boy who got her sent to a shrink and how she learned to keep the secret.

"Does anyone else know about your ability?" Chris asked.

"Lily and the chief."

"The chief?" Chris frowned.

"The police chief, Chief MacDonald."

"Wait a minute—is this the chief Walt was talking about, who wants to have me arrested?"

"Aren't you being a bit presumptuous?" Walt asked.

Chris frowned. "Presumptuous, how?"

"Calling me Walt. Did I give you permission to call me by my first name? Young people have no manners."

"I didn't hear you calling me Mr. Johnson," Chris countered.

"Your name's not Johnson."

"I haven't heard you call me Mr. Glandon either. Anyway, you died before you were thirty; that technically makes you the youngster, Wally."

"Have you forgotten the chair?" Walt warned.

Chris quickly put up his hands in defeat. "You're right. You have the power of the chair, Mr. Marlow."

"No, please call me Walt." Walt smiled smugly, leaning back in the sofa. The smile quickly faded. He leaned forward and glared at Chris.

"What's wrong now?" Chris asked.

"I just remember the other things you said. Exactly what does nerdy mean? Danielle wouldn't tell me."

"Oh…that." Chris smiled sheepishly.

Danielle's eyes widened. She started to laugh. "You were doing that on purpose! You knew he could hear you! You said all that stuff about him just to rile him!"

Chris shrugged and then glanced over to Walt, who glared at him through narrowed eyes. "In my defense, I had no idea you had mastered any spiritual powers."

"Spiritual powers?" Danielle repeated. "I always think of it as harnessing energy."

"I suppose that's the same thing," Chris told her.

"So do you always go around teasing poor defenseless spirits that way? Making fun of them?" Danielle asked in a scolding voice.

"No. To be honest, I've never been in a position like this. Never encountered a spirit who wasn't aware I could see him."

"Humm…interesting…" Walt studied Chris.

"Back to my original question—what was this about the chief wanting to arrest me?"

"Oh, right…Anna…Beatrice," Danielle said with a sigh.

"Anna? Beatrice?" Chris frowned.

"The woman who was just here, her body washed up on the beach yesterday. The chief showed up earlier today—twice, in fact—because he suspects the body is Anna's."

"That woman? Why, she looks nothing like Anna. Surely someone's told him that."

"That's the problem, Beatrice—that's the woman's name—apparently her husband threw her off the cliffs on Christmas day, and she fell face-first on the rocks. Her face is unrecognizable. And if you think about it, she's the general size and shape as Anna and has blond hair around the same length."

"What about fingerprints?"

"They ran them, but Beatrice must not be in the system." Danielle then explained to Chris about the chief's hopes of matching the blood on the rug to the dead woman and how that wouldn't be happening.

"I still don't understand what any of this has to do with me."

"Well, if that woman had proved to be Anna, you're on the top of the suspect list because of what Brian overheard at the diner."

"I didn't kill Anna," Chris reiterated.

"Maybe not. But if you could get her to return, clear up the mystery of the disappearance, then they'll leave you alone."

"That's not going to happen," Chris mumbled.

"You think they'll stay on your case even if Anna returns?"

"No, I meant Anna is not going to come back. That's not going to happen. But it has nothing to do with me. I can't control what Anna does."

"Then maybe you need to tell them where Anna went, if you know."

"I don't know." Chris shook his head. "Trust me, I really don't know where she went."

"Well, at least now that we know the woman who washed up on the beach is not Anna and that the blood they found on the rug isn't human blood, they really shouldn't be bothering you."

"Yeah, but how do we convince them the woman isn't Anna? You said yourself her fingerprints aren't in the system."

"No, but I can go to the chief, tell him I saw her spirit, give him her name…Oh, her name! What was her last name again? And her husband's name?" Danielle closed her eyes and tried to remember.

"Yeah, right, like you can just tell the police chief you saw the woman's ghost!"

"Shhh, Chris! I need to remember…what was her name?"

Danielle jumped up from the sofa and ran to the desk. She opened the desk drawer and pulled out a piece of paper and pen.

"Her name was Beatrice…Beatrice Montgomery, and her husband's name was…started with an H…Henry? No…Hugh?…Herbert!" Danielle quickly scribbled down the names.

"Can I talk now?" Chris asked impatiently.

Danielle folded the piece of paper and tucked it in her pocket. "Sure. What?"

"Knowing the name of the victim will help identify the body, but only if you can get the police chief to listen to you. How in the world are you going to convince him to check it out? You can't very well just march in there and announce her ghost gave you the information."

"Sure I can." Danielle smiled.

"You can?"

"I told you the chief knows I can see ghosts."

THIRTY-FOUR

Danielle dabbed the corner of her toast into the egg's yolk before taking a bite. Everyone at the table seemed to be talking at once, discussing their upcoming day, rehashing the events of the past week, and tallying up reasons to believe Patricia and Richard were probably siblings. She wasn't joining in on any of the conversations; her thoughts were elsewhere.

"Dani, are you going to answer the question?" Lily asked impatiently.

Danielle looked up from her plate. "Oh, I'm sorry. What were you asking?"

"Patricia wanted to know if you really thought Earthbound Spirits knew Stoddard's will wasn't fake."

"You were talking about Earthbound Spirits?" Danielle hadn't noticed the conversation turning in that direction. She glanced around, all eyes were on her. Lily sat at the dining room table with her and the guests of Marlow House.

Danielle set her fork on her plate and looked down the table at Richard, who silently waited for her answer. "I'm afraid I do. They had to have known. Clarence Renton prepared both wills for Isabella, and he became a member of the group after he went to prison. I really don't believe he would have kept that a secret from Morris, do you, Richard?"

"I always understood Mr. Renton was just eager to help Earthbound Spirits, and he made a poor decision."

Danielle smiled and picked up her fork again. "Oh, I believe Clarence made a number of poor decisions, yet I don't think that was one of them."

"You told me why you don't believe in Earthbound Spirits' ideologies," Richard said with a shy smile. Both he and Danielle were thinking of what she had told him—that she believed in ghosts. "Do you really have a specific reason? I mean, I understand just not believing. I remember once reading there are over four thousand religions in the world. Can't say I have a specific reason for not believing in them, maybe because I don't know anything about them."

"There are some things Earthbound Spirits may have gotten right—I believe there's something after this life. The reincarnation thing? Maybe, I don't know. Other religions believe in reincarnation. But I don't believe we should waste the time we have on earth trying to get to that other place. We'll get there soon enough. Our life here is a gift, and I don't believe we should squander it—or shorten it, like Clarence did. Unlike Earthbound Spirits, I do believe in a higher power—a God."

Patricia reached over and patted Richard's hand. "I believe in God, because he's answered my prayers."

"I think the biggest issue I have with Earthbound Spirits," Danielle continued, "is how Morris coerces his members to make large donations and leave all their money to the group after they die. And what does the group really do with the money?"

"Money means nothing. It's never brought me happiness," Richard insisted. "And if the money can help others find the truth after I'm gone, then isn't that the right thing to do?"

"If you want to find happiness now with your money, follow Chris's example, become a philanthropist. Help feed the hungry, get involved with a worthwhile environmental cause, create jobs—do something with your money that helps other people, here and now, in this life. I guarantee that will buy you a measure of happiness," Danielle suggested.

FLAMES FLICKERED and curled in the library fireplace. The

house was quiet. Walt lounged on the sofa, reading the book Danielle had given him for Christmas.

"Aren't you worried about someone walking in here and seeing that floating over the sofa?" Chris asked as he walked into the room.

Walt closed the book and set it on his lap. He looked up at Chris. "I knew it was you. Everyone else is gone."

"How do you know everyone is gone?" Chris headed for the fireplace to warm his hands.

"Danielle went down to the police station. Lily and Ian took Sadie for a walk on the beach, Richard took Patricia and Jessica out for ice cream, and Joanne has already gone home. It's just you and me and Max."

Standing before the fireplace, his back to Walt, Chris reached out and rubbed his hands together, warming them.

"What does a philanthropist do exactly?" Walt asked.

Chris stopped rubbing his hands together and turned from the fire, facing Walt. "In my case, you might say I just give away money."

"To whom, exactly?

Chris sat down facing Walt. "I've never set up my own foundation; instead I give to charities, ones I've researched and feel are legit."

"What happens when your money runs out?"

Chris grinned. "I really don't see that happening anytime soon."

"Where are you headed after you leave here?"

"I don't know yet. I was thinking of maybe sticking around here."

"You aren't planning to leave?" Walt frowned.

"I wasn't talking about living in Marlow House indefinitely. I was thinking of getting my own place somewhere in the area."

"Why?"

"You don't want me to stay?" Chris asked.

"I don't care what you do."

"Then why are you asking me what I'm going to do?"

"I'm curious. Doesn't mean I care." Walt shrugged.

Chris studied Walt for a minute. "So tell me, Walt, what's the deal with you and Danielle?"

"What kind of question is that?"

"Maybe I should be asking, why are you still here? Why haven't you moved on? If I had to guess, I'd say it had something to do with Danielle."

"Marlow House is my home."

"Does that mean you plan to stay here forever?"

"Of course not," Walt snapped.

"Hey, don't get defensive. I was just curious too. Then tell me, what's up with Joe? He seems to be a little territorial over Danielle."

"She dated him a few times when she first moved here."

"What happened? He obviously still has a thing for her."

"He arrested her for murder."

"Excuse me?"

"For her cousin's murder. Now that I think about it, for Stoddard's too. There might be a few other murders he arrested her for, but it's hard to keep them all straight."

"Are you joking?"

"I wish I was." Walt tossed the book on the coffee table and looked over at Chris. "Joe doesn't know about Danielle's—gift. And when certain things have happened because of it, he has a tendency to think the worst. I think he cares for her, but he has no faith in her."

"Sounds like a jerk."

Walt didn't comment.

"Is it true, does the police chief really know about Danielle?"

"If you mean how she can see spirits, yes."

DANIELLE PULLED her red Ford Flex into the Frederickport Police Department parking lot. She had called the chief earlier that morning, telling him when she would be in. He was under the impression she would be bringing along Chris, Richard, Patricia, and Lily to be interviewed again. Danielle didn't correct his misconception. She figured it would be easier to explain it all at once.

When she walked into the front office of the police station, she found the chief standing at the front desk with Joe and Brian. The three men stopped talking when she entered, and turned toward her.

Danielle glanced at the empty chair at the desk. "Where's Marcia?"

"She doesn't work here anymore." Joe glanced over Danielle's shoulder and then asked, "Where is everyone else? Did they take a separate car?"

"How long hasn't she been working here?" Danielle asked.

"I'm surprised you care; I thought you didn't like her," Brian said.

"It wasn't that I disliked her exactly; I just felt she was grossly incompetent. Her inability to relay a simple message almost got me killed."

"She's been gone for a couple weeks," the chief said. "So where is everyone?"

"I need to talk to you first, Chief." Danielle looked over at Brian and Joe and then back to the chief. "Alone."

"Since we have a dead body that looks like it might be your missing guest and Chris Glandon seemed to have an issue with her, I have to say this doesn't look good on him not coming in like he promised," Joe told her.

Danielle sighed. "Chris didn't promise anything—I did. He didn't even know the chief wanted him to come in today."

"You told me you were going to bring him with you." The chief sounded annoyed.

"Chief, please. In your office, alone," Danielle said impatiently.

Joe and Brian watched as Chief MacDonald motioned for Danielle to follow him.

"I don't get those two," Brian said when Danielle and MacDonald were out of earshot.

Joe frowned. "What do you mean?"

"They've become so—chummy. I can't help but wonder if there's something going on there."

"Would you stop saying that," Joe said impatiently. "Anyway, the chief's dating Carol Ann. Don't be ridiculous; he's not Danielle's type."

Brian snickered. "What is her type? You?"

MACDONALD CLOSED his office door and said, "This better be good, Danielle."

"I know who the dead body is. And it isn't Anna." Danielle remained standing and watched as the chief took a chair behind his desk.

He motioned for her to sit down. "Go on."

"Her name is Beatrice Montgomery, and she was traveling up the coast with her husband, Herbert, in a rented motor home. They fought, and he pushed her off a cliff into the ocean."

"You know this how?"

"Seriously, Chief? You can't figure it out?"

MacDonald sighed. "You talked to her?"

"Actually, it was your fault."

"My fault? How?" He frowned.

"Her spirit must have been hanging around her body when it was found on the beach. When I saw her, she was at that stage where she doesn't quite understand that she's dead. She tried to get the police to listen to her, and then she latched onto you."

"What do you mean?"

"She followed you back here, trying to get your attention. She went home with you, and then she followed you to Marlow House. She showed up after the last time you were there yesterday. Came walking through the fireplace in the library."

"Terrific." He let out a weary sigh and leaned back in his chair.

"Personally, I'm relieved. Oh, don't get me wrong, I feel sorry for Beatrice and all, but I really didn't want it to be Anna."

"I suppose I need to see if we can find anything on this Beatrice." The chief picked up the phone.

Danielle sat quietly and waited for the chief to finish his call. When he finally hung up, she said, "Oh, and about that blood on the rug Joe took from my place, it isn't human."

"What is it, vampire blood? Zombie?"

"Cute. No. Rat. My sweet cat killed a rat."

"From what I remember, your sweet cat about took my hand off."

"Oh, don't be such a baby. He's a sweetheart."

"Tell that to the rat."

Danielle shrugged.

"So what about your missing guest?"

"Probably the most likely scenario, she simply decided to leave. I think Anna is prone to impulsive acts—like showing up on my doorstep without a reservation just because she saw the ad. No planning. And when she felt like leaving, she just did. The only reason I ever called to make a police report was the storm. I was afraid she might be out in it somewhere, stranded."

"And you're sure the spirit you saw was the woman we found on the beach? After all, she wasn't recognizable."

"You told me she was wearing a nightgown. Any chance that nightgown was a blue floral pattern?"

"Yes." He nodded. "As a matter of fact it was."

"Then perhaps—"

The phone began to ring. He motioned to Danielle to hold her thought, and then he answered the call.

When he got off the phone he said, "Last night, a Herbert Montgomery filed a missing persons report in Astoria on his wife, Beatrice. Apparently, they had an argument on Christmas night; she stormed out of their motor home, wearing just her nightgown—a blue one."

"And he's just reporting it now? Christmas was four days ago."

"He said she's taken off before, but always comes back in a couple days. When she didn't return after three days, he figured he should report it."

"Seriously?" Danielle scoffed. "He expects the police to believe he didn't think there was anything odd about his wife wandering around in her nightgown for three days?"

"Hopefully we'll be able to come up with something to prove he was responsible for his wife's death. Thanks for all your help. Is there anything else?"

"Well, there is one thing," Danielle said hesitantly.

"What's that?"

"I think one of your sons may be like me."

"What do you mean?"

"He can see ghosts."

THIRTY-FIVE

Just as Danielle parked in front of Marlow House, she saw Richard drive off in his car. He was alone. When she walked into the library five minutes later, she asked Patricia where he had gone.

Patricia set the book she had been reading onto her lap and looked up at Danielle. "He got a phone call from someone from Earthbound Spirits—I think he said it was Cleve Mon…umm…I don't recall the last name."

"Ahhh…Cleve Monchique. He's Morris's right-hand man." Danielle sat down. "I got the impression Richard's been having some second thoughts about his involvement with that group."

"He has." Patricia smiled. "We've talked a lot about it the last few days. I think he was just searching for something after his parents died and he realized they'd lied to him all these years. I don't think it was the adoption that bothered him so much, but the fact that his adoptive parents made him think he was crazy— denying his real memories."

"I suppose adopted parents are no different from biological parents—there are good ones and bad ones."

"That's true. You can say the same about foster parents."

"I suppose you would know," Danielle said with a sigh. She then asked, "So where did Richard go, Earthbound Spirits' headquarters?"

"No. Cleve asked him to meet him at some café along the highway, midway between here and Earthbound Spirits' headquarters. Said he needed to discuss some upcoming event for the group."

"So Richard still feels attached to Earthbound Spirits?"

Patricia shook her head. "No. I think when Cleve called, Richard felt it might be the time to let them know he's having reservations. I have a feeling Richard is a little intimidated by Peter Morris and would rather discuss this with Cleve."

"Yeah, I get that Morris can be a little overwhelming."

Patricia chuckled. "Richard said this would be the easy way out."

"Sounds like this is more than just having reservations."

Patricia smiled up at Danielle. "I don't think Richard needs that group anymore."

ADAM NICHOLS SAT in the corner booth of the diner, fidgeting with an iPhone. Sitting across from him was Jason Baker, the diner's proprietor and the owner of the iPhone. He was also an old high school buddy of Adam's.

Jason anxiously watched Adam. "This is going to be great if it works."

"Hey, it'll work. If it wasn't for the camera I installed in my office, I might be in prison."

"I just want to be able to keep an eye on this place when I'm not here. See what's going on." Jason glanced around the diner. "Can't even see where we put the cameras."

"This is better than what I have. I got to get this app for myself."

"Jason, I need you back here!" a voice called out from the kitchen.

Grumbling, Jason stood up.

Holding the iPhone in one hand, Adam used his other hand to wave Jason toward the kitchen. "Go, see what they want. I'll figure this out."

A few minutes later, Adam grinned when a live feed came into focus on the iPhone. It was a view of an empty booth across the diner. From where he sat, it was impossible to see the booth, yet on the iPhone, he could clearly see the salt and pepper shakers sitting on the booth's table.

WHEN CLEVE ARRIVED at the diner, he was pleased to see it was practically empty. There was only one other customer. That man sat in a corner booth, his back to Cleve. The lunch rush had ended a few hours earlier, and it would be at least an hour before customers started showing up for dinner. Cleve intended to be gone by then. When the waitress showed up at the table, he ordered two drinks—a Pepsi for Richard and iced tea for himself. He remembered Richard liked Pepsi.

After the waitress brought the drinks and went back to the kitchen, Cleve glanced around. Aside from the man with his back to him, he was the only one in the diner. He glanced at his watch. Richard was supposed to arrive in fifteen minutes. He needed to hurry just in case he showed up early.

With shaky hands, Cleve pulled a small envelope out of his shirt pocket. He glanced around the room again. Confident he was alone, he tore open the envelope and then dumped its contents into the Pepsi.

Grabbing a spoon, he stirred the drink. Nervously, he pushed the Pepsi across the table and then picked up a paper napkin and wiped off the spoon. He folded the napkin and envelope together, stood up, walked to a nearby trash can, and disposed of the items.

Richard arrived ten minutes later. Cleve was already back at the booth, sipping his iced tea.

"I ordered you a Pepsi," Cleve said as Richard took a seat across from him.

"Thanks. I haven't had a Pepsi all week." Richard picked up the soda and took a gulp.

"How have things been going for you this week at Marlow House?" Cleve asked.

"Things haven't gone quite as I expected they would," Richard said with a smile.

"Peter tells me Danielle may not be quite ready to hear the truth."

"Danielle has her own beliefs. I'm not sure she would ever embrace Earthbound Spirits."

"Then I'm sincerely sorry for her." Cleve took another drink of tea. He glanced up when a server approached the table.

"Would you like to order now?" the server asked.

"No, we're just having drinks," Cleve told her. She nodded and walked away.

"The truth is, Cleve, I'm starting to have doubts."

"Doubts?" Cleve panicked. "Are you saying you no longer believe?"

"No, it's just I wonder if maybe instead of leaving Earthbound Spirits my estate or making my annual donation, the money would be best spent elsewhere. Danielle had a good point when she said money may not buy happiness, but by helping others, we can find happiness."

"So you're saying you aren't necessarily doubting the truth, you just want the freedom to spend your money on the good causes you choose as opposed to helping Earthbound Spirits spread the word?"

"I suppose that would…would that put me in bad standing with Earthbound Spirits?"

Cleve studied Richard for a moment. Finally, he reached across the table and patted his hand. "Of course not. Our biggest concern is helping you find the truth. While we would naturally welcome financial support from our members, we don't want to give the impression it's all about the money. So if you feel you need to spend your money elsewhere, then we understand."

"Really?"

"Of course."

Richard smiled. "I feel so much better. I knew Danielle was wrong. There is something else I need to tell you, which I feel better sharing with you now."

"What's that?"

"I think I've found my sister."

"Your sister?"

"I never talked to you about it. I assumed maybe Mr. Morris had discussed it with you. But after my parents died, I learned I had been adopted. What I didn't realize, I have a sister. And a niece."

"I suppose that means you'll want to change your will, to leave your estate to your sister instead of Earthbound Spirits."

"Do you understand?" Richard asked hesitantly.

"Of course. You should probably do that right away." Cleve smiled.

"I won't be able to do anything until after the New Year. With the holiday and all."

"Well, I certainly don't think anything is going to happen to you before then, so it'll be fine."

Richard winced and grabbed his forehead, massaging it a moment.

"Is everything okay?" Cleve asked.

"I just had a shooting pain in my head."

"Finish your Pepsi, and then maybe you should be heading back to Marlow House. It's already dark and the roads between here and there can be dangerous, especially if it starts raining again."

Richard rubbed his head again. "I think I will." He downed most of his Pepsi and then stood up, preparing to take out his wallet.

"No. I have it," Cleve insisted.

After Richard left the diner, Cleve looked around. The man still sat at the far booth, his back to Cleve. All the other tables and booths were empty, and the server was still back in the kitchen.

Cleve reached out and knocked over what remained of Richard's Pepsi. "Waitress!" Cleve called out. "I need a towel. I spilled my drink!" He glanced up, looking straight into the hidden camera.

ADAM STOOD up and looked at the front doorway of the diner where Cleve had just exited through. He scratched his head. Something did not feel right.

Jason walked out from the kitchen. "Sorry I took so long. There was a problem with the deep fryer."

"Hey, Jason, can I have a plastic bag?" Adam asked.

"A trash bag, why?"

"No. I was thinking of something like a ziplock bag."

HIS HEAD THROBBED. All Richard wanted to do was get back to Marlow House and lie down. He had experienced migraine headaches before, but this had to be his worst.

As he approached the curve along Pilgrim's Point, he began seeing double. Blinking his eyes, he found it difficult to breathe.

DARLENE GUSAROV WANTED to move on. Unfortunately, maneuvering Chuck Christiansen's car off Pilgrim's Point had indefinitely altered her travel plans. She had learned that killing someone when you were dead had consequences, just as it did when you were alive.

She would argue that if anyone had deserved to take a header off Pilgrim's Point, it was Chuck. After all, he had killed her first. Yet, to her eternal regret, revenge didn't work that way. Plus, there was that little matter of Stoddard. Killing her husband was her first mistake.

Darlene stood at the crest of Pilgrim's point, looking down into the darkness. It was where she had died. She could hear the breakers hitting the shore below. Something behind her made her turn around. It was headlights, coming her way. She watched as the car attached to the headlights weaved back and forth in her direction.

"Oh, please, am I going to get blamed for this one too?" Darlene said with disgust.

RICHARD FELT his head weaving back and forth, as if it were no longer attached. He wanted to pull over to the side of the road, but he couldn't seem to get his body to do what he wanted. It was as if his hands and feet were on some bizarre autopilot, acting independently of his brain.

Just as he felt his car careen off the highway, the driver's side door flew open. His eyes widened when he saw a woman who appeared to be hovering in midair alongside his car. Her hand reached in, grabbed him by the shirt, and jerked him from the vehicle. He landed along the side of the road just as his car hurled off the top of Pilgrim's Point to the surf below.

THIRTY-SIX

Outside, an ambulance's siren blared. It faded into the distance until Adam could no longer hear it. A few feet away, a young boy pounded on a vending machine in an attempt to free a Snickers bar. The boy's mother sat across the room from Adam, texting on her cellphone. On the opposite end of the room, a baby began to cry.

Adam glanced up at the wall clock over the sliding door leading to the parking lot. He had been sitting in the ER waiting room for over thirty minutes. Just as he was about to call Danielle and ask what was taking her so long, the sliding door opened and Danielle rushed in, with Chris and Patricia. He had met them both at the Christmas Eve open house. Adam stood up and started toward Danielle, meeting her halfway. They stood in the middle of the room.

"Adam, thanks for calling us," Danielle greeted him, slightly out of breath.

"Is he going to be okay?" Patricia asked.

"I think so," Adam told her. He turned to Danielle. "I recognized him from your party. I knew he was staying at Marlow House and wasn't sure who else to call."

"What happened?" Chris asked.

"I was coming home, just going past Pilgrim's Point, when a

woman flagged me down. I pulled over, and I found him. He was on the side of the road, unconscious."

"What did the woman say happened?" Patricia asked.

"That's the thing…ummm…" Adam looked at Danielle. "I checked his vitals, turned around to ask her what had happened, and she was gone."

"Gone?" Danielle asked.

Adam nodded. "And the really weird thing, I know you're going to think I'm nuts, but when I first saw her standing along the side of the road, with my headlights on her, I thought for a moment it was Darlene Gusarov."

"Darlene Gusarov?" Patricia looked at Danielle. "Is that someone you know?"

Danielle glanced from Adam to Chris. "Yes…Darlene was killed a few months back. They found her body at Pilgrim's Point."

Patricia responded with a startled gasp, yet she said nothing.

"You said on the phone, his car went over the cliff?" Chris asked.

"Yes. After I checked his vitals, I called for help. When the cops arrived, they found his car. It had driven off the side of the hill. Looks like he jumped out at the last minute."

Officer Brian Henderson seemed to appear out of nowhere. None of them had noticed him walking up, they had been so engrossed in what Adam was saying.

"Adam, I need to talk to you about that powder you found," Brian said. He then looked at the rest of the group. "And I would appreciate it if you all would stick around. I have some questions for you."

"Powder?" Danielle asked with a frown. She didn't get her answer because Brian led Adam off to a private corner in the waiting room.

"THE DOCTORS TELL me Winston would probably be dead right now if you hadn't given them that powder you saw him ingest," Brian told him. "Tell me exactly how you happen to have it."

"I was over at Jason Baker's diner, helping him install some security cameras. I was messing around with the app I downloaded on his phone when Cleve Monchique sat down in one of the booths."

"Monchique from Earthbound Spirits?"

"Yeah. I was testing the cameras when he sat down. From where he was sitting, all he could see was my back."

"But you could see him through the camera?"

Adam nodded. "I didn't recognize him at first. But I saw him do something I thought was strange."

"What?"

"He took a small envelope from his pocket and dumped something from it into the soda. I figured he was going to drink it, but he pushed it to the other side of the table, and a few minutes later Richard Winston came in. I recognized him from the Christmas Party at Marlow House. He drank it."

"So how did you get the envelope with the powder residue?"

"After Monchique dumped the powder in the glass, he stirred it with a spoon. Then he picked up a napkin and cleaned off the spoon. I thought that was strange. Then he got up and tossed the napkin and the envelope in the trash. Winston came in after that, and when he left, Cleve calmly knocked over the spiked drink, or what was left of it. Did it on purpose. And then he called the waitress to clean it up. After he left, I took the envelope out of the trash, stuck it in a plastic bag, and brought it with me."

"Why?"

"You mean why did I take it?" Adam asked.

"Yes."

"I have no idea."

"You explained this all to the doctor?" Brian asked.

"Yes, and the paramedics and cops at the scene. I was kind of freaked when I realized who it was, especially since I'd seen Monchique slip something in his drink."

Brian asked Adam several more questions, and then they walked back to where Danielle and the others waited. He opened his notebook. "When was the last time any of you saw Mr. Winston?"

"It was about four o'clock," Danielle told him. "When I got home this afternoon, I pulled up right as he was driving away."

"Did you talk to him?" Brian asked.

Danielle shook her head. "No."

Brian jotted something down in his notebook. "Did anyone talk to him before he left Marlow House? Did he say where he was going?"

"I was probably the last one to talk to him," Patricia said. "It was right before he left."

"Where was he going?"

"To some diner along the highway," Patricia told him.

"Did he say why he was going there?"

"He got a call from Cleve…umm…" Patricia looked at Danielle.

"Cleve Monchique," Danielle said.

"Yes, that's him. He called Richard and asked him to meet him at the diner. He said he needed to talk to him about some Earthbound Spirits event."

"I understand Mr. Winston is a member of Earthbound Spirits," Brian said.

"Yes, but he's been having second thoughts," Patricia explained.

"Oh crap, look who's here," Danielle whispered. They all turned toward the sliding door. Peter Morris had just walked in. They watched as Morris walked to the admittance desk.

Brian closed his notebook. "If you'll excuse me for a minute." He walked to Morris.

"I want to see Richard Winston," Morris was saying just as Brian reached him. "He was admitted tonight. Someone called me."

"Excuse me, Mr. Morris," Brian interrupted.

Morris turned to Brian. "Yes, Officer Henderson?"

"I don't think it would be a good idea if you see Mr. Winston right now."

"I would think that would be up to the doctor, not you. I'm Mr. Winston's spiritual advisor. He had my number as an emergency contact in his wallet, which is why they called me."

"As I said, I don't think it would be a good idea right now."

Morris narrowed his eyes and glared at Brian. "Officer Henderson, if Mr. Winston was a Catholic and I was a priest, would you be attempting to stop me from seeing my parishioner?"

"Under certain circumstances, yes," Brian snapped.

"As I said, it's really none of your business." Morris turned from Brian and faced the woman behind the desk. "I want to see Mr. Winston."

"I'll have to get the doctor," the woman said nervously. She picked up her phone.

"THAT'S the doctor working on Richard," Adam whispered when a man in a white physician's coat appeared in the admittance area.

"Let's see what he says about Richard," Chris suggested, leading the way toward the doctor.

"I'm afraid the officer is correct," the doctor was saying just as Danielle and the others showed up by Brian's side. "You cannot see Mr. Winston right now, Mr. Morris."

"I'm Mr. Winston's spiritual advisor. He had my name in his wallet to call in case of an emergency. You called me!"

"I don't know who called you, Mr. Morris. It certainly was not me. It possibly could have been someone from admitting." The doctor glanced over to the woman behind the counter.

"It wasn't me. I just came on duty."

"In any case," the doctor said, "the only one Mr. Winston wants to see right now is his sister."

"Sister? He doesn't have a sister!" Morris insisted.

"I'm his sister." Patricia spoke up. "Is he going to be all right?"

"You're Patricia?" the doctor asked.

"Yes."

The doctor took Patricia by the arm. "Come with me."

"Doctor!" Danielle called out.

The doctor paused and turned to face Danielle. "Yes?"

"Can you at least tell us if Richard is going to be okay?"

Instead of answering, the doctor looked at Patricia.

"They're with me," Patricia explained. "I'm sure my brother would want you to let them know how he's doing."

Looking from Patricia to Danielle, the doctor said, "He has a broken ankle from being thrown from the car. Right now, he needs his rest."

Danielle let out a sigh of relief. "Thank you, Doctor."

After the doctor walked away with Patricia, Brian turned to Peter and asked, "Can you tell me where we might find Cleve Monchique?"

"Cleve? Why do you need to talk to him?"

"I understand Mr. Winston's accident happened right after he left from a meeting with Mr. Monchique."

"Cleve mentioned they were going to meet for coffee this afternoon. But it wasn't a meeting exactly, just two friends getting together."

"We're going to need to talk to him. Do you know where we can find Mr. Monchique?"

"No. In fact, I tried calling him before I came over here, but he wasn't answering his phone," Peter explained.

A few minutes later, as Peter Morris made his way to his vehicle in the hospital parking lot, he heard a voice call out, "Mr. Morris!"

He paused a moment and turned to see who was shouting at him. A young nurse ran in his direction. He recognized her; she was a member of Earthbound Spirits. Yet he didn't remember her name —she was one of his less affluent members.

"Mr. Morris, I'm so glad I caught you!"

He reached out and took her hand, silently reading her name tag. "So good to see you, Cora."

"I just wanted to let you know I'm the one who called you to tell you Mr. Winston was here."

"Thank you, Cora." He patted her hand.

"I shouldn't be telling you this; we aren't supposed to discuss a patient's medical history. But I think you should know. I'm sure it's what Mr. Winston would want."

"What is it, dear?"

"I was in the hospital room when they brought him in. The man who found him told the doctor he saw someone put something into Mr. Winston's drink. The man was able to recover some of it, he gave it to the doctor, and they had it tested. Someone tried to poison Mr. Winston!"

"Do you know who?"

"No, he didn't say. But I overheard one of the officers who brought him in say something about how they knew who had tried to poison Mr. Winston and that it had been captured on video!"

"Video?"

"Sounded like some surveillance camera or something."

Peter patted the nurse's hand again. "Thank you for telling me. I'm just grateful the police know who did this to poor Richard. I'm sure they'll handle it."

Ten minutes later, Peter Morris sat alone in his black Mercedes. He picked up his cellphone and placed a call.

"I'm at the hospital. Apparently, someone has poisoned poor Richard Winston, but the doctor says he'll recover. I believe it's time for you to go home now; you've done all that you can do here. But before you go, don't forget to clean up."

THIRTY-SEVEN

On Tuesday morning, Danielle awoke to the sound of a mariachi band blaring on her clock radio. Groaning, she rolled over and grabbed hold of the radio's cord, jerking its plug from the wall.

"I swear, Walt! If you don't stop screwing with my radio, I'm going to kill you!"

"Too late." Walt chuckled when he appeared in her room. "But I didn't touch your radio."

"Yeah, right." Danielle sat up, rubbing her eyes.

"Well, technically I didn't touch it."

"See! I knew it was you." Danielle climbed out of bed and grabbed her robe.

"I am sorry. I honestly didn't mean to leave it on that channel, but I wasn't sure how to get it back to where it was."

"I guess I need to get you your own radio," Danielle grumbled.

"Do you think Richard is coming home today?"

"I don't know. I imagine Patricia will call the hospital this morning."

"Do you think Adam really saw Darlene?"

"Kind of sounds like she's haunting Pilgrim's Point. And I have to wonder, how exactly did he manage to get out of his car before it went off the side of the cliff?"

"Darlene doing good deeds?" Walt asked.

"Or penance."

"Perhaps. I suppose I should leave so you can get dressed."

"I would appreciate it."

Walt vanished.

Ten minutes later, Danielle stepped out from her bedroom into the hallway. She didn't hear anyone else up yet and guessed everyone in the house—except Walt and herself—was still sleeping. Of course, she didn't think Walt ever slept.

Quietly, she made her way downstairs to make coffee. Joanne wasn't due to show up for another fifteen minutes.

She thought of Richard and what Adam had told her the night before. Had Cleve really tried to poison Richard? Would this finally be the downfall of Earthbound Spirits? While Danielle considered the various possibilities, she barreled into the kitchen, paying little attention to her surroundings when she came face-to-face with an intruder: Cleve Monchique.

Danielle came to an abrupt halt and slowly started to back up, looking for something to grab to use as a weapon. "What are you doing here?"

"He lied to me," Cleve told her.

"I don't know what you're talking about, but I want you to leave."

"Did you know I arranged Clarence's death?" Cleve took a step toward her.

"You need to go. I'm not alone."

"I paid someone to kill Clarence. They drugged him first and then put him in the noose."

"Why are you telling me this?"

"I tried to kill Richard too. But that didn't work out. Someone saw me. Do you know who saw me?" He took another step in her direction.

Danielle shook her head. "I don't know anything about that. Please go."

"It was supposed to be the perfect murder weapon—an unde-tectable drug. One that only shows up on a tox screen if you specifi-cally test for it. But someone must have told them I gave Richard the drug. But who?"

"I'm going to scream!" Danielle warned.

"Why are you going to scream?" Lily asked as she walked into the kitchen.

Danielle pointed to Cleve.

"What's your problem?" Lily walked around Danielle and then walked through Cleve, making her way to the coffee maker. "Darn, you didn't make coffee yet." She turned to Danielle. Cleve stood between them.

"Don't you see him?" Danielle asked.

"See who?"

Danielle let out a sigh of relief. After a moment she announced, "Well, I have good news and bad news."

"What's the good news?" Lily and Cleve asked at the same time.

"The good news is I'm no longer worried about Cleve attacking me."

"What are you talking about?" Lily asked.

"I wasn't going to attack you." Cleve sounded insulted.

"The bad news—for Cleve, anyway—he's dead."

"Dead?" Lily glanced around. "Is he here?"

Danielle nodded and pointed to Cleve again.

"What does he want?" Lily asked.

Danielle looked at the ghost. "What do you want, Cleve?"

"I wanted you to know Peter Morris lied to me. He lied to all of us. I ended my life for nothing. This isn't how it's supposed to be."

"Did Peter know about Clarence, about what you tried to do to Richard?"

"Yes. He gave the orders. He told me to take my life. He said it was time for me to go home. But it wasn't supposed to be like this."

"Who blackmailed Darlene to lie about the will? Was that you or Peter?" Danielle asked.

"It was Peter. But I got him Isabella's wills—the original ones. Clarence told me where to find them. All his files were put in storage."

"How many others have there been?" Danielle asked.

"What do you mean?"

"Has Peter had anyone else killed?"

"No. I don't think so. But Clarence was getting demanding, threatening to tell the police Peter knew the truth about the wills. We were afraid Richard was going to change his will—and we had just lost another big benefactor."

"How did you know Richard was going to change his will?"

"He told me at the diner—but we had already decided it had to be done before Richard lost faith."

"I don't understand, before he lost faith?"

"We were taught that as long as a believer had faith in the truth when he died, he'd go on to his ultimate destination. I thought that's where I was sending Richard, before he lost faith."

"Why were you so sure he was losing faith?" Danielle asked.

"Because he found his sister."

"His sister? How did you know about that? Did Richard tell you?"

"No, not until we met at the café. But Richard had had extensive counseling in the beginning under Peter's supervision. Everyone does. The dreams he talked about—Peter wondered if they were suppressed memories, so he hired an investigator to look into his past—his family."

"Are you saying you knew Patricia was his sister all along?" Danielle asked.

"We didn't know the Patricia staying here was his sister—not at first."

"What is he saying?" Lily asked.

"They knew Richard had a sister out there somewhere."

"I was just trying to help Peter—to help Earthbound Spirits," Cleve said. "But the truth was a lie, and what am I supposed to do now?"

"You need to follow the light, if possible."

"And if that isn't possible? Will I be stuck here indefinitely, in this middle world existence?"

"You can't stay here, Cleve. But first—is there anything you can tell me that'll help us stop Morris from doing this to anyone else? You know now he's a fraud. Help us stop him."

Cleve shook his head. "There's nothing. I handled everything for him, he told me to clean up, and I did."

"There must be something…some way we can stop Morris."

"I was a fool." Cleve disappeared.

"Cleve?" Danielle looked around.

"Is he gone?" Lily asked.

"I think so." Danielle then went on to tell Lily everything Cleve had told her.

When Joanne arrived a few minutes later, Danielle told her what had happened to Richard the night before.

"I need to run down to the police station this morning, so if you and Lily can get breakfast for everyone, I would appreciate it," Danielle told her.

"Has there been news on Richard this morning?" Chris asked as he walked into the kitchen. He had overheard Danielle's last comment about going to the police station.

"No. But could you come up to the attic with me, Chris? I need to get something up there and wondered if you would help me get it down."

"You really don't need anything in the attic, do you?" Chris asked as he walked with Danielle up the attic stairs a few minutes later.

"No. But I need to tell you and Walt something, and I figured it would be easier if I did it at the same time."

They found Walt in the attic, watching the ocean through his spotting scope. The moment they walked into the room, Danielle announced, "I wanted you both to know Cleve is dead. He was here this morning; I thought you should both be aware in case he shows up again."

"Did Morris kill him?" Walt asked. Danielle went on to tell them about Cleve's recent visit and what she had learned.

"I'M SURPRISED to see you here so early," Joe greeted Danielle when she walked into the police station later that morning.

"I need to see the chief. I tried reaching him on his private cell-phone, but he isn't picking up, and when I called down here, they said he was on another call."

"He's been pretty busy this morning. We have a lot going on."

"Is he in his office?"

"Yeah, but like I said, he's tied up. Why don't you tell me what you need; maybe I can help you."

"Thanks, but I need to talk to him." Danielle turned from Joe and started walking to the chief's office.

Joe followed Danielle. "I told you he's busy right now."

"I heard you, Joe. But this is important."

When they reached the chief's office, Danielle knocked and then opened the door without waiting for an answer. The chief looked up from his desk.

"I'm sorry, Chief," Joe said. "I told her you were busy, but she insisted on seeing you."

"That's okay, Joe. Leave us alone." He waved Joe off.

"Cleve is dead," Danielle blurted out the moment Joe left the office and closed the door.

The chief sat at his desk, pen in hand, absently tapping the end of the pen against the desktop. "How do you know?"

"He visited me this morning."

The chief motioned for Danielle to sit down. "It looks like a suicide."

"He told me he killed himself. But Morris gave him the orders." Danielle sat down.

The chief tossed the pen aside and picked up a piece of paper from his desk. "This is a copy of the suicide note we found with his body."

"When did you find him?" Danielle asked.

"Early this morning. His car was parked down by the pier. He was inside, the suicide note on the passenger seat. Looks like it's in his own handwriting." The chief leaned over his desk and handed the note to Danielle.

"I'm sure it's his own handwriting." Danielle read the note. "He's taking responsibility for everything—even mentions Renton."

MacDonald leaned back in his chair and watched Danielle as she read the suicide note. "According to that, Morris had nothing to do with Renton's death or with the attempt on Richard's life. Cleve claims it was all him."

Danielle tossed the note back onto the desk. "He even mentioned Isabella's will, covering all the bases to protect Morris. But you know it's a lie."

"What did Cleve say about Morris's involvement?" the chief asked.

Danielle recounted her morning conversation with Cleve's ghost.

"Why would he cover for Morris like that, be willing to kill himself?"

"Was Cleve any different from a suicide bomber?" Danielle asked. "I promise you, when those guys get to the other side and discover there're no virgins waiting, they're just as pissed."

"I wish there was some way to tie Morris to this. Put him in jail where he belongs."

Danielle sighed. "I don't see how. According to Cleve, he handled everything for Morris. He protected him. I wish there was some way we could stop that charlatan."

"At this point, we have nothing to arrest him on. Cleve's suicide note is Morris's get-out-of-jail card. When Morris left the hospital last night, he drove to Astoria, had dinner at a restaurant, made a point of being seen. From what I understand, he was quite social. Checked into a motel there, claimed he was too tired to drive home. Called room service and the front desk numerous times during the night, claimed he didn't feel well."

"Establishing an alibi?" Danielle asked.

"Looks that way."

"How did Cleve kill himself?"

"Gunshot. The weapon was still in his hand. According to the coroner, he hadn't been dead long when they found him. Morris was still in Astoria."

"Maybe Morris didn't physically pull the trigger, but he killed him," Danielle said.

THIRTY-EIGHT

Danielle stopped by Adam Nichols's office on the way home from the police department. She found him sitting at his desk, looking at his computer.

"Knock, knock," she said from the doorway.

Adam glanced up and smiled, waving her in. "How's Richard doing this morning?" He turned off his computer monitor.

"I called home a minute ago. Looks like they're keeping him over for another day. But he should be able to come home tomorrow if everything is okay."

"That soon? I thought for sure they'd keep him longer than that."

Danielle sat down. "I wanted to stop by and thank you again for having the presence of mind to take that envelope out of the trash. According to the doctor, Richard could have died."

"Honestly, I have no idea what made me take it. I'm just glad I was able to help."

"Richard's guardian angel perhaps?" Danielle smiled.

Adam leaned forward, resting his elbows on the desktop. "I was serious last night when I told you what I saw. I swear it looked just like Darlene."

"Well, she was killed at that spot," Danielle reminded him.

"Do you believe in ghosts?"

Danielle smiled. "You tell me. You're the one who saw her."

Adam leaned back. "It all happened so fast. There she was, standing in the glow of the headlight. And then I saw Richard on the ground. I didn't know who it was at first, not until I got out of the car and took a closer look. But then she was gone. Whoever she was."

"You read about those sorts of things all the time. Some anonymous savior who appears out of nowhere, saves the day and then vanishes."

"Yeah, but that stuff doesn't happen to me!"

Danielle smiled, yet said nothing.

"When you came in here, I was trying to retrieve the video I took of Cleve Monchique spiking Richard's drink. But now I'm not so sure I took one. I thought I had, and I thought I loaded it to the Cloud, but I screwed up somehow. Nothing's there. So now it will be just Cleve's word against mine."

"I don't think you have to worry about that. I just came from the police department. Cleve is dead. He committed suicide early this morning and left a note. Confessed to everything—including Clarence's death."

"Are you saying Renton didn't commit suicide?"

Danielle nodded.

Adam let out a low whistle and leaned back. "*Damn.*"

WHEN DANIELLE CAME HOME, she found Lily and Chris standing in the downstairs bedroom, talking, while Joanne changed his sheets. Walt stood quietly in the corner, watching and smoking a cigar.

"What's up?" Danielle glanced around the room. She noticed Richard's suitcase sitting in the corner. Chris's duffle bag was nowhere in sight.

"I'm switching rooms with Richard; I didn't think you'd mind," Chris told her. "He's not going to be able to walk on that ankle for a while."

"That's probably a good idea. Where's Patricia? I didn't see her car when I drove up," Danielle asked.

"Chris just wants to be closer to your bedroom," Walt said between puffs.

For Joanne's sake, Danielle ignored both Walt's comment and the look of annoyance Chris flashed Walt.

"She went to the hospital to see Richard. Ian and Jessica went with her," Lily explained.

"I hope Richard has learned his lesson about that shady group!" Joanne said as she shoved a pillow into a fresh pillowcase. "He's a nice boy. Shame he's gotten mixed up with that bunch."

"I hope so too," Danielle agreed.

"I think Ian knows what his next story is going to be about," Lily told her.

"Earthbound Spirits?" Danielle asked.

"Yep."

Danielle smiled. "Maybe Morris got a pass with Cleve's suicide, but hopefully Earthbound Spirits won't fare as well after Ian finishes his investigation."

<hr>

THE HOSPITAL RELEASED Richard the next afternoon—on New Year's Eve. The doctor wanted him to stay off the ankle for a while, so Ian and Chris picked up a wheelchair and had it waiting for Richard when he returned to Marlow House.

Ian and Lily had made plans for New Year's Eve, which they decided to cancel—that was, until everyone talked them out of cancelling. When evening rolled around, the current residents of Marlow House—minus Lily—sat in the living room with a fire raging in the nearby hearth. Sadie napped by the fire while Max crawled around under the Christmas tree, batting at low-hanging ornaments.

"That was an excellent dinner," Patricia told Danielle.

Danielle's response was interrupted when the Christmas tree shook, diverting her attention.

"Max! Stop that, you're going to knock the tree over!" Walt scolded. Max stopped batting the ornament and then charged out from under the tree and raced from the room. The commotion woke Sadie. She lifted her head and looked toward the doorway just in time to see Max's tail disappear around the corner. Letting out a short bark, she jumped up and charged out of the room. The sound of their feet running down the hall, into the kitchen, and out the pet door into the backyard drifted into the living room.

Jessica peeked out the doorway into the entry. "Sadie isn't going to hurt Max, is she?"

Danielle laughed. "The real question is will Max hurt Sadie?"

When Jessica turned to Danielle with a concerned frown on her face, Danielle smiled and said, "No, they'll both be fine. Not sure how my bushes in the side yard will fare, but those two will be okay."

"I'm really sorry I've ruined everyone's New Year's Eve," Richard told them. He sat on a chair with his injured foot propped up on a stool.

Patricia stood up. "Don't be silly, we're just glad you're okay. And anyway, I have something I want to show you." Without telling anyone what that something was, Patricia left the room and ran upstairs. When she returned a few minutes later, she was carrying an overstuffed manila envelope.

"What's that?" Richard asked. Everyone looked at Patricia, waiting for an answer.

Patricia sat down on a chair next to Richard, the envelope on her lap. "Remember how I told you I stored our things in my car after I moved out of our apartment?"

Richard nodded. "I remember."

"I know there's always a chance someone will break into my car at the airport—steal our things. If that happened, I didn't want them to get this, so I brought this with me. I never really thought I would be bringing them out while I was here."

"What is it?" Chris asked.

Patricia smiled. "Old photographs. Really the only thing I have left of my…our parents. After Mom died, and we were taken into foster care, her things—well, they pretty much disappeared. I really have no idea what happened to them. She didn't have a lot. What she did have, it was gone."

"But they gave you the pictures?" Danielle asked.

Patricia looked over to Danielle. "Not exactly. I went back to the apartment after I turned eighteen. Of course, everything had changed. There had been a number of tenants since we moved out, and the guy who owned the apartment had sold it a few years before I returned. But there was one tenant still living at the apartment— an older woman who had been a friend of my mother's. She had the photographs, and she gave them to me."

"How did she happen to have them?" Danielle asked.

"I guess when they were cleaning out the apartment, she went in and started looking around. She saw the old photographs—they had been tossed in the trash—and she recovered them. She hoped I'd come back someday so she could give them to me."

"Can I see?" Jessica asked.

"Yes, we all can. I haven't looked at these pictures for years. It was always so painful. But now…" Patricia flashed Richard a smile. She opened the manila envelope. Inside were a number of smaller envelopes, each labeled with brief handwritten notations indicating what photographs were inside. The one labeled *Bobby and Patricia* she handed to Richard. The envelope marked *Mom and Dad's Wedding and Honeymoon*, she handed to Jessica. Curious, Danielle and Chris stood behind Richard, sneaking a look at his childhood photographs.

Walt wasn't particularly interested in looking through old pictures. He and his cigar vanished, retreating to Danielle's bedroom upstairs, the door closed, and the television turned on with the volume low.

"It's me!" Richard exclaimed.

Patricia glanced over and looked at the photograph he held. "That was taken about six months before Mom died."

"I have some pictures my parents—my adoptive parents—took of me when I was about that age. Must have been right after they got me. I have to be your brother! It looks just like the photos I have of me when I was that age!"

"Why do you have pictures of Anna's wedding?" Jessica asked. She sat cross-legged on the floor, holding several photographs in her hand.

"What are you talking about, Jessica? Those are your grandparents' wedding pictures. My mom and dad."

"No." Jessica shook her head. "This is Anna!"

"No, honey." Patricia grabbed a photograph out of her daughter's hand. "This is…oh my goodness, it does look like Anna!" Patricia stared at the photograph a moment.

"Let me see," Danielle asked. Patricia handed her the picture and then quickly flipped through the remaining wedding photographs. She shook her head in disbelief.

"This is amazing," Danielle said in awe. "Anna is a dead ringer for your mom."

Richard held a wedding picture in his hand, staring at it. "Do you realize the dress she's wearing in this picture is exactly like the dress Anna wore on Christmas night?"

"Let me see," Patricia said.

As Patricia, Richard, Jessica, and Danielle pored over the wedding and honeymoon pictures, amazed at the startling likeness between the two women, Chris stood silently by the fireplace, watching.

Danielle was about to say something to Chris when she looked up and realized he was not participating in the discussion—he was watching. By his expression, she knew he was not surprised at the uncanny likeness.

THIRTY-NINE

The clock struck midnight. Ian kissed Lily while Richard pressed a chaste kiss against his sister's cheek and then Danielle's. Chris was following suit, first giving Patricia a quick kiss, but when he got to Danielle, the kiss he initially intended for her cheek landed on her lips. He didn't linger; he could feel Walt watching. It was officially 2015.

Jessica had fallen asleep on the sofa. Not wanting to wake her, Chris offered to carry her upstairs.

"She's too heavy," Patricia protested.

"Don't be silly, there's no reason to wake her," he insisted.

Chris was halfway up the stairs when he began to regret his rash offer. The little girl was heavier than he had imagined, or perhaps he was just out of shape, he thought.

"You need a little help there?" Walt asked with a chuckle. He walked alongside Chris as they made their way up the stairs.

Chris flashed Walt a pained look. Walking ahead of them was Patricia, oblivious to Chris's discomfort.

After a few more steps, Walt let out a sigh and said, "I don't want you to drop the poor child."

To Chris's surprise, Jessica became light as an infant. For a brief moment he imagined he might drop her—the radical shift in weight had momentarily caused him to lose balance. But then he steadied himself and continued up the staircase with no difficulty. Glancing over to Walt, Chris understood what had just happened. The two men—one a spirit and one flesh and blood—carried the child together, up the stairs and to her room.

"WHAT'S GOING ON, Chris? Who is Anna?" Danielle demanded after everyone else had gone to bed. She found him in the parlor.

Walt appeared. "I'd like to know the answer to that question too."

Chris let out a sigh and sat down at the parlor desk. "I thought you would've figured it out by now. Anna is Trudy Ann, Patricia and Richard's birth mother."

"How is that even possible?" Danielle sat down and looked at Chris, waiting for his explanation.

"I'm definitely confused." Walt waved his hand for a cigar.

"The first time I met Richard was at his parents' funeral. I felt obligated to attend the funerals of all those who had died on the boating accident with my parents. That was my first mistake."

"First mistake?" Danielle asked.

"Since her death, Trudy was unable to find peace. I couldn't really blame her. Patricia bounced around from one foster home to the next, separated from the little brother she adored, and Richard ended up with the Winstons. Look up the definition of dysfunctional family in the dictionary and you'll find a picture of the Winston family."

"Are you saying their mother's spirit has been with them all these years?"

"Yes." Chris nodded. "She bounced between the two, watching them grow up, trying to get someone to help them. Trudy wanted to reunite her children. No one would listen, of course, because no one could see or hear her."

"But you could," Danielle said.

"She came to the Winstons' funeral with Richard. Of course, he had no idea his birth mother was by his side, like she so often was. When Trudy discovered I could see her—she wouldn't let me rest."

"What do you mean?" Walt asked.

"She began haunting me. Badgering me. Demanding I do something to help her children. She would barely let me sleep. I had no choice; I had to find some way to get them together."

"So what was the plan?" Danielle asked.

"First, I hired a private detective to find out what I could about the two. I really couldn't trust what Trudy told me; spirits are not always reliable."

"Exactly why did you look at me when you said that?" Walt asked with a scowl.

"Is that when you learned about Richard's involvement with Earthbound Spirits, or had Anna always known?" Danielle asked.

"He wasn't involved with them until after his parents' death—after Trudy latched onto me. From what I can tell, he was devastated when he learned the truth about the adoption, how his parents had lied to him all those years. He was vulnerable, looking for answers. Earthbound Spirits was there with answers, for a price."

"Was he really that upset to discover he was adopted?" Walt asked.

Chris shook his head. "It was not the adoption per se. But Trudy had seen what had gone on all those years, how the Winstons worked to erase his early memories. Remember, he was six years old when she died. He naturally remembered things, but for years they pounded into him that his memories were all his imagination."

"Like he was crazy," Danielle murmured.

"Yes. The way people want us to feel if we foolishly reveal we can see spirits," Chris told her.

"So you were behind Benevolent Charities, like I thought?" Danielle asked.

"Yes, but not for the reasons you assumed. I learned Richard had reservations here, and I figured if I could get Patricia here for Christmas, it would be one way to get them together, at least under the same roof. So I created the phony charity and threw in the gifts as incentives so she'd come. I had learned Patricia lost her job and was on the verge of being evicted—which did happen—so I figured she couldn't afford to pass up the trip."

"I'm not sure why you went through all this," Danielle said. "Wouldn't it have been easier to simply send them each an anonymous letter letting them know about each other? After all, it shouldn't be too difficult to prove they're related with a DNA test."

"Trust me, I offered to do that after Trudy first latched onto me. But Richard was in such a bad place, and the people he thought were his parents so betrayed him. Trudy was afraid if Patricia just showed up, he'd suspect her of just being there for his money, that she'd always known about him but had never tried to contact him. Trudy wanted to do something where they'd have a chance to get to know each other first."

"How was everyone able to see Anna? I don't understand," Danielle asked.

"Well, that makes two of us. Trudy coming here was not part of the plan. Honestly, I wasn't sure how I was going to get Richard and Patricia to see they were siblings. I just figured I'd improvise."

"You didn't know she was coming?" Danielle asked.

"No. That wasn't part of the plan. And when I first saw Anna, I didn't recognize her as Trudy—not until I looked into her eyes. The woman we saw as Anna was an image of Trudy as a newlywed, not how she looked when she died."

Danielle looked at Walt. "Well, I suppose that answers one of our questions."

"What question was that?" Walt asked.

"If a spirit could appear as a younger version of himself, or if you died at a really old age, whether your ghost self would always appear as an old man," Danielle explained, reminding Walt of a conversation they once had.

"That may explain how she appeared as a younger version of herself," Walt began. "It still doesn't explain how everyone could see her. And it wasn't an illusion, she appeared as flesh and blood."

Chris stood up and walked across the room to the window. Pushing the curtain aside, he looked out into the dark night. "I've wondered how she did that. And when she disappeared, I wondered where she went." He turned and faced Walt. "And she couldn't see you."

"Me?" Walt asked.

Chris nodded. "It's always been my experience that spirits can see each other. It's not like Danielle and me, where we can see spirits but Lily and the rest can't. Yet when Trudy was in this state—whatever state that might be—she couldn't see or hear Walt."

"You really didn't know she was leaving right after Christmas?" Danielle asked.

"I had no idea. Frankly, I was surprised when she disappeared, because Richard and Patricia still had not considered the possibility they were siblings. I just naturally assumed she would stick around until they did."

Danielle studied Chris for a moment and then asked,

"Remember when Brian said he heard you and Anna arguing at the diner? Why did he really think you threatened her life?"

Chris looked over at Danielle and smiled. "To be honest, I did say something about maybe I should just kill her. I understand why Brian misunderstood. But I was talking about killing someone who was already dead—who had taken on what appeared to be a flesh and blood body. Even then I wasn't serious, at least not how it sounded."

"If you haven't seen her since she disappeared, does that mean her spirit self has moved on?" Danielle asked.

"That's what I'm beginning to believe. If she just went back to how she was the last time I saw her at Dana Point, I would assume I could see her."

"Perhaps she has truly moved on," Danielle suggested.

Walt stood up and angrily asked, "I want to know how she did that. How did she become flesh and blood?" Walt disappeared.

Danielle stared at where Walt had been standing right before he vanished. "Why is Walt so upset?"

Chris smiled. "I think I know."

"Why?"

"I think he would like to be able to do what Trudy did—to come back as a flesh and blood person, if only for a brief time."

"Why would he want that? What would be the point if he could only come back for a few days?"

Chris reached out and grabbed Danielle's right hand, gently squeezing her fingertips. He looked into her eyes. "For you, of course."

"Me?"

"He may be a ghost, Danielle. But I think he's in love with you."

"GOOD MORNING, Joanne! I haven't seen you since last year!" Jessica greeted her with a giggle.

Joanne set the platter of biscuits on the table. "Has it been that long? I swear, it seems like just yesterday!" She winked at the child and handed her a fresh biscuit and then headed back to the kitchen to get the rest of the breakfast.

Jessica giggled again. Tearing off a piece of the warm biscuit, she popped it in her mouth.

"How are you feeling this morning, Richard?" Ian asked as he sat down at the table, joining the occupants of Marlow House for breakfast.

"Much better, thank you. I can't believe we go home tomorrow." Richard grabbed a biscuit for himself and then passed the platter down the table. "In spite of my two nights in the hospital, I can honestly say this has been one of my best Christmases."

Patricia reached over and patted Richard's hand. "I second that!"

Joanne returned to the dining room with more platters of food and began passing them around the table.

"Well, I'm going to miss you all," Danielle told them. "I've really enjoyed sharing Christmas with all of you—it helped me not miss my own family quite as much."

"It feels like family around this table," Lily said. Danielle flashed her a smile.

"Do you fly back to Arizona in the morning?" Chris asked Patricia.

Patricia looked over at Richard. "Should we tell them now?"

"What?" Lily asked.

"Richard's going to need some help. It'll be a while until he gets walking again. Jessica and I are going home with him."

"I'm sending someone to pick up her car at the airport," Richard explained. "We're going to be pretty busy these next few days, getting Jessica enrolled in school, getting them both settled in. And severing all ties with Earthbound Spirits. I already called my attorney."

"About your will?" Lily asked.

"After that incident with Cleve, I realized I can't be too careful. That last day in the hospital I called my attorney at his home. He faxed me some papers to sign, making sure Earthbound Spirits doesn't get a penny of my money if something were to happen to me before I get my new will finalized."

Walt appeared in the room. He lounged casually against the buffet, listening.

"I just want Richard safe!" Patricia said.

Danielle grinned. "I'm happy for you both."

"I'm still trying to understand the uncanny resemblance between our mother and Anna," Patricia said.

"I think Anna was Grandma," Jessica said with conviction.

Patricia smiled at her daughter. "She definitely looked like Mom."

"And you never noticed the resemblance when Anna was here?" Lily asked.

Patricia shook her head. "No. Mom went gray at a very young age. I think she was completely gray by the time she turned thirty-five. Her illness those last few months really aged her. Unfortunately, that's how I tend to remember her."

Richard looked over at his sister. "I like to think Jessica is onto something."

"Maybe she is…" Patricia returned her brother's smile.

"What are your plans, Chris?" Richard asked a few moments later.

Walt studied Chris. "Yes, what are your plans?"

"At Danielle's open house, I met one of her friends, Adam Nichols."

Lily raised her brows. "Adam?"

"He mentioned he owned a property rental company in town, and Ian said that's who he got his house through. So I thought I'd go talk to him tomorrow, see what he has available."

"Weren't you planning to check out tomorrow?" Lily asked, flashing Danielle a grin.

Chris looked over to Danielle. "I was hoping Danielle would be willing to rent me a room until I can find something more permanent."

Walt stood up straight. "You're staying here?"

"I like Frederickport. It rather grows on you—especially the people."

"Gee, Dani, you think you can rent Chris a room for a few more days?" Lily asked mischievously.

"Certainly. We'd love to have you." Danielle grinned.

"Fine, but he moves back downstairs!" Walt said before he disappeared.

FORTY

Bundled up in a quilt, Danielle sat in the swing in front of Marlow House. The toe of her right sneaker repeatedly pushed against the damp ground, keeping the swing in motion. It was chilly outside. Not surprising, considering it was New Year's Day. Inside the house, the occupants watched football in the living room—all except Jessica, who was in the kitchen, finishing her paint by numbers picture she had started several days earlier.

On Danielle's lap was Max snuggled beneath the quilt, his black nose and whiskers peeking out from the blanket's folds.

"What're you doing out here in the cold?" a familiar voice called out from the direction of the street.

Danielle looked up and smiled. "Happy New Year's, Chief." She scooted over in the swing, making room for him. When he sat down, Max reached out with his paw, giving him a swat before retreating back under the quilt.

"Nice to see you too, Max." MacDonald chuckled.

"Why aren't you home watching football?"

"Thought I'd stop by and see how Mr. Winston is doing."

"He's doing great. They're all going home in the morning. I'm going to miss them. Well, all but Chris. He's decided to stay in Frederickport."

"Really? Is he staying with you?"

"Only until he can find something more permanent. He's meeting with Adam tomorrow to see what he has."

The chief leaned back in the swing and looked across the street. His foot moved in unison with Danielle's, keeping the swing in motion. "I don't imagine Joe's going to be thrilled with that."

"Joe? What does Joe have to do with it?"

"For some reason, he feels responsible for you. Doesn't seem to like this Chris character, especially when he found out he was using an alias, and after what Brian overheard at the diner. And then of course, we have your missing guest, who remains MIA."

"Actually," Danielle said with a sigh, "I can explain all that."

"You can?"

"I know now what happened to Anna—well, at least I have an idea. I can tell you, but of course it's not something I can tell Joe, so I imagine he'll continue having his suspicions."

"Are you saying this has something to do with…ghosts?"

Danielle nodded and then proceeded to tell the chief the truth about Anna—and Chris—and what had happened over the last two weeks. When she was done telling her story, neither one said anything, but they sat quietly on the swing, pushing it to and fro.

"Do you really believe this Anna was the spirit Trudy, who Chris claimed to have seen?" the chief finally asked.

"You never saw Anna, Chief. But those pictures Patricia showed us of her mother—even a dress she was wearing in one was identical to what Anna wore on Christmas."

"So now spirits can take the solid form of a living person?"

Danielle shrugged. "I think Walt—or Chris—can't remember which one, said something about Anna appearing in a flesh and blood form. But maybe she didn't. It could be her energy creating the illusion, like with Walt. Just in this case, everyone could see her. Maybe it's no different than Darlene. Just that her appearance lasted longer."

"Darlene? What does this have to do with Darlene?"

"Lily can't normally see spirits, but she saw Darlene. And by the way, so did Adam Nichols. I don't think Darlene has moved on. I think she's haunting Pilgrim's Point."

"What makes you say that?"

"I don't think Adam said anything to the cops when they showed up the other night after the accident. But Adam told me he saw a woman standing by Richard—she looked just like Darlene.

And then she disappeared. I think Darlene may have pulled Richard out of his car."

"Everyone seems to be seeing ghosts…even Evan," the chief grumbled.

"Your son? Did you talk to him about what I told you?"

"Oh yeah…" The chief sighed.

"What happened?"

"I told the boys I knew one of them threw a toy truck at a woman in our house—and that I wanted to talk to the guilty party —privately. I lied, told them I already knew which one had done it, but I wanted the guilty one to fess up, and if he did, he wouldn't get in trouble."

"And that worked?"

"Yeah. I'm a cop, remember? I scare people. Especially little boys."

Danielle laughed. "You bully."

"Actually, I felt like crap. The poor kid, seeing some woman just appear like that."

"He told you?"

"Yeah. Later that night, Evan came into my room. Told me he did it, but that she had scared him. He said it always scares him when *they* show up like that."

"*They?*"

MacDonald closed his eyes and leaned back. "Yep."

"Oh my…Evan is like me and Chris."

MacDonald opened his eyes and turned to Danielle. "The real reason I stopped by, I wanted to know if you'd help me with Evan. I don't want this to mess the poor kid up."

"Like it did with me?"

"I think you turned out okay."

DANIELLE REMOVED the elastic band from her braid and tossed it onto the bedroom dresser. She stared into the mirror and combed her fingers through her hair, unbraiding it. When it was fairly smooth, she picked up her brush.

After Danielle pulled the brush through her hair, Walt appeared and asked, "A hundred strokes."

"Excuse me?" Danielle stopped brushing and looked at Walt.

"Don't women give their hair a hundred strokes each night to keep it beautiful?"

Danielle grinned mischievously. "I read somewhere the real reason women used to do that was to get rid of lice."

Walt frowned. "You certainly do know how to ruin a lovely picture."

Danielle grinned and started brushing her hair again.

"Now when I see you brushing your hair, I'm going to be thinking of lice crawling out of your scalp!"

"Ewww, gross!" Danielle tossed the brush on the dresser and headed for bed.

"Yes, but you started it. I was being nice."

"True. I can be a brat." Danielle climbed into bed and scooted to one side so Walt could sit next to her.

"Yes, you can." He sat on the edge of the mattress and watched as Danielle snuggled down under the bedding, pulling the blanket up to her chin.

"It'll seem a little quiet around here after tomorrow," Walt said.

"I know. Of course, Chris'll still be here."

"*Downstairs.*"

Danielle grinned. "Sometimes I think you think you're my dad."

"Hardly. I'm younger than you," Walt reminded her.

"Now I really feel old!"

Walt chuckled. He then asked, "Do you think Richard will ever go back to using his real name?"

"I don't know; I wondered that myself."

"If you think about it, all these years he's been using the name of his adoptive parents' first child."

"I know…a dead child's name." Danielle yawned.

Walt quietly watched as Danielle closed her eyes.

"I had a nice Christmas." Danielle yawned again. "And it was wonderful seeing Richard and Patricia find each other, but can I tell you a secret?"

"Certainly, you can tell me anything," Walt said, his tone no longer teasing.

"It made me really miss my family. It's hardest at Christmastime. I miss my mom and dad so much. I even miss Cheryl."

"I'm sorry, Danielle."

"Oh, I guess that's life—and death."

"I haven't given you your Christmas present yet," Walt told her.

"Christmas? Christmas is over." Once again, Danielle yawned.

"Remember, I told you Christmas isn't over until the fifth of January."

"Okay," Danielle murmured, already half-asleep. "Night, Walt…"

SHE HEARD carolers in the distance singing "Jingle Bells." Opening her eyes, Danielle stood in the middle of a snow-covered field. The only clouds in the blue sky were white and puffy. Stretching out before her were two rows of Christmas trees, reminding her in some bizarre way of Oz's yellow brick road. Instead of yellow bricks creating a road, the path wound through two rows of pine trees, their branches dripping with red and gold glass balls.

In spite of the snow, it wasn't cold, which was a good thing since she was only dressed in black leggings, boots, and an oversized Christmas sweater, sporting a felt patchwork rendition of Rudolph the Red Nose Reindeer.

Wondering where she was, she glanced around and was about to shout *hello, is anyone here,* when Walt appeared. He wore what he typically wore when not dream hopping, a suit circa 1920.

"Walt, where are we?"

"I'm here to give you your Christmas present." He took her hand and began leading her down the path between the two rows of Christmas trees.

"Are you taking me to meet Santa? To the North Pole?"

"No. Something better."

"Better than meeting Santa?" Danielle teased.

"I think you'll like this better." He squeezed her hand. "By the way, I understand now how Trudy came for Christmas as Anna."

"How?"

"Christmas magic."

"Christmas magic?" she asked.

"Yes, Danielle. Can't you feel it? Christmas is a magical time, and if you have faith, anything is possible."

In the next moment, the snow turned to pavement and the Christmas trees disappeared. She stood on the sidewalk in front of a familiar ranch-style house. A Christmas wreath hung on its front door.

"My house!" Danielle cried out. "That's where I grew up!" Excited, she looked up and down the street. It was just as she remembered.

"Come, Danielle, they're waiting." Walt led her by the hand, up the walkway to the front door of the house she had once lived in.

"Who's waiting?"

"You'll see." Walt squeezed her hand again.

In the next moment, the house's front door opened and Walt gently pushed her inside. The scent of pine and peppermint filled her head. Once again, she could hear the faint sound of Christmas carols, but this time it sounded as if it was coming from the radio. Instead of "Jingle Bells," it was Bing Crosby singing "I'll be Home for Christmas."

Standing in the entry hall of the house she had grown up in, she turned around, looking for Walt. But he was gone, and the front door was closed.

"Walt?" she called out.

"Danielle! We've been waiting for you!" a woman's voice called out. Danielle turned and came face-to-face with her mother. Mrs. Boatman wore her Christmas apron over jeans and a T-shirt. In her hand she held Danielle's Santa apron. She handed it to Danielle and said, "Dear, put your apron on!"

"Mom?" Danielle whispered.

"Is that my little girl?" a man's voice boomed.

In the next moment, Danielle found herself wrapped in her father's strong arms. His bear hug was soon replaced by her mother's more tender embrace. Closing her eyes, Danielle caught a whiff of Diva, her mother's favorite perfume. She breathed deeply, savoring the fragrance.

"Danielle's here!" another voice shouted.

"They're anxious to see you," her mother whispered, breaking away from the embrace.

With tear-filled eyes, Danielle turned to the new voices—it was her aunt Susan, uncle Carl, and cousin Sean. They were all wearing their Christmas aprons, the ones she had brought home from Cheryl's. Everyone was talking at once. They led her into the kitchen, where a roasted turkey rested on a cutting board, waiting to be carved. On the kitchen table were bowls and platters filled with her favorite holiday foods.

"After dinner Cheryl wants to make graham cracker houses," her mother told her.

"Cheryl, look who's here!" Uncle Carl shouted.

Danielle turned and came face to face with her cousin Cheryl. To Danielle's surprise, Cheryl hadn't changed—she still wore too much makeup, and her blouse revealed a bit too much cleavage, yet Danielle thought she looked wonderful.

Blue eyes twinkling, Cheryl opened her arms. Danielle laughed and threw her arms around her cousin. The two women hugged. "We miss you, Dani Boo," Cheryl whispered. "Someday we'll all be together again, but for now, enjoy your life. You have a long one ahead of you. *Merry Christmas.*"

RETURN TO MARLOW HOUSE IN

THE GHOST OF VALENTINE PAST

HAUNTING DANIELLE, BOOK 7

A romantic weekend at Marlow House Bed and Breakfast turns deadly when Earthbound Spirits' founder, Peter Morris, is murdered. Plenty of people had a reason to want the man dead—especially Danielle's current guests.

But it isn't Morris's ghost distracting Danielle on this deadly Valentine's Day weekend, it's her late husband, Lucas. She has her hands full with suitors coming from all directions—both living and dead—while she tries to figure out if there's a killer in Marlow House.

NON-FICTION BY
BOBBI ANN JOHNSON HOLMES

Havasu Palms, A Hostile Takeover
Where the Road Ends, Recipes & Remembrances
Motherhood, a book of poetry
The Story of the Christmas Village